MURDER IN STYLE

MURDER IN STYLE

Emma Lou Fetta

COACHWHIP PUBLICATIONS
Greenville, Ohio

Murder in Style, by Emma Lou Fetta
© 2014 Coachwhip Publications
Introduction © 2014 Curtis Evans. First appeared in *CADS* 67 (March 2014).
No claim made on public domain material.

Murder in Style first published 1939.

ISBN 1-61646-232-9
ISBN-13 978-1-61646-232-1

Cover Image: Woman in Red © Blanaru

CoachwhipBooks.com

CONTENTS

INTRODUCTION

Emma Lou Fetta
High School Yearbook Photo

KILLER FASHIONS
THE DETECTIVE NOVELS OF EMMA LOU FETTA
CURTIS EVANS

I. MANNERS AND MURDERS IN THE
GOLDEN AGE OF DETECTIVE FICTION

IF ONE IS ASKED to think of Golden Age detective novels set in the fashion design world, English Crime Queen Margery Allingham's *The Fashion in Shrouds* (1938) surely comes to mind, but likely very few people have heard of American author Emma Lou Fetta's *Murder in Style* (1939), a detective novel set in the New York fashion industry that followed on the haute couture heels of Allingham's *Shrouds* by just one year. Nor is it probable that mystery fans will be familiar with Fetta's two subsequent detective novels, *Murder on the Face of It* (1940) and *Dressed to Kill* (1941). Yet the sophisticated mysteries of Emma Lou Fetta, like those of Margery Allingham, are noteworthy in that they clearly reflect the development within the crime fiction genre of the "novel of manners" style, in which authors place at least as much emphasis on the study of social customs and values as the matter of *whodunit*.[1]

This signal development in mystery writing was apparent to observers at the time, at least in regard to English detective fiction. In a 1939 article in the *Saturday Review of Literature*, "The Golden Age of English Detection," Marxist writer (and later Labour politician) John Strachey, after writing dismissively of the modern

---

[1] Another Golden Age (or near Golden Age) English fashion world detective novel that comes to mind is Christianna Brand's debut mystery, *Death in High Heels* (1941).

English novel, turned with relief to detective fiction. He concluded that in the hands of the best English crime writers, detective fiction was taking the place of the mainstream English novel: "Here suddenly we come to a field of literature—if you can call it that— which is genuinely flourishing. Here are a dozen or so authors at work, turning out books which you find that your friends have read and are eager to discuss. . . . I have myself little doubt that some of these detective novels are far better jobs, on any account, than are nine tenths of the more pretentious and ambitious highbrow novels."[2]

The detective novels that Strachey lauded in "The Golden Age of English Detection" were not those which placed primary emphasis on murder puzzles, but rather those which he believed displayed literary merits comparable to what he had once found in mainstream fiction. For example, Strachey took disdainful notice of traditionalist mystery author Freeman Wills Crofts, a former railway engineer, for what Strachey saw as Crofts' "bleak attention to the mechanics of the detective story" and "ostentatious refusal to have anything to do with literary frivols." The crime writers whom Strachey came not to bury but to praise in his essay were Margery Allingham, Michael Innes and Nicholas Blake. Of Allingham's *The Fashion in Shrouds* specifically, Strachey avowed that the novel, while not "her best as a detective story," was a fine piece of literary workmanship, with "really good social observation of a certain set which exists within the English plutocracy." Heinemann, the English publisher of *Shrouds*, struck a similar note in its blurb for the book, trumpeting that Allingham had produced "a convincingly realistic novel of modern times" and "a powerful modern novel which has something to say about the world in which we live."[3]

Traditionalist puzzle fans carped about mystery fiction more concerned with love interest and literary quotations than clue analysis, but mystery critics and reviewers for the most part were

[2] John Strachey, "The Golden Age of English Detection," *Saturday Review of Literature* 19 (7 January 1939): 12-13.

[3] Strachey, "Golden Age," 13.

enchanted by the manners school of detective fiction. Today such writing largely is seen by critics outside the community of detective fiction aficionados as the demesne of a handful of English "Crime Queens" (Allingham, Dorothy L. Sayers, and Ngaio Marsh), plus a few male courtiers like Innes and Blake. American detective fiction often is assumed to have contrastingly consisted mostly of tough, masculine tales by hard-boiled writers like Raymond Chandler. For example, in Lucy Worsley's regrettably superficial *A Very British Murder: The Story of a National Obsession* (the companion volume to the 2013 British television series), Worsley, a historian and BBC presenter, pronounces that "by complete contrast to the suave British sleuth, his American counterpart was tough." She then goes on to treat Chandler's hard-boiled P.I. Phillip Marlowe as representative of all American sleuthdom.[4] Of course, readers (if not necessarily BBC presenters) know that American Golden Age mystery was in fact a "gorgeous mosaic," with different types of detectives, including not only hard-nosed private investigators and no-nonsense cops but flippant gentlemen-about-town, prying spinsters and clever couples.

In the three detective novels that she published from 1939 (the year John Strachey's "The Golden Age of English Detection" appeared) to 1941, *Murder in Style*, *Murder on the Face of It*, and *Dressed to Kill*, Emma Lou Fetta introduced two bright new sleuths to American readers, fashion designer Susan Yates and assistant district attorney Lyle Curtis, and established herself briefly as a more-than-capable exponent of the manners movement in detective fiction, joining not only the British Crime Queens Allingham, Sayers, and Marsh but such American writers as Mary Roberts Rinehart, Mignon Eberhart, and Leslie Ford, who shared with the British Crime Queens a penchant for keen social observation in wealthy and sophisticated environments.

Fetta's debut novel, *Murder in Style*, was praised as "the first mystery story in the fashion business" (the reviewer either meant

---

[4] Lucy Worsley, *A Very British Murder: The Story of a National Obsession* (London: BBC Books, 2013), 279.

first *American* mystery story or must have been unfamiliar with Allingham's *Shrouds*) while her second, *Murder on the Face of It*, was lauded for its "smart, sophisticated New York background reminiscent of that of the play *The Women*" (Clare Booth Luce's hit 1936 comedy of manners about Manhattan socialites that was adapted into a classic film in 1939). When Fetta's third novel, *Dressed to Kill*, was published, the author was pronounced to have "joined the ranks of feminine mystery story writers who know what feminine readers like." Fetta's mysteries, it was declared, "had even more appeal for the ladies than the works of Leslie Ford and Mignon Eberhart."[5]

In a notice in the "Book Nook" of the *West Palm Beach Post*, a reviewer of Fetta's *Murder on the Face of It* summarized the unique feminine appeal of the author's crime tales:

> Emma Lou Fetta's mysteries are inevitably designed to appeal much more to feminine readers than to men. Here is the type of detective stories most women dote on: plenty of atmosphere and subplots, not too gory, all giving the impression of being a story with a mystery, rather than a mystery story. It is all generously flavored with much feminine froth— fashions, love affairs, intrigue. The mystery is finally solved by a knowledge of fashion designing."[6]

Shorn of some characteristic period sexism ("feminine froth"), there is much of truth in this judgment, I think, particularly the idea that Fetta's tales give the impression of being stories with mysteries, rather than pure mystery puzzles bereft of those qualities that Willard Huntingdon Wright (the traditionalist mystery writer S. S. Van Dine) dogmatically dismissed as "literary dallying" and "atmospheric preoccupations." The appearance of Emma

[5] *Milwaukee Journal*, 10 September 1939, 12; *West Palm Beach Post*, 16 June 1940, 2, 15 June 1941, 3.

[6] *West Palm Beach Post*, 16 June 1940, 2.

Lou Fetta's stylish detective novels between 1939 and 1941 indicates that the move in mystery fiction during the late Golden Age away from the "humdrum," puzzle-focused, traditional tale toward the manners mystery was not a phenomenon confined within the bounds of England.

II. EMMA LOU FETTA, FASHION AND FEMINISM

EMMA LOU FETTA was well-placed to write mysteries set within the New York fashion world, for when she published her first detective novel in 1939, she had been the "press chairman" of the Fashion Group, a New York body of female fashion professionals that promoted both the fashion business and the women who made careers from that business, since the group's founding in 1930.[7] At the time she joined the Fashion Group, Fetta also worked with the Rayon Institute of America. She published the book *Molecules to Modes: Sources and Uses of Rayon* in 1929 and during the late 1920s and 1930s wrote about fashion matters in a nationally syndicated column. Her professional life commenced in the early 1920s, when she started working as a journalist for the *Indianapolis Star* and the *Cincinnati Enquirer,* contributing stories on a myriad of subjects, including overseas news (she traveled extensively in Europe after the First World War, reporting on social conditions in England, France, Germany, and Italy).

Emma Louise Fetta was born in 1898 in the town of Richmond, Indiana, the daughter of Robert Henry and Ellena (Fulghum) Fetta. Robert Fetta, the son of a market gardener who in 1846 had migrated with his family to the United States from Germany at the age of three, was a mechanic and entrepreneur who patented a mechanism for use in steam boilers and founded the Fetta Water Softener Company. Ellena (Fulghum) Fetta was the daughter of Jesse Parker Fulghum, who was, like his son-in-law, a talented mechanic. Fulghum is said to have "taken out about forty patents, having

---

[7] The Fashion Group is still existence today. See its website at www.fgi.org. As in the case of England's Detection Club, the founding members-to-be of the Fashion Group began meeting informally at meals in 1928, forming an official organization two years later.

secured more patents on agricultural implements than any other man in the west."[8]

In 1917, Emma Lou Fetta graduated from Richmond High School, where she was a member, appropriately enough, of the writers' club, as well as the staff of the *Pierian* (the school year-book), the dramatic society, and the school orchestra. Her year-book photo reveals an attractive, intelligent and earnest-looking young woman. After graduation she took voice lessons in Rio de Janeiro, but her father suffered serious financial reverses, filing for bankruptcy in 1922.

With her parents no longer comfortably circumstanced, Fetta pursued a career in journalism and made a substantial success of herself. By 1928 she had moved to New York, where she worked with the Fashion Group and maintained her syndicated column. She also married advertising executive George Walling Minster of New York and Wilton, Connecticut, with whom she had a daughter. In New York, she kept as her professional name Emma Lou Fetta, though at home in Wilton she was known as Mrs. Walling Minster.[9]

In a 1929 newspaper article Fetta addressed a subject that clearly was of great importance to her: the rise of the professional woman in the United States. "The interests of [American] woman-kind are broadening," Fetta approvingly announced:

> It is no uncommon thing to find [at a New York woman's club meeting or party] an eminently successful woman lawyer, a well-known woman artist or sculptor, a celebrated actress, a prominent woman politician, a distinguished orchestra leader, a woman editor, a woman detective, a scientific woman

8 For information on the Fulgham family see *Biographical and Genealogical History of Wayne, Fayette, Union and Franklin Counties, Indiana*, Vol. I (Chicago: Lewis, 1899). On the Fettas, see *History of Wayne County, Indiana*, Vol. II (Chicago: Inter-State, 1884).

9 *Indianapolis Star*, 6 January 1922, 9; *New York Times*, 12 July 1935. Robert H. Fetta died in 1935 at the Wilton home of his daughter and son-in-law. At the time of his death he designed furniture.

farmer, women from advertising and publicity fields, a woman broker or banker, women from manufacturing fields (all manner of these), and, of course, doctors, scientists and experts in such work as textiles, cookery, employment, gardening, interior decoration, office management or the like—or rather the unlike!

Furthermore, she added with a fine feminist flourish, "the modern woman specialist is not content to stop short at being simply efficient in one line or another, but . . . unlike the proverbial 'tired businessman' who seeks relaxation in trivial interests . . . must have her collateral important interests." Fetta specifically praised a woman newspaper editor who had authored a children's book inspiring, "through the fairy story medium, an interest in cookery."[10]

Fetta's interest in promoting careers for women is evident in her work with the Fashion Group, but also, most pertinently to this article, in her detective fiction. Clearly Fetta wanted to entertain with her mysteries, but it appears that she also wanted to appealingly portray for her readers the world of women professionals. Moreover, not only do her books present readers with extremely capable career women, they also offer a woman, fashion designer Susan Yates, who is one-half—and the better half at that—of a talented sleuthing team. Fetta's books succeed on dual levels, providing interesting murder problems to solve while also offering fascinating glimpses of the lives of New York career women at the close of the thirties and dawn of the forties. Although it is this latter aspect of her books that prompted contemporary mystery reviewers to brand them primarily feminine fare, in fact male reviewers enjoyed them too. For example, the influential Judge Lynch (William C. Weber) of the *Saturday Review* rendered the verdicts "excellent" on *Murder in Style*, "ultra-stylish number" on *Murder*

---

[10] (Huntingdon) *Daily News*, 10 July 1929, 4. Ironically, in the 1930s a publisher's line of detective fiction was promoted as part of the "Tired Businessman's Library."

on the Face of It and "slithery" (yes, it is meant as a compliment) on *Dressed to Kill*.[11]

III. EMMA LOU FETTA AND DETECTIVE FICTION

WHEN COMMENTING on the comparative skills of Emma Lou Fetta's series sleuths, Susan Yates and Lyle Curtis, a character in Fetta's second mystery novel, *Murder on the Face of It*, gives us what seems the author's own credo concerning her view of the relationship between men and women in the professional world: Women are just as capable as men, but should work with men, rather than try to supplant them. The character elaborates this philosophy as follows:

> "It seems to me it's about time you and Lyle decided you make a pretty good sleuthing team. Why don't you stop passing bouquets back and forth after every victory? Everyone who thinks women can't really do anything will say Lyle did it all anyway, and those who are so keen about women's rights that they forget men have any will say he never could have pulled it off without you. My personal opinion is a smart man and a smart woman can beat a single-sex approach any time."[12]

Susan Yates and Lyle Curtis first meet, appropriately enough, in Fetta's debut mystery, *Murder in Style*, in which death strikes during a meeting of the Tomorrow Club, an organization obviously based on the Fashion Group. As one of the members of the Tomorrow Club, Susan Yates is conveniently on hand when a sister member drops dead from poison at a luncheon round table (the set-up somewhat resembles Agatha Christie's 1945 detective novel, *Sparkling Cyanide*). Naturally the clever and curious Miss Yates soon turns amateur sleuth.

---

11 *Saturday Review*, 12 August 1939, 20, 51 June 1940, 20, 24 May 1941, 20. "Highly seasoned yarn of evil in Manhattan luxury professions," was how the Judge aptly summed up Fetta's *Dressed to Kill*.

12 Emma Lou Fetta, *Murder on the Face of It* (New York: Doubleday, Doran, 1940), 279.

The dead woman, Nancy Pierce ("a very vivid blonde") is one of those classic detective fiction murderees who seems to live for giving everyone she knows ample motives to compass her imminent death. Those with reason to wish Nancy Pierce ill include other Tomorrow Club members (besides Susan Yates herself, Lucinda Mason, Caroline Semmer, Vivian Peabody, Hortense Culbertson, "five delightfully dressed women...famous in America wherever fashions were worn"); Tom Benchley, the Club's newly-hired public relations man; Howard Pierce, Nancy's lawyer spouse; Linwood Semmer, a society doctor; and Ethan Van Weck and Colonel Stanley Gamberson, a husband and a fiancée, respectively, with whom naughty Nancy may have been canoodling. Then there is the ripe redheaded receptionist Ruby Holt, waiter Mike, and bartender Lucien—just what do they know about these high hats that they are not telling?

Susan Yates has reason not to like the envious and nasty-minded Nancy Pierce, who has been poisonously gossiping about her all around town:

> "I always say Susan Yates has the *most* interesting views, messing around with all those odd people, and anarchists and all. It's a wonder to me you do manage to keep best families and leading capitalists' wives. I mean, I don't suppose there'd be much money in making clothes for nihilists and people on relief."
>
> Susan counted three, holding her breath, and then she said calmly:
>
> "Nancy, I'm not an anarchist, nor a nihilist, nor a Lesbian. Please, for the love of heaven, don't go round telling people so."[13]

---

[13] Emma Lou Fetta, *Murder in Style* (New York: Doubleday, Doran, 1939),15. Earlier Yates complains to Tom Benchley, "Nancy apparently made up some fantastic tale about all my clients being queer. Got my nice dowager suspicious I'd begin making trousers for her any minute. Delicate thing to straighten out." Fetta, *Style*, 9.

Like the other women in the Tomorrow Club, Yates could not stand Pierce, but she cannot agree with others that Pierce's death was self-inflicted. "Women like Nancy drive others to suicide," she tartly observes at one point. "They don't commit it themselves." Soon she is looking into the suspicious circumstances of Pierce's death, along with her old friend Tom Benchley and a new man in her life, assistant district attorney Lyle Curtis. "A well-tailored man in his early thirties, who had level gray eyes and a pleasant, warm voice," Yates thinks when observing Curtis. "Behind the surface effects of good clothes and a cheerful manner," she senses that he has "quick muscles and a flexible, straight-thinking mind."[14]

As seen through the eyes of the waiter Mike, Yates has many commendable qualities herself: "Miss Susan Yates was Mike's favorite customer. Mike liked the way her brown eyes were set so nice and level in her face. She was a real lady. A famous designer, too. Made clothes for all the swells. Take the suit she had on now. No ordinary stuff. Green it was, the color of pine trees. Nice hat. The last word, of course, but not crazy like some."[15] It is the level-headed and keen-minded Yates who, with Curtis' help, ultimately solves the Tomorrow Club murder puzzle, though not before a second victim, this one unoffending, dies by another's hand.

Murder in Style is an impressive first mystery outing, with interesting and amusing characters and an intriguing, fairly-clued poisoning problem with good mechanics in its carrying out and emotional resonance in its solution. In Fetta's second detective novel, *Murder on the Face of It*, the setting and characters continue to hold reader interest, while the plot is impressively complex, comparing well with the magnificent convolutions of such puzzle masters as Christie and Crofts. In this tale Susan Yates is returning from France to New York (and Lyle Curtis) aboard the *SS Island of England*, on the eve of the German invasion of Poland. On board with her are two friends from *Murder in Style* (in an unusual twist, the pair, who were murder suspects in the first

14 Ibid., 47, 78.

15 Ibid. 2.

novel, again become murder suspects in the second one). During the voyage, Alma Peters, "empress of the American cosmetic industry," is found dead in her cabin, seemingly of a self-inflicted gunshot wound. Yates naturally is dubious, but officialdom accepts this suicide theory, given that the cosmetics empress seemingly had ample reason to do away with herself, as she was facing prosecution in New York for recently uncovered defalcations from her own company.

After Yates arrives in New York the mystery plot treads water somewhat, though empathetic readers will enjoy following the complications in the love lives of Yates and Curtis and reacquainting themselves with several other characters from the first novel, including the appealing Ruby Holt, who now works for Yates. When one of the passengers from Yates' voyage aboard *Island of England* is found slain in the apartment of another passenger from that voyage, however, a murder investigation finally kicks into high gear. Though Curtis plays an important role in the sleuthing, it is again Yates who hits on the complete solution of a complex series of crimes (in a pleasing touch the fashion sketches that are instrumental in Yates' deductions are included in the text).

Fetta's final mystery, *Dressed to Kill*, takes readers into the advertising business (the field of Fetta's husband), although this is not done with the same depth of Fetta's treatment of the fashion industry in her first two novels. The book opens in fine classical form with a skiing weekend house party of New York professionals at a New Hampshire country estate (complete with a proper butler, Baggs, and a comical cook, Mrs. Bumpet) owned by Lawrence Stratfield, dilettante artist and man-of-wealth. Stratfield's guests are Oliver Penbroke, president of the Oliver Penbroke Advertising Agency; Peter Sutton and David Barron, of the rival Sutton & Barron's Advertising Agency; Sutton's lovely and willful twenty-one year old daughter, Joan; handsome young Hinkle Conway, Joan's romantic interest and a copy-writer in Sutton & Barron's; Hazel Manchester, a "beauty-and-charm columnist"; and, last but not least, the novel's murderee, the beautiful and scheming Prunella Parton, another Sutton & Barron's copy-writer

(Prunella's half-sister, newspaper journalist Carol Parton, also crashes the party).

Prunella survives an explosion that wrecks her bedroom suite, only to be bludgeoned to death in the New Hampshire–New York Express Pullman car in which the house party host and guests were returning to New York (plans of both the New Hampshire country house and the NHNY Pullman car are provided). Lyle Curtis is brought into the case, the train having reached New York City when Prunella's body is discovered. No fool he, Curtis immediately seeks out the expert assistance of Susan Yates, poor Prunella having been found dressed in a most unfashionable combination of long woolen underwear and a dazzling red evening gown.

In *Dressed to Kill*, Emma Lou Fetta has fashioned another entertaining mystery with an impressively complex plot. There are some creative clues and an exciting finish (though somewhat disappointingly Yates tumbles to the identity of the culprit through a convenient coincidence). Throughout the novel Yates and Curtis are openly talking of marriage. I will let future readers find out for themselves just how the author leaves things between her two sleuths in her final published detective novel.

Unlike Margery Allingham's *The Fashion in Shrouds*, the mysteries of Emma Lou Fetta offer an unambiguously positive portrayal of the working world of women on the eve of the Second World War. Lyle Curtis is a man at ease with Susan Yates' professional and amateur sleuthing success and Yates does not see marriage as a blessed escape from career stresses, since she juggles detecting and designing alike with aplomb. As Yates, contemplating her scheme to ensnare a murderer in *Dressed to Kill*, thinks at one point, "she was used to taking chances. She had taken one chance or another every day of her life since she had put a pair of shears into a fifty-dollar-a-yard material to cut her first custom-made gown. She took a chance by being a businesswoman."[16] One might say that Susan Yates (and Emma Lou Fetta) dressed for success.

[16] Emma Lou Fetta, *Dressed to Kill* (New York: Doubleday, Doran, 1941), 258.

MURDER IN STYLE

The intelligent so rarely come
intellectual + the person; the
say so rarely either. So when a
friends manage the same time
mere "print booker" is honored
to say: To the Hoopers —
E. L. F.

An inscription by Emma Lou Fetta from
a copy of *Murder in Style* acquired from a
sale at the Chattanooga (TN) Public Library.

PERSONS CHIEFLY INVOLVED
IN THE "MURDER IN STYLE" CASE

Lyle Curtis . . . . . Assistant District Attorney

Susan Yates . . . . . Internationally Known American Fashion Designer

Thomas Benchley . . . . . Publicity Man

Lucinda Mason . . . . . Successful Decorator

Ethan Van Weck . . . . . Miss Mason's Socially Prominent Husband

Nancy Pierce . . . . . A Very Vivid Blonde

Howard Pierce . . . . . Nancy's Lawyer Husband

Olga Hotchkiss . . . . . Howard Pierce's Secretary

Caroline Semmer . . . . . A Drab Bird in a Nest of Peacocks

Dr. Linwood Semmer . . . . . Nancy's Park Avenue Physician

Vivian Peabody . . . . . Internationally Known Fashion Editor

Colonel Stanley Gamberson . . . . . Miss Peabody's Fiancé

Hortense Culbertson . . . . . Radio Commentator, Former Fiancée of Tom Benchley

Ruby Holt . . . . . A Redhead

Mike . . . . . A Waiter

Lucien . . . . . A Bartender

Randolph Scofield . . . . . District Attorney

Dr. Mordecai Dugan . . . . . Medical Examiner

Sergeant McQuire . . . . . Police Sergeant Lent to D.A.'s Office

Sergeant Withers . . . . . Of the District Attorney's Office

Inspector Beller . . . . . Of the Police Department

Possessiveness—sometimes quaintly called love—
makes most of the complications in the world.

CHAPTER ONE

THE DOCTOR'S EYES, bright like a bantam rooster's, were wary and quick, but his attitude was in the Hotel Eden's tradition of courtesy. He was behaving, Susan Yates thought, as if he recognized that the five delightfully dressed women watching him were famous wherever in America fashions were worn; as if he knew that, in their nervous world of silhouettes, decor and fashionable colors, people did not faint and make a fuss. When he spoke, his words sounded in the best possible taste.

"This young woman has not fainted," he said. "She is dead." He began rubbing his hands with a fat, professional gesture and added apologetically: "Shocking. Shocking." But his eyes retained their look of wariness.

AN HOUR BEFORE, rain had been falling in torrents, blown jaggedly between mid-town Manhattan skyscrapers, spitting and hammering at the windows of the Hotel Eden's bar. Inside, there were silver palm trees under an azure, star-sprinkled ceiling. Although it was only just past noon, more people would have been drifting in except for the deluge.

Lucien, rubbing energetically at an invisible speck on a Napoleon brandy glass, pondered philosophically that you couldn't beat Nature. She could still do more damage to business than politics could. Lucien was French and quick. His eyes darted about over the nearly empty bar. They rested for a moment on the man in his middle thirties who sat on the divan facing the Forty-eighth Street entrance. To him, the man looked clever but weak; and he had hardly touched his drink. Thus, among other things, he was not a desirable customer. Down the long, L-shaped room, in the angle leading to the Madison Avenue doors sat a different kind of man, square-jawed and sharp-eyed, with a pretty girl in blue and lots of sables. They sat close together and spoke in low tones, except when Mike, flicking his napkin at unoccupied tables, drew near hoping for another order. Then they frowned and stopped talking.

Only the tall young man hunched over the bar, quietly dispatching old fashioneds was, Lucien felt, doing justice to his talents as a mixer. At that, business wasn't good enough to feed capsule food to one of those North Pole expeditions. This he considered dispassionately.

Suddenly, borne in from Forty-eighth Street on a particularly wild gust of wind, a young woman who looked both very healthy and very fashionable bombarded the revolving door and came to a neat standstill inside. She smiled at Mike who rushed up, his expression a wealth of satisfaction. Miss Susan Yates was Mike's favorite customer. Mike liked the way her brown eyes were set so nice and level in her face. She was a real lady. A famous designer, too. Made clothes for all the swells. Take the suit she had on now. No ordinary stuff. Green it was, the color of pine trees. Nice hat. The last word, of course, but not crazy like some.

As a matter of fact, Susan's appearance was as perfect as a fine sculptor's work.

Mike gently took charge of her umbrella—also pine colored. He was no longer a table flicker but a person of responsibilities, saying good morning and that it was a nasty day. Miss Yates agreed with another smile; and without looking around moved on to the bar where she stopped beside the tall young man, inquiring: "Is New York's most promising publicity expert remolding the universe or merely taking it apart?"

Thomas Benchley started and unwound himself from the bar stool.

"Hi, Susan!" he saluted, and pulling out a stool for her, he grinned: "Furrowed brow indicated concern over whether America's foremost fashion designer was standing me up."

"Horrid thought. Am I that late?" Miss Yates consulted her watch. "Only ten minutes. A miracle, but I apologize. A lady client, weight one hundred and sixty-five pounds, braved the slightly inclement weather to explain that she doesn't look at all the way my slimmest mannequin did in the gown she insisted on ordering. I try to tell them— Morning, Lucien—yes, a dry martini, please. Very dry."

Tom said: "Another old fashioned for me," and Susan eyed him with mild inquiry. Lightly, she quoted:

> "If on my theme I rightly think,
> There are five reasons why men drink—
> Good wine, a friend, because they're dry,
> Or lest they should be by and by—
> Or any other reason why."

She laughed and added: "The last line's my question."

"Getting up courage," muttered Mr. Benchley not without pathos.

With a half-troubled second glance, Miss Yates said she had never thought the Tomorrow Club frightening enough to upset the famous Benchley nerve.

"Benchley," insisted the young man objectively, "is nevertheless intimidated. Delighted and all that to be doing the publicity for the annual show and fashion promenade of the world's most exclusive fashion club—how's that for copy?—but thinking of being cooped up in a mass gathering of females gets him unstrung. At heart, he's a lone wolf."

Susan admitted she had had, upon occasion, mild attacks of Tomorrow Club claustrophobia herself, but suggested that he consider the members individually. "Look at our individual charm. Our genius. Our intelligence. It's only the fissures and mountains we create in joint activities that scare people to death."

"Many major casualties?" inquired Mr. Benchley, attacking another old fashioned and not looking relieved.

"Emotional casualties, my child, are rarely traced to their bitter ends—or beginnings. Before we concentrated some of the cream of the fashion business in America in an exclusive little club, our temperaments did not show up so gaudily. Most of us in large masses or alone manage beautifully. But there's something about a *small* group of *talented* people. When the six members of our annual show committee get together they become enmeshed in each other's hair. I'll lay odds on it that up in the Eden ballroom this moment my five colleagues are making bedlam sound like a bedtime story."

Mr. Thomas Benchley gulped. "Look here, have I got to hang around up there?"

"How else will you catch our words of wisdom?"

"Stick by me!" he groaned.

Susan hastened to point out that he had other friends at court. "You've met our eminent president and chairwoman, Miss Vivian Peabody—"

Mr. Benchley interrupted by groaning again. "I have. When I went up to her regal office at *For Ladies* magazine to get the job, I thought I was a debonair man about town. By the time those raven locks and that patrician profile had finished with me, I felt like an old glove turned inside out and held up to light for holes."

"It's Vivian Peabody's poise. A concentrated supply of poise isn't contagious."

"It's poisonous. But I'll tell you, my girl, there's weight if not contagion in your Miss Vivian Peabody's grand manner. She ought always to be called Miss Peabody. Period. Like the elder Mrs. Astor. Period. The weight in her suavely efficient tolerance! In the hypnotic effect of those long white hands with that thousand-carat ruby! Weight enough to drown you. By the way, can that ruby mean some intrepid guy actually had the nerve to ask her to marry him?"

Susan laughed. "Colonel Gamberson, late of the U.S. Army."

Mr. Benchley generously sampled his drink and looked incredulous. "Doubtless he was fully armed. I wasn't."

"But Tom," Susan reasoned, "Vivian Peabody—*Miss* Peabody, period—must have liked you or she, of all people, would not have hired you. It won't mean, of course, *carte blanche* for your devious profession. All fifty of our members, if they have a chance, will undertake to edit your verbs. All six celebrated members of the show committee will certainly forbid your use of a single good publicity angle. We'll accuse you of blowing your own horn instead of ours; and when the job's done you'll have a curious feeling you've been apologized for all about the town for unfortunate lack of even turniplike mentality. But rejoice. You've been hired."

"Your cheering words," Tom Benchley said, "are like money to a man starving at sea. Which reminds me, how's the club's credit?"

"Above reproach. We're too well-known, exclusive and affluent not to pay our bills. Except for our hard-working secretary-treasurer, Miss Caroline Semmer, our personal incomes would put many a member of café society to shame. Some of our members even *are* café society. Take Lucinda Mason, decorator for half New York and Long Island. Her husband is even better than the café crowd. He's old Ethan Van Weck. By better, I mean an older line of ancestors accounted for."

With a spartan air, Tom said that their club credit being sound, the committee members might line up once an hour and insult him. "I won't care."

"You will," prophesied Susan. "You will. I've just indicated how much more dangerous six females are than six hundred. We six, as representatives of Tomorrow, have a painful sense of humor. Because we're talented and famous, we can get away with tying a publicity expert's hands behind his back and laughing and laughing."

"You don't?" begged Mr. Benchley.

In a different tone, which she tried to make casual, Susan remarked: "There's someone else on the committee whom you know—Hortense Culbertson. Did you know that?"

Tom nodded, and Susan let it go at that. Tom's engagement to Hortense Culbertson, the radio commentator, had been abruptly terminated a year before. It was common knowledge that the breadth of New York had lain between them since; and she suspected the old fashioneds were fortification against that reunion more than anything else. Hortense, of course, would be seemingly at perfect ease. The lovely voice that interpreted fashions to a million radio listeners each day would greet him without a tremor, which would tie poor Tom's tongue all the more.

An irritated voice at Susan's elbow intruded. "It's a sedative I need, but I'll try a cocktail first."

Looking up, Susan responded with mock gravity: "Miss Mason in person! Lucinda, your name fluttered from my lips just a moment ago. This is Thomas Benchley. Miss Mason, Tom, is our scenic designer for the show as well as the rest I told you about decorator extraordinary."

Lucinda Mason nodded at Tom with green-cast eyes, put her large suede handbag on the bar, clutched a small Pomeranian more firmly under one arm, and settled her big-boned elegance on a bar stool. "I don't care," she declared irritably, "if you said I was a man-eating Yak. I still couldn't compete with Nancy Pierce." Placing the Pomeranian in her lap where it did very well in matching her tweeds, she purred into one of its cars: "Poor darling. Did that horrible female almost kill you?"

"What has Nancy been doing to G. B.?" asked Susan, regarding the dog with friendly amusement.

"Deliberately kicking him, and telling me not to be quaint—quaint, my dear!—when I objected."

Susan remonstrated mildly. "Oh surely she didn't do it deliberately."

Lucinda finished demanding a drink of Lucien and turned back to them. "Well, it was dark, I had the lights out testing the desert scene—but that cat can see in the dark." She sniffed, gathered G. B. protectively in her arms again, and hissed: "There she is now. I really can't see a fox cape for business hours—"

Susan and Tom followed Lucinda's venomous look to the lobby corridor door.

"What a very vivid female," intoned Mr. Benchley incredulously.

A blonde, ornate young woman whose fox cape was topped by a hat supporting an assemblage of varicolored birds, stood prettily poised just outside the metal-bound, glass door, as if contemplating whether her entrance would cause a worth-while stir. Evidently she decided against it or saw someone it was not her pleasure to see, because she turned and disappeared as abruptly as she had arrived.

"What did you say the name was?" requested Mr. Benchley, his mouth propped open in simulated bewilderment.

Susan chuckled. "Nancy Pierce. Wife of the well-known corporation lawyer, and a very vigorous character in the fashion world. Her unofficial function on the committee is glamor chairman. Upstairs you may observe her inserting glamor into the show with fire-hose technique."

Tom remarked that he would rather have another drink.

"Do you no good if Nancy decides she can use you," advised Miss Mason. "She'll use you, drunk or sober. And you'll go not too quietly insane in the process. At least, everyone she's ever been associated with has."

Susan frowned and said quietly that perhaps Nancy did have an uncomfortable habit of uncovering other people's weaknesses and making something of them.

"Uncomfortable habit!" scoffed Lucinda. "There's general chaos wherever she is and you know it, Susan Yates."

In a virtuous tone, Mr. Benchley inquired: "Beyond stepping on dogs and squirting glamor, what does she do?"

Before Lucinda Mason could answer, Susan said lightly: "Nancy was emancipated too abruptly from the old-fashioned kind of purely personal feminine competitiveness. She hasn't learned that as a business competitor it's *what* you do, not *you* that's competitive. In the environment of professional competitiveness, Nancy is—well, a little unpredictable."

"Can't stand anybody to have a good job, a good client, or a man—good or bad." Miss Mason suddenly sounded more amused than irritated. She turned to Tom: "Nancy Pierce hit New York as a jewel designer. But she soon found need for broader horizons. She's trying several at the moment including"—and Miss Mason looked at Susan meaningly—"some sort of a mysterious onslaught on Vivian Peabody's publisher at *For Ladies* magazine."

Torn whistled. "The publishing patriarch himself? She goes high."

Lucinda Mason shrugged again. "I suppose not even Nancy Pierce could have the nerve to hope actually to steal Vivian's editorship of the magazine. Vivian has practically made it single-handed the power it is in the fashion business. But Nancy is up to some sculduggery in that quarter. She is doing what is so pleasantly known as 'contacting' the patriarch, as you call him, Mr. Benchley. And besides that, Nancy's trying to grab Hortense Culbertson's television chance which everyone knows is rightfully Hortense's with her great national following over the air."

Tom looked up quickly over the rim of his glass, but he observed casually enough: "This Pierce dame sounds charming. Wonder somebody doesn't push her off a bridge."

"Compliment to her subtlety," observed Susan dryly. The decorator snorted. "Well Lucinda, call it what you like, but people are a bit afraid of Nancy Pierce's tongue. I am myself."

"You?" Miss Mason exploded, and insisted on an explanation.

Still lightly, Miss Yates said: "Oh, my clashing of swords with Nancy was over commissions on the purchases of one of my oldest clients—an old girl who was coming to me long before Nancy arrived in New York. She claimed she'd sent her to me. When I wasn't submissive, Nancy apparently made up some fantastic tale about all my clients being queer. Got my nice dowager suspicious I'd begin making trousers for her any minute. Delicate thing to straighten out."

Torn shuddered. Lucinda Mason sat for a moment with narrowed green eyes, saying nothing. Glancing at her watch, Susan exclaimed: "We should all be upstairs adding at least to the general confusion." But Lucinda nodded toward the corridor door, and demanded:

"Why? The committee seems to be drifting this way. There's Caroline Semmer looking like badly beaten eggs."

A small woman of withered plumpness stood just inside the door peering nearsightedly around the room. Her eyes lighted with sudden perplexity on the divan opposite the Forty-eighth Street entrance. Her features, Tom thought, though neatly enough arranged had the pinched look of someone about to sneeze. She was plump in a squatty way, and neither old nor young—perhaps forty, perhaps fifty—he decided.

"Mother hen come to gather in the chicks," Miss Mason murmured. And Tom, remembering suddenly that Caroline Semmer was the name of the club's secretary-treasurer—and thus the check dispensing department, decided he had better look sober. Glancing at the older woman's clothes, he secretly marveled that the same kind worn with such grace by Susan and the big-boned, elegant Miss Mason could so intensify the newcomer's plainness. She seemed to wear fashionable attire as a kind of label testifying to her connection with the fashion business; and while he'd soon, Tom supposed, be carrying around the same brooding expression, he'd be damned if he'd buy a new tweed coat. Hunching his shoulders further into the relic now taut across his back, he asked Susan under his breath if the old girl's hat was a flashlight camera, or what? Shushing him as Miss Semmer came alongside, Susan rose and shook hands while Tom unwrapped his long legs and achieved a dignified standing posture.

"Have a drink?" Miss Yates asked the older woman, but the newcomer replied with an apologetic laugh that she was afraid she *never* did until evening; especially when there was *so* much to do.

Lucinda Mason demanded: "How *is* the madhouse upstairs?"

"Well—quieter," and Miss Semmer sighed. "The committee is a little scattered. That's what brought me down here—to urge you all to come back to the ballroom. So much to decide. The stagehands are working on your sets, Miss Mason, but we must start the meeting."

The decorator descended from her stool, clutching G. B. who emitted a bark hopefully. "All right," she agreed. "Only La Pierce better stay out of my hair." Abruptly, she turned to the revolving door, and added: "It seems to have stopped pouring for a minute. I better take G. B. for an airing first. See you all upstairs." With that, she allowed the delighted dog to lead her from the bar.

Miss Semmer sighed again and moved away, too. Susan and Tom dropped back on their stools. "Finish our drinks first, can't we?" he begged. Looking over his shoulder, he asked: "Who's the next roundup?" Susan turned, and Mr. Benchley indicated with a discreet thumb the divan where sat the solitary man with the whisky sour. Miss Caroline Semmer's squat figure was retreating from them in his direction. Turning, Susan saw the excellently tailored figure rise and greet Miss Semmer with thinly veiled exasperation. They exchanged a few low-voiced words, the woman's "flashlight camera" hat, as Tom had called it, bobbing indecisively as she spoke. After a moment the man sank back on the divan listening but apparently not inviting Miss Semmer to be seated. His face remained clouded with annoyance.

"That," explained Susan reflectively, "would be Caroline's bachelor brother, a Park Avenue specialist. You must remember the publicity about him, Tom. He became a society doctor practically overnight by the happy accident of saving the De Morgan oil heiress's life. They were both in the same air crash, remember? To me, he looks a gloomy soul, and he ought to be ashamed treating poor Caroline so rudely in public. He's her pride and joy. Veritable passion she has for him. She'll tell you by the hour how he would have achieved the highest pinnacles of professional success, De Morgans or no. Wonder what brings him here this noon? I should think he'd be busy patting pale hands on Park Avenue counterpanes." She laughed thoughtfully. "You see," she said turning to Tom again, "Linwood Semmer and I have a good many of the same customers—except I haven't saved an heiress yet. My clothes are far too becoming."

Tom Benchley interrupted: "Linwood Semmer? So that's the grouch's name? Sure, I've heard of him—but not in the same breath with men like my late governor. Semmer, though, was a classmate of a pal of mine—Lyle Curtis, first assistant on the district attorney's staff. Lyle suspects him of putting perfume in his tonics. He says Semmer's a chronic grump but that the idle rich like it because it makes their toe twitchings and other minor complaints seem monumentally important." Tom stared at the brother and sister again. "Your secretary-treasurer doesn't look infected with gaiety, either. What'd she do, swallow a pair of scissors as a child?"

"Just Caroline Semmer's perennial inferiority complex. On her ultimate tombstone should go the words: 'A life spent doing and apologizing.' But we lead her a mangy existence as we will you, my lamb—in case those old fashioneds have obliterated my warning. Caroline is the only full-time officer in the club. It's her only job and our trouble-loving avocation. So we all say: 'Oh, Caroline can do it' about everything routine or dull. Poor thing—a drab bird in a nest of peacocks. But she tries her best to look smart and spends enough on her clothes, I should think, to come to me for them. I'd give her a professional cut besides. Oh, hummm. Nancy Pierce probably told her the Lesbian tale and scared her to death. Come on, let's go up to the peacocks." Susan slid from the bar stool. "No more stalling, my boy. Caroline Semmer is right—it's ridiculous holding up the meeting by dawdling about. As a matter of fact, I should be in my own workshop this moment, scissors in cloth, mouth full of pins."

Tom Benchley sighed, gulped the last of his drink, and with sepulchral mutterings loped at her side. Reaching the corridor, they were turning toward the ballroom elevators when a honeyed voice exclaimed from the Ladies' Room door: "Susan, darling!"

They both turned to face the glamorous Nancy Pierce who was coyly gathering her red fox cape about her, and looking from Susan to Tom with bright demanding eyes.

Inwardly amused, Miss Yates presented Mr. Benchley and watched Nancy's panorama of tricks: her extended hand and slightly withdrawn body, her lashes lowered and as quickly raised in a look of wide-eyed frankness, her almost unnoticeable step nearer to Tom, and childishly uptilted face, the quick intake and expulsion of breath through her nostrils, ending in a rippling laugh.

Alarm written on his face, Tom, as quickly as possible, acknowledged the introduction and backed off. Nancy laughed again, her mouth going at once more soft and more cruel.

Susan thought: "Mouths do give you away," and asked aloud: "Are you going to or from the rehearsal, Nancy?"

Her lips pouting invitingly at Mr. Benchley, Mrs. Pierce said in the tone of a child who has played too long and too hard: "I'm escaping, darling. Simply escaping for a few little moments of peace, hoping someone will buy me a drink and let me see the world has gallant men as well as mad, mad women."

"Well," exclaimed Mr. Benchley hastily, "if you'll excuse me, I must be reporting to your president, Miss Peabody." And he escaped, coattail flying, in the direction of the ballroom elevator rack.

Nancy dropped her pout, also her honeyed tone, and demanded: "Who's the sophomore? The Tomorrow Club's official droop? What a devastating man! I ask you, darling!"

Miss Yates said Tom was going to do the show's publicity, and that he was all right, just in a hurry. Nancy Pierce sighed, murmuring something about "hurry, hurry, hurry, these dreadful American men." Then she expostulated that if Susan also was going to the ballroom she would find the place a "perfectly hideous mess."

Susan said: "Well, if we all concentrate, perhaps we can keep peace and order. After all, we are six adult women, not a class of boarding-school girls."

"That's what you think," snapped Nancy Pierce sharply. "You should have heard Lucinda and her dog howling a while ago. Too, too silly. And Vivian Peabody spent the entire morning shooting looks—nice murderous ones—at poor little me."

With an effort, Susan asked evenly: "Goodness, Nancy, what have you been doing to Vivian?"

"Doing? Don't be quaint, my angel. If a woman can't hold her fiancé, is it my fault? And if Lucinda Mason—a decorator gone stage-mad, if you ask *me*—can't keep the ballroom lights on or off two consecutive seconds, am *I* to blame?"

"Heavens! Man? Lights? What are you talking about, Nancy?"

"I'm trying to tell you. During one of Lucinda Mason's murky moments, when she had simply *all* the lights out, I collided with our august president's fiancé, Colonel Stanley Gamberson. Then the Mason idiot suddenly turned *all* the ballroom lights *on*. Well, all I can say is that Vivian Peabody should have Stanley Gamberson trained to stick to his homework instead of dragging him around places to see *her* being military. Or else," and Mrs. Pierce's vivid blue eyes narrowed, "she should be terribly, terribly sure of herself and him—instead of blindly condescending all over the place. I mean, having a vulgarly large ruby engagement ring isn't having your man all the way to the altar. Not by any means."

Susan sighed. "Oh come," she cried, "Vivian doesn't mean to be condescending. She's a grand gal, Nancy, and a very able president."

Nancy Pierce paid no attention to Susan's interruption. Her eyes still narrowed, she said: "Now that Vivian has finally succeeded in getting a fiancé I suppose she can't resist waving him around in public, hoping everybody will see the 'Don't Touch' tags." Pausing she demanded irrelevantly: "Whatever are you staring at, Susan? Oh, my new fox cape! Divine, isn't it? Of course, if you hadn't been so stingy with little Nancy about commissions, I should probably be coming to *you* for some of my wardrobe—for little things at least." She eyed Miss Yates with enjoyment, and added: "If only to hear your *views*, my lamb. I always say Susan Yates has the *most* interesting views, messing around with all those odd people, and anarchists and all. It's a wonder to me you do manage to keep best families and leading capitalists' wives. I mean, I don't suppose there'd be much money in making clothes for nihilists and people on relief."

Susan counted three, holding her breath, then she said calmly: "Nancy, I'm not an anarchist, nor a nihilist, nor a Lesbian. Please, for the love of heaven, don't go round telling people so."

"Oh," purred Mrs. Pierce, all honey again, "so glad, darling. I'll say you definitely told me you weren't. That is," and she paused thoughtfully, "if you'll tell Vivian the Colonel Gamberson episode this morning was just an accident. I always think that for most people ignorance is such bliss; and actually she looked at me with those superior black eyes of hers simply fiendishly all the rest of the morning. I can't do my best work when people are glaring and glowering. It's too, too silly."

Susan thought: "Well an armed truce is better than none." Aloud she said grimly: "I'll tell her. No use having her peace of mind disturbed either. We have to pull together or we'll never put the show over."

With another purring sound, Nancy murmured: "Dependable Susan. How right you are. Of course, I'm a tremendous believer in co-operation. Simply tremendous." Then she tucked her huge handbag even more tightly under her arm, smiled faintly and added: "Now I really *shall* have to have a drink. Au revoir." She turned and sailed on to the bar entrance. Susan stared after her for a long moment, then hurried toward the ballroom elevators.

CHAPTER TWO

DEPRIVED ON THEIR departure of entertaining whiffs of Susan and Tom's conversation, Mike had looked about for other game in the again nearly deserted bar. Dr. Semmer's whisky sour was still, he noticed, scarcely touched. There was no glass at all before Miss Semmer who had finally sat down apparently both unasked and unwanted. Mike moved solicitously near. Miss Semmer stopped talking, glanced up at him primly and said:

"I'm not drinking anything, thank you."

So Mike had to go away. He took up his stand near the bar, and observed that whatever Miss Semmer was telling her brother did not seem to be improving his disposition. Mike caught a few thin words: "Ballroom . . . testing lights . . . dog . . . such a sweet girl . . . couldn't have been intentional. . . ." But Dr. Semmer's sulkiness continued. A muscle in his cheek began to twitch. Presently the sister stood up, put a fond, ungloved hand tenderly on his shoulder and said loudly enough for Mike to catch: "My, how I've been chattering on! You know I never can gossip about anything with the club members. It wouldn't be diplomatic, you—"

Mike thought Dr. Semmer's interruption didn't make much sense considering the length of time he'd been over one whisky sour. Dr. Semmer was saying with crisp irritation: "People come into bars, Caroline, to drink. If you aren't drinking, there's really no point being here—"

Miss Semmer broke out in a little rash of apologetic murmurs. "But I was just going, dear. I know you probably came in to think

39

over some case and be alone—and—and I only came in to look for
strayed committee members, saw you—and—it was such a pleasant surprise."

"No doubt," the doctor replied peevishly, but she didn't seem
to notice his tone, gave his shoulder another soft pat and started
on her hat-bobbing way back across the room toward the lobby
corridor. There Miss Semmer encountered the blonde young
woman in the red fox cape who had just put a hand on the corridor
side of the chromium-bound glass door. Nancy Pierce pushed the
door open without even seeing Caroline Semmer. Her eyes were
lost in some apparently entertaining thought which had brought a
narrowed curl to her full lips. Miss Semmer slowed up as if weigh-
ing the idea of speaking to her, then apparently decided against it
and disappeared.

The Gallic Lucien remarked to Mike: "Never will their meeting
start, it seems. Here comes another—the job-and-man-snatching-
one Miss Yates and the tall guy talked about."

Mike nodded and pointed out: "She's making for the doc. I
wondered what he was waiting for. But she can't steal him from
nobody. He ain't married." Mike started in pursuit of the blonde's
undoubted order, and over Mrs. Pierce's shoulder got it:

"Manhattan. Hurry it!"

Waiting at the bar for the drink to be mixed, Mike saw that Dr.
Semmer was doing the talking now. The blonde young woman was
taking off her gloves, putting them with her big handbag by her
side, and hunching her shoulders gracefully from under the fox
cape. She wasn't even trying to talk, but was listening with a cool
look as if the doctor was plain funny. Mike approached with the
cocktail and overheard Semmer saying a little frantically:

"Last night at my place, you solemnly promised to give me your
decision today. For God's sake, Nancy, have you no sense of responsibility?"

Paying no attention to the waiter, Nancy Pierce snapped: "You
sound old enough to be my grandfather—just as you did last night.
And let me tell you something: I didn't meet you here to be handed
a behavior program or to be bawled out. Skip it!"

Mike set down the glass and retired a suitable distance, his ears attentive; but to his regret, he had to miss the next half minute of the conversation while taking a wet overcoat from a red-nosed man in tweeds who had just come through the revolving door from Forty-eighth Street. Red Nose took a seat at the bar, and Mike turned to hear the physician saying to the blonde with sudden loudness: "Just leave my profession out of it, will you?"

Nancy Pierce's tone was also strident. "Don't be quaint," she said.

Mike noticed that the square-jawed man and his pretty companion, still seated quietly in the "L" down near the Madison Avenue doors, were peering around, their attention attracted by the raised voices. Then Dr. Semmer pushed the table back angrily and stood up. For a long moment he stood looking down at the blonde woman, bitterness sharp in his eyes. He slammed his hat on his head, then, and without waiting to pay his check, grabbed up his coat and stalked out of the Forty-eighth Street door. Mike stood hesitant. Red Nose at the bar had turned around to stare, too. The blonde girl rolled her eyes at him as if she might start crying; but Mike decided that wasn't likely. After a second, this opinion was borne out. The young woman, with a pretty pouting expression, rose and walked up to the bar where she slid onto a stool next a startled Red Nose. But she said so confidingly: "In a foul mood, wasn't he?" that the tweed-clad man unbent a little.

Quickly the blonde followed up this slight advantage. "You're Ethan Van Weck, Lucinda Mason's husband, aren't you? I'm Nancy Pierce—another Tomorrower, alas? Shall I have a cocktail with you until my poor face stops being red?" It was, Mike saw, not red at all. She laughed like a nice-sounding bell while Red Nose fumbled with his tie, cleared his throat, looked into her uptilted blue eyes and succumbed.

"Most c-certainly, my d-dear young woman," he stammered. "Quite. B-bartender, something for this little lady to drink."

Nancy ordered another manhattan, and Lucien and Mike exchanged covert glances meaning: "Pickups not allowed in the Hotel Eden—but what can we do?" Then Lucien shrugged, deciding the morality of the situation lay in the fact that the young woman knew the Old One's wife. Hadn't he with his own ears heard Miss Mason none too flatteringly confirm this? But, as he prepared the drink, Lucien kept an alert ear on the conversation thenceforth led by the blonde.

Meanwhile, Mike saw that the couple at the other end of the room were showing activity. The man motioned sharply for his check. Mike went over with it. Square Jaw seemed suddenly in a big hurry. He didn't wait for change, but slapped some bills on the tray, said: "Oke," and rushed off out one of the Madison Avenue doors. His companion lingered, however, fooling around with a lipstick and then her compact. She adjusted her furs, then put some more lipstick on. Mike's attention was thus annoyingly divided between the pair at the bar and the girl who might turn out to expect the change to be brought to her. Sometimes dames did after a gent had left. You couldn't be sure.

At this moment, the door from the corridor swung open and the hesitant figure of Dr. Semmer's sister reappeared. She looked nearsightedly in the direction of the divan where her brother had been sitting. Indecisively, she crossed the room, stopping just short of the table in apparent surprise at finding him no longer there. But she went on up to the table, stooped down and began looking for something apparently under it. Before Mike could reach her, she came up, grasping a pair of black gloves.

"Thank you," Miss Semmer replied to his offer of help, "I found them." She started back across the room straightening the fingers of her gloves absent-mindedly. But as she came abreast of Nancy's and Van Weck's backs, Ethan chortled loudly over something the girl had said, and Miss Semmer glanced at him primly. At that instant, Nancy whirled round on her stool gesturing with her cocktail glass, spied Caroline, and exclaimed a little shrilly: "Now don't be too, too silly, Carry, and tell me I should be up at that hideous meeting. I'm fed up with the damn place, and I'm having fun here!"

Miss Semmer glanced from Nancy to Van Weck, hesitated before his rude stare and flushing, said sedately: "But I didn't know you *weren't* upstairs, Mrs. Pierce. I just came in for some gloves I'd dropped—and I'm sure—"

Nancy yawned audibly, glanced disinterestedly at Caroline's apologetically outstretched hands and dismissed the matter by saying: "Well, I scarcely suspected it was your garters." She turned back to Van Weck, laughing provocatively.

Caroline Semmer hesitated a brief second, flushing over Mrs. Pierce's remark, and giving Van Weck's back a disapproving look of sudden recognition. Then she turned and hurried away, her hat bobbing futilely.

The girl at the Madison Avenue end of the room was standing up when Mike turned around. She hesitated a moment, glanced at her watch and sat down once more, choosing a position that gave her a better view of the bar. Catching Mike's eyes she signaled, and he went to her suspecting the worst about the change, but she said pleasantly: "Bring me a straight whisky and a glass of water. Here, pay the check for it at the same time, please. I'll be going right afterwards." She put money on the table. Mike beamed and went off. The girl in the sables pulled her round felt hat a little lower over her eyes. From under it she watched the tableau between Nancy and Van Weck. With narrowed eyes she observed Mrs. Pierce permit the man to order her another drink. Mike was bringing the straight whisky across the room, when Nancy slipped from her stool and crossed to the divan where her lavish fox cape advertised its owner's somewhat dramatic chic. She reached for her handbag and drew from it a small, flat, white box returning with it in her hand to the bar counter. There she opened it and showed its content to her red-nosed companion.

Mike delivered his order and came back to the bar. When he reached it, he glanced back at the young woman in the distant corner. Her whisky glass was empty and, adjusting her sables, the girl was just going out one of the Madison Avenue doors.

CHAPTER THREE

SUSAN WAS STILL SMILING wryly over her conversation with Nancy Pierce when the elevator deposited her on the top floor of the Hotel Eden. There, waiting for a down elevator, was Hortense Culbertson, the pretty radio commentator. She was looking her best in black-and-yellow tweeds with a tiny sailor hat decorated with little-girl ribbons that hung down her back. "Poor Tom!" thought Susan, and said: "Hello, Hortense. Are you fleeing from the holocaust?"

"I'm fresh out of cigarettes," smiled Miss Culbertson. "Was just going down to the lobby for some. Have you any?"

Investigating her handbag, Susan said: "Not one. I'll go down with you." Ashamed of herself, she thought it would be a good opportunity to discover what effect Tom's appearance had had on Hortense. But while they had nearly five minutes of privacy waiting for the ballroom elevator to come up again, Hortense prettily refused to be pumped. When they reached the lobby floor Miss Culbertson stopped suddenly and said: "Susan, get me a tin of Chesterfields, will you? I think I'll dash into the Ladies' for a moment." She disappeared and Susan went on to the cigarette counter to make her purchases. Then she walked up and down the corridor waiting for Hortense. Pausing at the Madison Avenue end on one of her jaunts back and forth, Susan looked out upon the bleak day. At that moment, Lucinda Mason strode past led by an eager G. B. straining on his leash. Susan turned and sauntered back, looking through the glass door of the bar as she passed it. Caroline Semmer was standing at the bar talking to Nancy Pierce and a man in casual tweeds. With a start of amusement Susan recognized the man as Ethan Van Weck, Lucinda Mason's husband, and wondered if Lucinda, marching square-shouldered and determined in the slush outside, knew that her Ethan was cocktailing with the Yellow Peril of the fashion world. Then Caroline Semmer turned and came out of the bar, her face flushed, and holding tightly her pair of black gloves. "Miss Yates!" exclaimed Miss Semmer stopping short. "Are you still down here? I thought you had gone upstairs. Oh, dear, we'll never get the meeting started."

"So sorry, Caroline. We're an unreliable committee, aren't we? I did go up, though. Came back with Miss Culbertson for some cigarettes. I'm waiting for her now; but we'll be right up."

Miss Semmer looked at her with patient reproval etched on her face, then broke into a trot toward the elevators, calling "Up!" in her tremulous voice as the doors threatened to close. They did close but behind Miss Semmer's chunky figure just as Hortense Culbertson emerged from the Ladies' Room.

"Come on!" urged Susan. "I've just been delicately chastised by Carry Semmer for not being at the meeting." As they hurried on, Susan glanced at Mr. Benchley's former fiancée and noticed with amusement that although Miss Culbertson had been impersonal and noncommittal on the subject of Tom's predicted presence at the luncheon meeting, she had just given her complexion a thorough going-over.

Upstairs, the famous Eden ballroom was looking tired and tawdry, its mirrors and gilt unreal as a woman in evening clothes at high noon. A long wooden runway for the fashion promenade of their show bisected the room. Workmen in overalls were setting up painted cardboard sets on the stage. Just behind the footlights, a striking, dark-eyed woman in black and white was waving at Susan and the radio commentator. It was Vivian Peabody, the club's president, Colonel Gamberson's fine ruby sparkling on one of her justly celebrated white hands. Miss Peabody's voice sounded melodiously imperious, and annoyed in an Olympian fashion. "Come along you two—we want to start the meeting over luncheon right away." Her black eyes were impatient.

To the right of the stage, and some distance from it, a white-covered table was laid for seven. A waiter was making preparations to serve a plate luncheon which one glance assured Susan was guaranteed to be nonfattening. Tom Benchley stood at the table gazing down upon the waiter's delicate preparations in evident disapproval. Without raising his eyes as Susan and Hortense Culbertson came up, he asked rather loudly: "Is that sawdust or seaweed?" But this effort at banter failed him as he looked up and met Miss Culbertson's eyes. "Hello. How are you?" he mumbled. Miss Culbertson was trying to make her cameo face look casual.

"Very well, thank you," she said. "How are you, Tom?"

Interrupting this, Miss Peabody, her black eyes still impatient, came up and took a seat, saying: "Everyone! Please sit down." Miss Semmer slipped modestly into a chair opposite the club President across the round table. Susan dropped down on the chair nearest her, and Tom came hastily around the table to sit on her left. Hortense Culbertson seated herself on the other side of Miss Semmer. In a second, Lucinda Mason came striding in behind G. B. and slipping into the place between the radio commentator and Miss Peabody, announced:

"Sorry I'm late. It started raining again while I was walking G. B. Had to take him into the Ladies' and dry him off with paper towels. Poor lamb, he catches cold so easily." She placed the Pomeranian on the floor by her side, detached his leash, and fed him a lump of sugar.

Miss Peabody demanded of the table at large: "Where is Nancy Pierce?"

Susan replied: "Having a quick one in the bar, I believe. Let's not wait for her. I for one am starved." The luncheon party settled down to scattered talk. Conversation ran on handsomely from the subject of whether Lucinda Mason, with her decorator's lavishness, was not letting the club in for too much expense with her stage-sets to why on earth Hortense Culbertson, who was doing the script, wanted a desert scene instead of a ski slide; then back again through a gamut of complaints, countercomplaints, "divines" and "simply ghastlies."

Some minutes later into the midst of this, Nancy Pierce made a languorous entrance, and sat down between Miss Peabody and Susan Yates.

Susan said: "Hello." Everyone else eyed Mrs. Pierce with much the same cordiality which would be accorded a precocious infant at a debutante dance. The waiter brought Nancy her plate of non-fattening luncheon. She took her time about arranging herself; put her handbag on the table in front of her plate, slipped out of her fox cape with the waiter's aid; made arch motions with her shoulders and finally nibbled a bit of food languidly. Presently, arousing herself from this self-conscious pose, she spoke in Susan's ear. "What's happening? Have we decided anything?"

"No," said Susan. "Just a brave communal effort for which, thank heaven, my social consciousness prepares me."

"Really?" exclaimed Mrs. Pierce. "*I* didn't know you were a so-cialite." She brightened perceptibly. Susan gave her a sidelong glance of amused disgust. Nancy was looking around the table, and apparently finding that no one was paying the slightest attention, lowered her voice and said: "It actually never occurred to me before. I suppose you're from the Nelson Yates family?"

"He was my grandfather," Susan answered with blunt brevity.

Nancy cooed. "Then, darling, you can tell me if Ethan Van Weck is in the Social Register."

This demand struck Susan as so disgustingly tasteless that she promptly considered it unasked. But it took her thoughts to the green-eyed Lucinda, dog adorer, and talented decorator, whom she had known for many years. She knew all about Lucinda's tedious acquisition of a credible culture; knew that her big bones indicated strong stock if not a gentle line of ancestors. She knew that the well-born Ethan had found it a very comfortable arrangement to marry the financially successful decorator and have his debts and mortgages paid off. It was true that Ethan was not resplendently bright, but in family ways he had been useful luster for the ambitious Lucinda; more an institution, perhaps, than a husband, like acquiring a piece of the Hall of Fame or part of the Morgan Library. And what of it? Lucinda had an advantage over many people. She always knew exactly what she wanted. Susan neither particularly liked nor at all disliked her. If she was dedicated heart and soul to a complete career, she was but another human being in a world where weakness rarely seemed an asset.

Looking up, Susan caught Nancy's eyes on her curiously. "I asked you a question, dearest. You've been looking as if you were sailing over Mount Everest or something."

"Have I?" smiled Susan, suddenly realizing that perhaps the world had to have its quota of Nancy Pierces too; only Nancy Pierces grabbed, and Lucinda Masons worked hard every step of their way.

Nancy pouted. "I asked you about Ethan Van Weck. Is he in the Social Register?"

"You put me," murmured Susan, "in the awkward position of saying I can't see what earthly difference it makes, but, yes, he is." She looked away for a moment, then continued without change of tone. "There's a very fine exhibit of jewel settings at the Metropolitan Museum just now. It would interest you, I think."

Nancy, not missing the inference, looked momentarily deflated; but this exceptional mood of accepting reproval passed, and she snapped inelegantly: "I'm frying other fish at the moment." Then, as if to prove her determination to accept no social spanking from Susan, she returned to the subject of Mr. Van Weck, and explained with loquacious detail what she termed his rescue of her from an idiotic episode with Dr. Linwood Semmer.

Susan was only half listening, but it occurred to her to glance across the table to see if Lucinda Mason could hear Nancy's rambling conversation. But Miss Mason appeared to be absorbed in some attractive opinions of her own which she was pouring into Vivian Peabody's right ear. In Susan's ear Mrs. Pierce's tone grew suddenly confidential: "Imagine! He just walked out on me! Men can be such a nuisance. Of course, when Linwood brought me through pneumonia last year I—my husband and I were terribly appreciative; but my dear he's so childish! That's his dear sister Caroline's doing. She's always babied him to death. Well, he was being particularly dull this morning. Finally, I said: 'My dear man, don't go on this way with *me*. Go and tell it at the Park Avenue bedsides.' And it made him simply livid." Nancy paused to scrutinize Susan a moment, and observed: "I don't suppose you've studied men the way I have; but I don't see anything atrocious in saying *that!* But it made him simply go up like a rocket, yipping about my leaving his profession out of it. Can you *imagine?* Then, my dear, he walked right out of the bar without so much as paying his check." She laughed unexpectedly and nastily. "Poor old Caroline would sleep better tonight if she'd seen it—her precious itsy baby brother saved from wicked married woman!"

Susan had to admit to herself that Nancy was an outrageous mimic. She had sounded exactly like Caroline Semmer. Then her tone changed suddenly to competent brittleness, and she said darkly: "Not that he won't be mooning round again at the snap of a finger."

Fortuitously, their president's voice spoke to the table at large in commanding tone. "We must start conferring as we eat, or we'll never finish. Hortense Culbertson is trying to tell us something about the script for Scene I." Miss Peabody pounded with her fork.

Immediately the general buzz of conversation began again. The radio commentator rustled some papers and her cameo face looked annoyed. Vivian Peabody pounded once more with her fork. Spottily, the conversations subsided, some left in midair, others ebbing into whispering retreat. Then came a dead silence—of the kind which proclaimed itself but a hiatus, Susan thought.

The silence was short lived. Squaring her broad shoulders, and laughing, Lucinda Mason caroled: "Our famous suspended-motion act!"

"Please!" chided Miss Peabody turning to the decorator at her side.

Carefully not looking at Mr. Benchley, Hortense Culbertson began. "Who and for what purpose suggested 'On the Wheel of Fashion' as the show's title? That's what I want to talk about."

Caroline Semmer was referring to some shorthand notes beside her plate. Clearing her throat she said; "Mrs. Pierce suggested it, I believe." Miss Culbertson's pretty face continued to look annoyed, and Lucinda Mason's green eyes narrowed as she glared around at Nancy Pierce. Lucinda said she didn't see how one could be *on* a wheel of fashion or any kind of wheel. Indignantly, Mrs. Pierce pointed out that you could be on a bicycle. Wasn't that a wheel? Or a Ferris wheel!

President Peabody reminded her frigidly that they weren't using Ferris wheels or bicycles.

"We could," insisted Nancy, "as easily as some of the other stupid props Hortense has lined up; and if we want to call it 'On the Wheel—'"

"We don't. At least I don't," broke in Lucinda Mason decisively and Susan caught her regarding Nancy Pierce again as if she were a worm on a pin.

Then everyone began talking at once. Susan glanced at Tom to see how he was taking their committee meeting and found the tall young man's eyes staring at Hortense Culbertson with a transfixed expression of infatuation. Suddenly he glanced past Susan to Mrs. Pierce, and his look, like a new stereopticon slide, became a very different one filled with determined resentment.

Vivian Peabody held up the long-fingered hand on which Colonel Gamberson's ruby sparkled and said energetically to the waiter standing at interested attention: "You need not wait. Leave water and glasses, please, and go." The waiter bowed, expeditiously conformed and withdrew with obvious regret.

Miss Semmer's apologetic voice was saying: "I had thought 'Skirting Fashion' might be nice because of the interest in skirts this year."

"That's cute!" shouted Lucinda Mason in the presidential ear. "Vivian, did you hear what Caroline suggested? It's darling, don't you think? Oh, didn't you hear? Caroline suggested 'Skirting Fashion.' Not bad, is it?"

But what Miss Peabody thought was lost to Susan in the general renewal of conversations. At last, however, with only Nancy Pierce hotly dissenting, they decided that just "Skirts" was an amusing *double entendre* and competent title for the show.

Irritably, Nancy began to dig about in the vastness of her chic handbag. Eying her, Lucinda Mason wanted to know if she was looking for smelling salts.

"Lucinda, my sweet," murmured Mrs. Pierce still scratching around in her bag, "do compound jokes with more of a point."

Unexpectedly, Caroline Semmer said: "Dear me, it wasn't a joke. It was a jibe, I should think." Everybody but Nancy laughed at so untypical a *bon mot* from their frumpy secretary. That broke the tension momentarily; but Nancy Pierce interrupted their laughter to demand of herself aloud: "Now where in hell did I put those capsules?"

Hortense Culbertson's precise and liquid radio voice revived the air of irritation by asking too sweetly: "Do you take your vitamin capsules for anemia, my dear?"

At that moment and with some ceremony, Mrs. Pierce brought forth from her handbag a flat, square box, setting it on the table before her. "No," she answered Hortense, "but you'll find them awfully good for it."

Temperately Susan asked what the capsules were, and Nancy explained that they were made of cod-liver oil and were excellent for making you feel fit all winter.

Also conciliatory, Caroline Semmer's thin voice murmured: "Probably I should take them—I've really been feeling so tired lately." She peered shortsightedly across the table at the box. "But they look so enormous. How do you manage to swallow them, Mrs. Pierce?"

"Heavens! It's no trick. Quite simple, really," Nancy added with more elegance and then, immediately forgetting the elegance, said in a scoffing tone: "They look bigger than they feel."

"Might I try one?" asked Caroline Semmer timidly. "If I bought a whole box and then couldn't get them down—"

Everyone laughed, and Nancy pushed the box across the table saying: "Sure. Go ahead." Miss Semmer reached for it and studied the label. Then she took a capsule, put it gingerly in her mouth, and swallowed it down with a gulp of water. Beaming at Nancy, she said: "Why, it's not difficult at all. Thank you so much. I shall certainly have to get some right away." She closed the box tidily and handed it back.

Pleased at the attention thus settled on herself, Nancy opened the box again and with her index finger proceeded to count aloud: "One, two, three!" Picking up the third capsule, she placed it between her scarlet lips and swallowed it with the aid of her glass of water. She replaced the glass on the table with a typically studied gesture of rhythmic motion, closed the box and put it back in her handbag.

Susan thought: "What a graceful fool she is!" and aloud asked Nancy if she always went through the counting ceremonial when choosing a dose. "My goodness," she said, "there must be two dozen capsules to ponder about. Why the third? What is it, obi and black magic?"

Nancy Pierce shrugged. "Oh, you realists; always convinced that anyone having a pet superstition must be mad."

"Not at all," smiled Susan. "Man is born to superstitions. Something about race memories. I was just curious."

Nancy became affable. "It's an old Persian belief—or Parisian, I forget which. A chant, they called it. 'Third from the end, puts you on the mend!' Only I take the third from the beginning. It's easier. Anyway, I'm practically never sick and I've taken pills and things that way for ages. So there you are. There might be something in it!"

Lucinda Mason, listening from across the table, rose saying nastily: "But, of course, you've got to know how to count." She came around the table and looked over Nancy's shoulder at the box lid. "Derived from halibut livers," she read stentoriously. "Listen, everybody. Each capsule contains not less than 8500 Vitamin A units and 145 Vitamin D units. They are soluble in—"

"The stomach, we hope," Tom Benchley muttered at Susan's side.

"Oh, hush, everyone," commanded Vivian Peabody. "This isn't a kindergarten. We are trying to settle something important. If you girls don't stop private conversations—and clowning—we might as well call the meeting off."

Lucinda subsided. "I'm sorry. You're right," she agreed amiably. "Only, according to our cod liver expert," and she eyed Nancy's back speculatively before leaving it, "vitamins *are* really vital." Someone at the table emitted a feverish laugh, and Susan, who was powdering her nose, looked up quickly. No one appeared at that moment in the least amused. Lucinda was going back to her place looking suddenly thoughtful, murmuring: "Vitamins are vital," as if it were an idea for a decorative scheme. Susan turned her attention to her vanity case and pondered: "Now that was queer. Somebody laughed as if she were about to have a nice, old-fashioned attack of hysterics. And then nothing happens. We must have a member with a secret cod-liver oil phobia. I believe I've got a phobia myself about this meeting. I don't like the edgy nerves around this table. Ballrooms are built for midnight parties, lights, laughter; not a lot of overtired females at high noon." She regarded herself wryly in the vanity's mirror, then put it away, and with effort brought her attention back to the table. President Vivian Peabody was saying decisively, and with evident irony, "Then, since no one has any special fault to find with 'Skirts,' suppose we consider it the working title. Mr. Benchley can use it in his publicity."

"And what if we change it? What if we get a really brilliant idea?" Nancy wanted to know.

"Then," explained Miss Peabody with restraint, "Mr. Benchley can get out another news release saying we've renamed the show— as they often do in the theater. You could do that easily, couldn't you, Mr. Benchley?"

"Good idea, matter of fact. Get two stories instead of one out of it," Tom acquiesced with heartiness.

"Exactly," said Miss Peabody. "And now we can get to the sets. Lucinda, will you show us Scene One?"

Lucinda Mason said: "Very simple. It's all set up. But the lighting is what is important." She raised her voice and called: "Electrician! Lights for Scene One, please."

A man's voice called hoarsely and unintelligibly from backstage, and the ballroom lights blinked and went out. The stage was still well lighted, but after another brief delay, its lights were lowered.

For a moment, the entire room and stage were in darkness. Then gradually a ruddy glow of muted radiance began to appear on the distant backdrop, increasing very slowly in intensity. The background displayed a desert with one palm tree dimly outlined in an expanse of sand.

"The sun is supposed to rise now," Lucinda Mason whispered, "but they haven't quite got the hang of it yet. Just be patient."

Through the inkiness at the table, Susan faintly heard the same brief, hysterical laugh she had heard before. But in the darkness everyone was talking at once with familiar argumentativeness, and again she could not locate the sound.

Somewhere under the table G. B. began to whine, and she could hear Lucinda saying: "Hush, baby." At the same moment, Susan felt against her hands, lying clasped on the tablecloth, a slight vibration, as if some object had been dropped on the table. It was not repeated, and, her eyes on the stage, she presumed that someone had raised and set down again the water jug left by the waiter.

At that moment, while the ballroom itself remained blanketed in darkness, two things happened: the footlights came on vividly, illuminating only the stage, and one of the workmen began to pound a nail somewhere backstage. Conversation momentarily ceased while they concentrated even more closely on the stage arrangement. In the pause, Susan realized afterward, she had heard, close at hand, an odd gurgling sound, but at the time she put it down again to the water jug and someone pouring a drink. The footlights went out, throwing the stage again into darkness, and then, in the background, a tropical sun began to rise. The man with the hammer stopped pounding.

Except for G. B.'s intermittent whining, there was no sound for a minute until Lucinda Mason said through the blackness "How do you all like it?"

"Grand!" Vivian Peabody and Hortense Culbertson assured her in unison, and pleased murmurs were repeated around the table. The general amiability was too marked not to be suspicious, Susan thought, and said aloud:

"I think it's quite lovely, Lucinda."

Vivian Peabody added, rather extravagantly for her: "Lucinda, You've really done a good job with it."

"Realer than real," commented Mr. Benchley.

Susan became oddly, alertly conscious that Nancy Pierce was remaining remarkably quiet; and Nancy always at least had a criticism to make. The lights on the stage were growing a little stronger causing a faint glow to spread over the luncheon table. Susan turned to Nancy. Then with a quick intake of her breath, she called across the table to Lucinda.

"Lucinda! Lights! Nancy seems to have fainted."

"What?" cried Miss Mason incredulously, then she shouted to the distant electrician: "Lights. Lights!"

In a second illumination came in a sudden, brash glare. Susan saw sprawled on the table at her right a golden head and a white hand and wrist. Nancy's other arm was flung out toward Miss Peabody.

For a second, there was complete cessation of sound around the table, then gasps and a babble of incoherent, questioning voices. Susan, pushing back her chair, stood up to lean over Nancy. The girl's cheek pressed against the tablecloth was as white as it, and her mouth gaped unnaturally.

CHAPTER FOUR

"W HAT ON EARTH 's the matter with her?" Lucinda Mason demanded shrilly, and got to her feet, clasping the back of her chair.

Hortense Culbertson gasped and leaned forward, as though hypnotized by the sight. Her eyes then turned, unconsciously, to Tom Benchley across the table. He returned her look for a long moment, and muttered: "Don't be frightened, Horty. She's probably just fainted." He pushed his chair back from the table, said: "I'll get a doctor," and ran for the door.

Susan glanced on around the table to where Caroline Semmer's trim figure sat as if riveted to her chair, her eyes staring unbelievingly at the prostrate form. Looking at her, Susan had a sudden foolish desire to see herself in a mirror, but abandoned so ridiculous an idea, and turned her attention to Lucinda Mason, who, her interesting green eyes bright and startled, was saying:

"Good heavens! Is she sick? Or is she just trying to attract attention again?" Susan realized that from where Lucinda sat, she could not see the gaping mouth.

For the first time in the history of the Tomorrow Club, you could have heard a pin drop. Then Vivian Peabody, who had been staring at Nancy as though she were in a trance, rose quickly to her feet. Vivian's black eyes looked disturbed and somehow angry in their inscrutable depths. Susan remembered with queer intensity that Vivian hated to see women place themselves in a weak position, hated any exhibition of frailty in females. Certainly there was nothing sympathetic in Vivian's stiff, erect figure as she put a tentative hand on the still shoulder.

Tom Benchley came running back, calling, "The doctor's coming—is she any better?" For a full moment, no one answered. Then Hortense Culbertson cried frantically: "She looks *dead!*"

Benchley came over to Nancy, peered at her and then said in an odd tone: "Hell. Better not touch her, Miss Peabody." They all stared with their various expressions of startled anxiety at the still form. At Benchley's peremptory command, Miss Peabody stopped trying to rouse the girl, looking somehow surprised at herself for obeying so readily.

Susan wanted a drink badly. She stretched out her hand for an untouched glass of water on the table. Someone—it was Vivian—slapped her wrist away from it, and Benchley said: "I wouldn't touch that. You don't know what's—affected Mrs. Pierce. Maybe something she's eaten or drunk off this table."

Lucinda Mason shrieked hysterically: "Eaten or drunk—"

"Stop that, Lucinda," commanded Miss Peabody, regaining control of her masterfulness. She turned to Tom, drew him aside, and forming the words with tense lips, said: "We mustn't lose our heads, Mr. Benchley! Is the doctor coming at once?"

Tom, whose eyes had returned to Hortense Culbertson, nodded. "A waiter went right off to get him," he told Miss Peabody.

Susan glanced at Hortense. She was staring at Tom, her eyes touched with a queer mixture of fright and affection.

"Queer time to patch up a lovers' quarrel," Susan thought, "but good heavens, they certainly have." She looked down at the still figure, her eyes traveling from the head to the feet. Its supreme stillness, its awkward position, both so unlike Nancy Pierce, were, it occurred to her, terrifying in the way that all unaccountable happenings are; terrifying not so much in themselves as because the beholder cannot comprehend their cause.

Lucinda Mason was now saying: "God!" for the third time, as if repetition would some way help. Caroline Semmer rose suddenly from her position of frozen surprise, hesitated a moment, and then walked around the table with unusual determination, saying wildly to no one in particular: "Goodness! Why doesn't someone *do* something!"

She went around Susan, circling the frighteningly quiet figure of Nancy Pierce. Susan made way for her. Still muttering to no one in particular, Caroline Semmer was saying: "It's *insane*, not *doing* anything. We don't know how *soon* the doctor will come."

Before Benchley, whose back was turned, could stop her, Miss Semmer leaned down and began tugging at the inert shoulders—like a frail mother trying to lift quite a big child, Susan thought. Her efforts suddenly brought Nancy upright, shoulders back against the chair. Seeing the gaping mouth and staring eyes, Lucinda Mason shrieked again and Caroline began rubbing Nancy's white hands. Benchley, turning at Lucinda's shriek, commanded: "Stop that, Miss Semmer. Wait till the doctor comes."

Caroline turned hurt, determined eyes to him, and almost in a whisper insisted: "It isn't human not to do *anything*."

Fortunately, at that moment, one of the ballroom doors burst open to admit a suave little man with a black bag, and behind him a gentleman in morning coat and striped trousers.

While the doctor placed his bag on the floor and began his examination, the man in the morning coat—the hotel manager—made clicking noises in his throat and soothing gestures with his hands. Susan, watching the doctor, saw him let a limp wrist fall, and gently push Nancy's eyelids up. Then, with an oddly final motion, he smoothed them down again. Straightening, he looked around the circle. It was then Susan noticed that his eyes, bright like a bantam rooster's, were wary and quick in his inspection of their faces, although his attitude was in the Eden's impeccable tradition. When he spoke it occurred to her as being ridiculous that he managed to make his words sound in such excellent taste. Still eying them he said: "This young woman has not fainted. She is dead." And then apologetically: "Shocking. Shocking."

Hortense screamed, and Susan felt her own breath catching in her lungs and coming out in uneven gasps. The hotel manager came around the table, hands fluttering. "Most unfortunate. So many cases of heart failure these days," he said pacifyingly. The doctor pulled down his cuffs. "This young woman has been poisoned. I must notify the police," he announced in a more businesslike tone.

LATER, WHEN SUSAN tried to remember exactly what everyone had said in the ensuing babel of voices, she found she couldn't. Imbedded, however, in her memory was a recollection of the doctor stepping back purposefully from the corpse, and the hotel manager stooping and picking up a white paper from the floor at Nancy's feet. Vivian Peabody and Tom Benchley had both reached out for it.

"What's that? Let me see it," Vivian had commanded, taking the paper from the hotel manager's hand. Tom had leaned over her shoulder as she had read what was written on it. Then there had appeared in Vivian's eyes a suddenly weary expression. Tom's eyes had held a curious expression, too. Immediately, Lucinda Mason had grabbed the paper, and from her it had traveled around the table. When it had reached Susan, she had been dumfounded to find it a typewritten note saying:

> I am a thief. Whatever the reasons that drove me to it, I admit that I have committed a crime. This is the only way to save myself from being handed over to the police.

CHAPTER FIVE

TOGETHER IN AN inappropriately elaborate jade and gold reception room off the ballroom, the five women and Mr. Benchley were waiting. Mr. Benchley was pacing the floor. They did not entirely know what they were waiting for; something, muttered by the police inspector, about "necessary evidence at the time of a sudden death." After the confusion of the doctor's tasteful announcement that Nancy was dead, and the subsequent discovery by the hotel manager of the typewritten note, the hotel's representatives, while continuing to distribute an air of deepest sympathy, had nevertheless become very efficient in standing unobtrusive guard over the corpse until the ambulance doctor and police followed by the medical examiner had arrived. Then Police Inspector Beller, after a few cursory questions, had glanced at their distinguished attire and ushered them into the jade and gold room. At the open door a policeman lounged, one attentive but approving eye on them; one on what was going on outside in the ballroom. They could see only each other, and for a second time in the history of the Tomorrow Club no one seemed inclined toward conversation.

Suddenly, Mr. Benchley stopped his pacing. He addressed Miss Peabody: "As your publicity man I ought to be doing something—I ought at least to be making this as little unpleasant as possible. If they'd only let me at a telephone, I could call a friend of mine— Lyle Curtis, an assistant district attorney. I don't know whether he would come into a case like this officially or not—but, well, he's a gentleman as well as a very smart egg, and—"

Miss Peabody eyed him and made a crisp gesture with the hand that bore Colonel Gamberson's sparkling ruby. "We could demand our lawyers if we were being put to real—ah—inconvenience. I suppose there's a certain necessary routine in cases of suicide." She eyed Mr. Benchley again as if speculating on the efficiency of any suggestion of his, then turned to the others and inquired: "Would the rest of you like to have Mr. Benchley get this Mr. Curtis up here—just in case there's to be an investigation or anything of the sort? We don't want the club's name dragged around in police courts, of course."

No one objected or for that matter especially agreed, but there was a general murmur of accepting the Curtis idea as not objectionable, and Tom went up to the policeman at the door and made his request. The policeman shrugged then turned toward the ballroom.

"Sam," he bawled, "tell the inspector—" Sam apparently drew nearer because they couldn't hear the rest which was a loud mumble. Tom stuck his head out of the door, and more loud mumbling followed. Then heavy feet moved away. Tom brought his head back into the room and the policeman returned to his strategic position.

"They'll call him," Tom said. "I'm not allowed near a telephone." He came to the center of the room, lowered his voice and added, jerking his head over his shoulder: "Howard Pierce has arrived."

"Poor Mr. Pierce," moaned Caroline Semmer, "how terrible for him. Is he very distressed?"

Benchley dropped into a chair next to Hortense Culbertson and said: "He looks more mad than anything else. Seems to be disagreeing with the inspector over something—over the suicide note, it looked to me."

"Well, it at least is clear," said Vivian Peabody firmly.

"I," said Susan reflectively, "don't find it clear at all. It seems so unlike Nancy."

"Not at all," sniffed Lucinda Mason, her green eyes thoughtful. "I should think that Nancy, in contemplation of the Great Beyond, would find only two things to regret: that shades, presumably,

cannot exercise sex appeal; and that she would have to stop talking. A suicide note would be her way of keeping on talking after
she was dead. I don't know what she'd do about the other. . . ." and
Lucinda lapsed into sudden, uncomfortable silence. Mr. Howard
Pierce had appeared in the doorway.

He did indeed, thought Susan, look more angry than bereaved.
His hard, square jaw was set in stern lines, white against the angry flush of his cheeks; and his strong, predatory nose loomed
above a mouth set thin with displeasure and doubt. With a curt
gesture, he cut short the murmur of condolences that greeted him,
and said:

"All of you feel all right?" They gaped at him, and he went on
impatiently: "You're not sick? You feel well? That damn fool hotel
manager is trying to make me believe it was an accident. If it was,
then one of you may have been poisoned too." Hortense Culbertson
gasped and then subsided into a look of white-faced terror as Vivian
Peabody sent her a stern glance.

"I feel quite well, though naturally upset," said Vivian, who
looked perfectly calm. "None of the rest of us seems to be ill." She
surveyed them all with an imperious look that dared them to be sick.

"Did you all have exactly the same lunch Nancy had?" demanded Mr. Pierce.

"We must have," said Lucinda Mason. "It was a plate lunch—
we didn't order from a bill of fare. Unless Nancy ordered something special . . . ?"

"No," said Vivian firmly. "I sat next to her and I saw what she
was eating. It was exactly what the rest of us had—only she hardly
touched hers."

"Might it not have been something she ate earlier in the day,
perhaps?" asked Miss Semmer tremulously.

"Apparently not," said Howard Pierce. "According to the doctor, and to the story you all have told of how suddenly she died,
she must have taken poison at lunch." Hortense Culbertson moaned,
and Tom whispered:

"Buck up, darling—you're all right."

"Oh," said Susan suddenly, "but of course—I knew there was something . . ."

Howard Pierce whirled around. "What?"

"She took a capsule after lunch," said Susan slowly. "That was something no one else had."

"Except Caroline," Lucinda reminded her. They all turned to Caroline Semmer with the slow motion of suspended thought. Caroline flushed, then grew pale, and fluttered her hands.

"Oh, dear," she whispered, "do you think—oh, dear—I—I think I'd like a glass of water." Tom Benchley leaped for the door and shouted "Doctor!" Susan hurried over to Caroline and took her hand. "There," she said, as though speaking to a child, "you're all right—I'm sure you're all right." Hortense was staring at Caroline as though she were seeing a ghost. Vivian and Lucinda peered over Susan's shoulder and conferred in low tones.

The medical examiner appeared in the doorway with the inspector at his heels.

"What's the trouble?" snapped the inspector.

Susan rose from her knees and said: "I just remembered that Mrs. Pierce took a capsule after lunch—which was the one thing she had the rest of us didn't have—except Miss Semmer. She had one of Mrs. Pierce's capsules. She's mostly frightened, I think."

The medical examiner was taking Caroline's pulse; then he bent and lifted her eyelids gently, as Susan had seen the hotel doctor do with Nancy.

"Feel any nausea?" he asked. Caroline shook her head. "Any pain? Any burning in the stomach? No? Well, then, you're probably all right." Caroline Semmer sat, white and trembling, looking at him like a frightened dog. He gave her a closer look and said: "We'll give you something anyway, just to make sure, and so you'll not be anxious." Crossing the room he spoke to the hotel manager: "Get me some baking soda, half a dozen limes and some castile soap," he said. "And let me have an empty room and bath." Returning to Caroline, he half lifted her from her chair with one hand under her elbow, and propelled her gently to the door, saying:

"Have I your permission, Inspector?" The inspector nodded, and asked: "Could it have been the capsule?"

"Might have been," the medical examiner said tersely, hunching one shoulder toward the ballroom. "No sense taking any chances with this lady. Will you want her again? Well, I'll bring her back as soon as I can—though she ought to go home after this." He disappeared through the door, still propelling the wan Miss Semmer. The inspector stood looking after them for a moment, then came into the room.

"Well, now," he said. "Suppose we try to get a few facts about this. Then I won't have to keep you ladies any longer." He turned to the door again, barked: "Mulrooney!" and settled himself in a Louis XV chair, somewhat gingerly, waved his hand and said: "Sit down, ladies." They sat. The inspector took a cigar from his pocket and bit off the end. A policeman, evidently the desired Mulrooney, came in with a pencil and notebook and established himself at a small table near the inspector. That worthy lit his cigar, took two puffs, looked toward the door, opened his mouth, closed it again and struggled to his feet, saying: "Good afternoon, Mr. Curtis."

Susan who had been watching the inspector with fascination turned also to the door. A well-tailored man in his early thirties, who had level gray eyes and a pleasant, warm voice, greeted the inspector then shook hands with Tom Benchley. Behind the surface effects of good clothes and a cheerful manner, Susan sensed quick muscles and a flexible, straight-thinking mind. He looked wholly masculine.

Tom made general introductions which the newcomer acknowledged, and, as his eyes rested on Susan, she suddenly wondered when she had powdered her nose last.

Without preamble, Howard Pierce asked: "What are you doing here, Curtis?" Tom Benchley hastened to explain.

Amused at her own feminine impulse regarding a shiny nose, Susan glanced around the group. Everyone's eyes were on Assistant District Attorney Lyle Curtis. Even the patrician Vivian Peabody was sitting straighter in her chair. Lucinda Mason had gotten busy at once with her lipstick, and Hortense Culbertson,

who had seemed of them all the most obviously shaken by the trag-
edy in the ballroom, had turned her eyes from Tom to Curtis with
a look of reassurance.

The inspector began speaking: "Just about to try to straighten
this business out, Mr. Curtis. I gave you the idea of what it was all
about over the phone—haven't done much since but examine the body."

The assistant district attorney nodded. "I'll just sit and listen,
then, since I'm not here officially." He dropped into a chair next to
Susan with a smile that asked: "May I?" and she found herself
smiling back. He was really a very attractive young man.

"Now," said the inspector, "we'll need names and addresses
first, if you please. Suppose you start." He pointed a finger at Vivian
Peabody, who raised perfect eyebrows, and replied smoothly:

"Vivian Peabody, 817 Park Avenue." Mulrooney wrote indus-
triously in his notebook.

"Any occupation?" asked the inspector.

Vivian looked outraged. "Editor of the fashion magazine, *For
Ladies*," she snapped. "Address 19 East Forty-eighth Street."

"Married?"

"Single."

"Thank you," said the inspector. "You next, please."

Hortense gulped and said in a small but musical voice: "Hortense Culbertson, 51 Gramercy Park. I'm a radio commentator at
Consolidated Broadcasting."

"Married?"

"Single," Hortense replied, not looking at Tom.

"You, miss?"

"Lucinda Mason, interior decorator at 585 Madison Avenue.
In private life, Mrs. Ethan Van Weck, Glen Cove, Long Island." The
inspector nodded and looked at Susan.

"Susan Yates, dress designer. My shop is at 18 East Fifty-sev-
enth Street. I live at 10 East Sixty-second. I'm not married."

"Thank you, Miss Yates," said the inspector.

Tom was next. "Thomas A. Benchley, publicity and public relations counsel." He winked at Susan. "At home at 30 West Fifty-
second Street. Office at 60 East Forty-second Street."

Mr. Pierce rose abruptly from his corner and said: "Inspector, would you mind asking me whatever it is now, and then letting me go? I have a—great many things to be attended to."

"Naturally," agreed the inspector. "Of course, Mr. Pierce. You are the husband of the—ah, what is your occupation, Mr. Pierce?"

"Lawyer—at 30 Wall Street. Home address 12 Beckman Place. You can reach me there if you have any more questions." He rose, but the inspector held up a hand.

"Just a moment, if you don't mind, Mr. Pierce. You have seen the note we found, which would indicate that the, ah, that Mrs. Pierce may have taken her own life."

"That's nonsense," Howard Pierce began angrily, but the inspector held up his hand again.

"If you please, Mr. Pierce. I must, nevertheless, ask you if your wife seemed perfectly normal when last you saw her?"

"Perfectly," said Mr. Pierce.

"When was that?"

"Last night at dinner. After dinner I had—business to attend to downtown. This morning, I left for the office before my wife was up."

"Do you know if Mrs. Pierce went out after dinner?"

"I don't know."

"Was she in her usual spirits at dinner last night? Did she seem distressed or unhappy?"

"Not at all," said Mr. Pierce sharply. "She was perfectly normal and in the best of spirits. You're barking up the wrong tree, Inspector. I saw that suicide note, but just the same, my wife did not commit suicide. She was murdered, and I intend to find out by whom if you do not."

Hortense Culbertson again gasped, and the suave Vivian looked shocked. Susan wondered why she herself reacted to that statement with so little surprise. It seemed somehow, in the back of her mind, she had been expecting this all along. She darted a look at Lyle Curtis, and finding that young man's eyes on her, turned away to the inspector again, who was saying soothingly:

"Now, now, Mr. Pierce, we have no evidence of murder. You are naturally upset. I assure you that if any such evidence is found, we will of course do our utmost. But at the moment . . ."

Howard Pierce cut him short. "Evidence or not, she was murdered. May I speak to Mr. Curtis privately for a moment?" The inspector looked anything but pleased, but nodded, and Pierce drew Lyle Curtis out of the door with him.

"If you have any evidence to give, Mr. Pierce," the inspector called after him, "I should hear it, too."

"I have none," Howard Pierce said over his shoulder. "That is not what I want to tell Mr. Curtis." Susan could see the two of them just outside the open door, but she could not hear what Pierce was saying to Curtis with such incisive gestures of his large, square hands. She saw Lyle Curtis nod once or twice, then turn to the door.

"Finished with Mr. Pierce, Inspector?" he asked. The inspector nodded, and with a final inaudible word to Curtis, Howard Pierce departed. The assistant D. A. came back and resumed his seat next to Susan.

The inspector was sitting in painful concentration of his cigar. He looked up to bark at the policeman at the door: "Go ask the doctor if the other lady is well enough to come back." As the policeman departed the inspector suddenly snapped his fingers and swore. "I forgot to ask Pierce who his wife's doctor was."

"I can tell you that," said Vivian Peabody. "It was Doctor Linwood Semmer. I don't know his address, but his sister—the one with the doctor—will be able to tell you."

Lyle Curtis had exclaimed half under his breath at the mention of Semmer's name. Benchley called out to him: "Didn't you go to school with him, Lyle?"

Curtis nodded, and said:

"But I don't know his address. You'll have to ask his sister anyway, Inspector."

Caroline Semmer appeared at that moment, very white, leaning on the doctor's arm. The medical examiner said:

"Don't keep her any longer than you have to, Inspector. She's very weak."

The inspector nodded, and Lyle Curtis rushed forward to lower Caroline solicitously into a chair. She flushed apologetically and murmured: "Oh, thank you—I'll be quite all right. I just feel a bit nervous, you know."

"Well, at least you know you're out of danger now," the medical examiner pointed out bluntly. "Need the body any longer, Inspector? If not, we'll take it along." The inspector said: "Go ahead," nodded to the departing doctor, and turned to Caroline Semmer.

"I shan't keep you long, miss," he said. "I have just a few questions to ask. May I have your name, address and occupation, if any?"

Caroline Semmer gave an apologetic cough and said: "Miss Caroline Semmer, Tompkins Road, White Plains, New York. I am the secretary-treasurer of the Tomorrow Club, whose offices are in this hotel."

"And will you give me your brother's address, please, Miss Semmer?"

The pinched face above the plump little body looked dumfounded. "My brother!" Miss Semmer cried. "What has Linwood to do with this?"

"I understand he was Mrs. Pierce's regular physician," explained the inspector. "The medical examiner will want to consult him about Mrs. Pierce's general state of health. Routine, Miss Semmer."

Caroline looked infinitely relieved. "I see," she said, and gave her brother's office address as 1012 Park Avenue. The inspector nodded and relit his cigar.

After a moment he said: "Now you people all know about the note found on the floor by the body? A suicide note?"

They nodded, and Lucinda Mason gurgled: "Oh yes, we all read it."

"And handled it," nodded the inspector peevishly. "But I meant, you all know it was there when you found her dead?"

Susan said slowly, "No-o, I don't seem to remember seeing it when I first tried to rouse Nancy."

The inspector eyed her with an expression which said women either saw too much or nothing at all. "According to the hotel manager," he said, "it was by her right foot."

Caroline Semmer's hesitant voice said: "It's just possible I may have seen it." She paused. "You know how difficult it is to recall afterward what seemed a mere—triviality at the time. Especially," she raised one hand to stem an embarrassed cough, "especially when such a horrible thing has happened in the meanwhile. That is, I mean, it seems to me I saw something fall. I *think* I thought at the time it was a handkerchief, or something. Anyway, I have the definite feeling that I *meant* to call Nancy's attention to something. Then my own attention must have been diverted for I'm sure I didn't. Dear me, I wish I could be sure."

"When was this, Miss Semmer?" asked the inspector.

"Why—it must have been when she was looking in her bag for her capsules," said Miss Semmer, "although I can't remember exactly."

"Did anyone else notice anything?" asked the inspector. But if anyone had, it remained unrevealed. Susan found herself going maddeningly hot and cold with an indefinite memory of something she couldn't put a mental finger on. She decided finally she needed time to think over everything quietly by herself: the whole of the latter half of the luncheon, that queer hysterical laugh, how each of them had looked when the lights went up, what they had all done in the following moments. There was something nagging at her memory—something said or done, something she had seen or not seen which she should have. But what it was she could not remember.

CHAPTER SIX

MISS SEMMER'S RECOLLECTION that she might have seen something white fall from Nancy Pierce's handbag had apparently taken all their minds back to the minutes preceding the discovery of the slumped body. Looking around the little jade and gold room, Susan saw that all their expressions were a little faraway and thoughtful; and she wondered if each of them had, perhaps—as she had—a troublesomely nagging memory of some little detail scarcely noticed at the time and now misplaced. In the turmoil of the subsequent event of Nancy's death, she felt they all must have felt a deep sense of shock—however much they had disliked the girl.

Suddenly, Miss Peabody sat forward and commanded the inspector's attention with her compelling black eyes. "Mrs. Pierce," she announced firmly, "must have been suffering from a mental state none of us even guessed. Our psychologists have not arrived yet at a definition of what is normal in humans; but, in my opinion, no normal person commits suicide."

Inspector Beller nodded ponderously, and Vivian went on:

"Of course, it is nonsense to believe that Nancy Pierce had committed a robbery. Her husband is a rich man; and she herself, from time to time, made very sizable incomes. The theft idea must have been a neurotic fixation in Mrs. Pierce's mind."

"It does sound ridiculous," Lucinda Mason agreed. And Miss Semmer nodded her head and said in the tone of a mother defending a child: "No one could possibly have thought such a thing of the poor woman."

At this Hortense Culbertson opened her delicately formed lips to say something, but the inspector who had evidently been chewing over Miss Peabody's words rumbled a question: "Any of you suspect she wasn't right in her head?"

There was a shocked silence before Lucinda remarked slowly: "It would have accounted for her often filthy behavior—kicking dogs and things—"

Miss Peabody looked at Lucinda reprimandingly and said quickly: "Miss Mason does not realize quite how ruthless that sounds, Inspector. What she means to say, I feel certain, is that we all knew Mrs. Pierce was high strung. Her behavior was sometimes impetuous. But I am convinced it occurred to none of us to think of her as mentally unbalanced."

"I," Hortense Culbertson remarked slowly, "always thought she was particularly *well* balanced—enough to get everything she wanted."

Inspector Beller absorbed this with cautious eyes, then his expression brightened. "She was hasty, high strung, thoughts always turned in on herself, as they say, eh?"

Miss Peabody answered as the radio commentator again opened her pretty mouth. "That is a fair picture, Inspector. Very fair. And it suggests an introspective state of mind capable perhaps of turning into morbid apprehension—a fixation that she had committed some crime. We—her acquaintances—naturally only saw her sometimes extravagant energy." Vivian stared into space for a moment. Then said: "We should all use our knowledge of psychology with associates as well as employees. But we forget." For once Miss Peabody looked almost apologetic.

The inspector looked the same way and said hastily: "Well, we don't have to have a clinical discussion, miss. That's for doctors, alienists and such. Anyway," and he brightened, "you can't psychoanalyze a corpse." He sounded definitely pleased. "I just wanted to get it straight whether the deceased had seemed upset or anything lately—especially today."

Lucinda's green eyes were narrowed in thought. "I don't know that it helps," she said, "but she acted to me especially gay today—as if she had put something over on somebody."

Dolorously, Miss Semmer murmured: "She did seem in very high spirits, almost as if she—I can't quite find the word for it—"

"Feverish?" pounced Inspector Beller.

"Well," Caroline considered doubtfully, "that seems a little strong." She coughed and leaned back in her chair again looking far from well.

Apprehensively, the inspector cast a look in her direction. "I guess we're keeping you here too long, miss. You better get home to bed—that is, if there's nothing else you want to tell me."

Miss Semmer sat forward at this and tried to look vigorous with poor success. "I really feel very much better," she insisted. "But I do feel I should be in the office. So many people will be calling up."

"Nonsense, Caroline," Miss Peabody admonished her. "You go home and to bed. Mr. Benchley will take care of reporters and other calls can wait."

After a trifle more demurring, Miss Semmer was led off to a taxi on the arm of a plain-clothes man called in from the ballroom. The latter was endeavoring to look fatherly and able to cope with Caroline's somewhat shattered nervous system. Meanwhile, the inspector leaned over and spoke in an undertone to Mulrooney, his expression and gestures indicating that the case was too clear cut and self evident for much more time to be wasted on it. Lyle Curtis watched this byplay in silence. Then the inspector turned back to them and said: "We'll just check up on the matter of the capsules and that will be all." Everyone looked relieved except the assistant district attorney whose expression remained quietly alert and faintly puzzled. "When," the inspector rumbled on, "did the deceased take some capsules?"

As his question was posed to the room at large, Susan waited a moment for someone else to answer. When no one did, she said that Mrs. Pierce had taken a capsule, only one, directly after her luncheon.

"How soon was that before the lights went out? Do you remember?"

Susan did. "Just a few moments before."

The inspector looked pleased.

Tom Benchley said: "Before that her capsule box was in her purse, and her purse was right on the table in front of her plate."

The inspector wanted to know if everyone agreed and they all nodded Then he asked: "And the room was fully lighted until after the deceased swallowed the capsule, eh?"

They nodded once more, and Susan found herself suddenly describing the scene in greater detail than the inspector had specifically requested:

"I think that part is very clear in all our minds, Inspector," she heard herself saying. "Just before we were ready to look at the stage-sets, Mrs. Pierce took a box of capsules from her handbag and put them on the table. As Mr. Benchley said, she had laid her handbag in full view of all of us when she first sat down. No one but Mrs. Pierce herself and Miss Semmer touched the box. Mrs. Pierce pushed it over for Miss Semmer to try a capsule, which she did with all of us watching idiotically because Caroline—Miss Semmer—had said she didn't know whether she could swallow anything so big. Immediately afterward, Miss Semmer handed the box back to Mrs. Pierce who also took a capsule and swallowed it; then closed the box and put it back in her handbag. A few moments after that the lights were lowered."

With waning interest, the inspector relit his cigar, puffed a moment in thought, then inquired how long the lights had stayed out.

Lucinda Mason answered. "At most four or five minutes. There was a little trouble about the sun."

"The what?"

Lucinda explained, but an artificial solar system turned out to hold no attractions for the inspector. He turned again to Susan Yates as if her sudden burst of details might or might not be suspicious. "You screamed, didn't you?" he barked unexpectedly.

Susan admitted that that must be the right word for it.

"Why?"

"Because I thought something was wrong with Nancy."

"What made you think so?"

"I tried to speak to her—leaned toward her. There was a faint glow from the stage just then. I could see she was slumped over."

"Everybody agree about that glow?" demanded the inspector, but his hope seemed to have dimmed that there would be denials and when his question received a general chorus of agreement, he nodded placidly.

"The same kind of glow there is in the theater when an act is on," amplified Lucinda Mason. "You know, you can see your neighbors, but never can read your program. But half the time—ninety-nine per cent of the time—you don't see your neighbors because your eyes are concentrated on the stage."

The inspector grunted and asked, his eye roving to Miss Peabody, if the deceased had been dead when the lights had come on.

The president of the Tomorrow Club answered with poised dignity. "We have no idea. We saw, of course, that she appeared to be unconscious. After a moment of shock I stood up to try to rouse her. Then Mr. Benchley went for a house doctor. We did not—and could not know—she was dead until the hotel physician arrived and examined Mrs. Pierce."

Looking fully content, the inspector rose. "O.K. There's nothing more, I guess, unless someone has something to say." No one apparently feeling thus inclined, the inspector and his Mulrooney gathered themselves together, the latter rising like a smaller shadow behind his superior. "Looks like a plain case of suicide," rumbled the inspector matter-of-factly. "Of course, it's possible I might have to call on you again for further evidence on the woman's state of mind. But nothing more now, thanks." Followed by his smaller shadow Inspector Beller, looking solid, unimaginative and well pleased with himself, trod on the feet of a cat from the room.

Glances were exchanged briefly between the others. Glances of relief and weariness. Susan stood up. They all stood up. Beside Susan, Lyle Curtis said: "Bit of a strain."

"Certainly very upsetting." She was still wondering idiotically if her nose was shiny, and taking out her compact verified the suspicion. Curtis had faced the group. In a casual voice, he was saying:

"I'd like to keep you all for just a few minutes. I'm not here in any official capacity, you know, but Mr. Pierce tells me he is somewhat upset by the police's theory of suicide. I'm not certain how you all feel—" He paused waiting for some expression of opinion and got only rather rigid glances. "But in any case," Curtis continued after a moment, "Mr. Pierce told me outside a while ago that if suicide is the official verdict, he intends to ask the district attorney's office to investigate further." Pausing again, his eyes traveled around the little group. "I imagine, some of you may agree with his point of view. In any case, there are several things I might later want to know. Perhaps we can go over a few points now while they are fresh in all your minds."

No one spoke for a moment. Then Hortense Culbertson, who had been consulting her wrist watch, said: "I go on the air, Mr. Curtis, at five-thirty. It's four now. Will you need me long?"

"Half an hour at the most," smiled the assistant district attorney. His eyes remained on Miss Culbertson for a long second, then he addressed them all: "What I'd especially like to know now is as much as possible about Mrs. Pierce's movements today. Who can tell me where she was before she arrived here at the Eden?"

Silence again for several seconds. Abruptly, Miss Peabody replied: "I only know that she was here at eleven-thirty."

"She couldn't have been much of anyplace else," Lucinda Mason remarked, "because she never got up, unless she had to, until ten-thirty."

"So. She was here at eleven-thirty." He then skillfully led them through the Colonel Gamberson episode during which Miss Peabody remained tight lipped. In detail, Lucinda gave her version of the dog episode. No one disagreed. Then Curtis asked: "Mrs. Pierce, you say, left the ballroom about half-past twelve? Know where she went?"

"To the bar," said Susan dryly.

"Know whom she was meeting there?" hazarded the assistant D. A.

Again no one replied, so Curtis returned to the narrative of the morning, leading them to answer his questions in their own ways, until he came to the taking of the capsule. "You say," he asked, "that she fished around in her handbag for some time before she found her box? As though to attract notice to the fact that she was about to take a capsule—perhaps a poisoned one?"

Miss Peabody said: "How could we have had any such idea?"

But Miss Mason broke in: "She always did that—dropped her things all over the place, making a devastating racket if possible, and managing to call attention to herself. That's what she did this noon, and before that on the stage this morning. You remember, Vivian! All the stagehands were on the floor looking for her lipstick."

Unexpectedly Miss Culbertson said she didn't remember that, but Miss Mason reminded her that at the time she had said Nancy Pierce's name would be mud if she ever dropped all her chattel at a broadcast.

Curtis asked: "What was she looking for in her bag on the stage?"

Miss Peabody answered. "For the capsule box itself. I had sneezed. It was incredibly dusty on the stage. But Mrs. Pierce decided—ah, suggested that I might be taking cold."

"Did she find her box?"

"Oh yes, opened it and invited me to inspect the capsules."

"Were all of you there at the time?"

"Yes, we were inspecting the sets."

Susan reminded Miss Peabody that she hadn't been there, and the club's president said: "That's right, my dear. You hadn't come yet. I remember. But Lucinda and Hortense and I were. Was Caroline Semmer there?" She looked in turn at Miss Mason and Miss Culbertson.

Lucinda shrugged. "I suppose so. Caroline's always self-effacingly present when there's work to be done. Poor thing. The medical examiner must have given her a walloping, nasty dose a while ago. Though, believe me, if I'd taken one of those capsules I'd be demanding drastic treatment, and I don't mean maybe."

Curtis eyed Miss Mason quietly during this digression, then asked amiably: "Can you recall what the box of capsules looked like—when you saw it on the stage? I mean, was it full? How were the capsules placed?"

Lucinda looked a trifle vague, and Miss Peabody answered crisply: "It was almost full. I recall distinctly there were only two capsules left in the first row, and I think the other rows were completely full. I know it was that way when Mrs. Pierce opened the box at the luncheon table—and it appeared precisely the same to me." The look in the fashion editor's eyes suggested that no one would dare dispute her capacity for recalling details accurately. Curtis' look lingered on her handsome profile.

"Then Mrs. Pierce did not take a capsule when she showed you the box on the stage?" he asked.

"Certainly not. Vitamin capsules are taken after meals."

Mildly, Hortense Culbertson said: "Not necessarily, Vivian."

"Nancy," Lucinda Mason joined in, "took them after meals. I know she did. I've had to lunch with her a lot over details of the show. She always dragged out her box after lunch. I'd ragged her before about 'vitamins being vital.' Of course, this noon I was really trying to be annoying because of her having stepped on G. B."

"On what?"

"Her dog," explained Susan.

Curtis smiled. "A George Bernard Shaw namesake?" And Lucinda smiled back and nodded affirmatively. Without a change of tone the assistant D. A. asked: "And when did you last lunch with Mrs. Pierce, Miss Mason?" Lucinda who was busy with her lipstick again looked over the tiny mirror she had dragged out. She seemed to have caught the implication in the question, mildly as it had been asked. Dabbing some paste on her lips, she smiled a little wickedly and said:

"Ten days ago, and I have an alibi for every meal I've eaten since. I hope that doesn't make me guilty of having contrived to give Nancy a poisoned capsule."

Mr. Curtis said softly: "We don't know the capsules were poisoned, do we?"

Lucinda laughed again. "Caught out on another limb! Goodness! But let me assure you I haven't time to go about murdering blonde cats."

Vivian gave Miss Mason a sharp look of reproof, and Lucinda subsided.

Then Mr. Curtis asked if Mrs. Pierce had seemed to hesitate over taking a capsule that noon; and Susan described Nancy's "every third" ritual. He inquired if they had all known of this custom

of hers. Every head shook. "Not even you, Miss Mason? You didn't
notice it when she took capsules after the luncheons you'd been
having together?" Lucinda pondered, then shook her head again
and said:

"For all of me, she may have gone through some mumbo-jumbo,
but I didn't take it in, if she did."

"But you all heard it at the table today?" insisted the assistant
district attorney, and they agreed. After that Curtis asked for a
description of the seating arrangement at the luncheon table, and
Susan, taking a notebook from her handbag, offered to draw it for
him. Her trained designer's fingers drew a nearly perfect circle and
surrounded it with names. "Like this," she said handing it over to
Curtis:

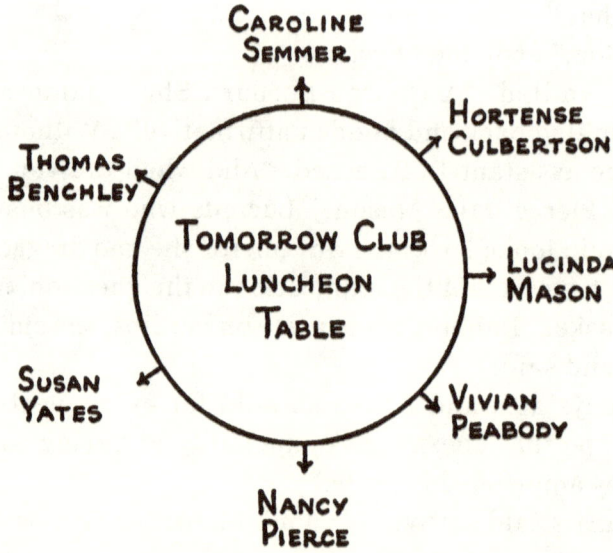

After scanning it with interested eyes, the assistant district
attorney put Susan's diagram carefully away in his wallet, and
proceeded to acquire from them various other scattered details of
the strange luncheon up to the arrival of the ambulance doctor,
Inspector Beller and his men, and the medical examiner.

Presently he inquired conversationally: "It was the hotel manager, wasn't it, who found the suicide note? How did it happen none

of the rest of you had spied it?" That was a point which had been indefinably troubling Susan. She said so.

"It is queer," she said, "that we hadn't, because whether Nancy dropped it on purpose or unintentionally, it must have been there when I went around her after the lights came on—and—and the funny part is I did look down at the floor then to make certain I wouldn't step on Miss Mason's dog. G. B. had been whining under the table. And now I remember I did notice Nancy's feet."

"Her feet?"

"Yes, they were crossed over each other in a way she had. They looked so—so natural. That is, in contrast to the crumpled way she looked otherwise."

Curtis raised an eyebrow. "Crossed over each other?" he repeated, and Susan nodded. Still in his conversational tone, he said: "The house physician tells me they were flat on the floor when he examined Mrs. Pierce."

With crisp authority Miss Peabody explained: "At first, as I explained to the inspector, we didn't know but that Nancy had simply fainted. We tried, naturally, to revive her. In touching her it seems more than probable we jarred her feet apart. Rigor mortis, I've always been led to understand, does not set in at once. Do you find this trivial point important, Mr. Curtis? Otherwise, I'm certain you realize we are all very busy people—" She paused and glanced meaningly at her watch.

The assistant district attorney smiled briefly. "Probably not," he said as if his interest in the case was waning rapidly.

The radio commentator was glancing with a worried frown at her watch, too. Curtis stood up. His tone was even more affable. "I think I need not detain any of you any more—today, at least." He glanced carelessly at his own watch, and added: "Miss Culbertson will be in good time for her broadcast." Looking at Hortense he went on: "Being late on the air is practically a national offense, I understand."

Hortense smiled wryly and gave him a grateful look. "It's indefensible," she said.

"Heavens!" exclaimed Lucinda Mason. "It's four-thirty and G. B. hasn't been out since one o'clock." Gathering up the immediately excited Pomeranian, she made her way purposefully to the door, calling indelicately cheerful farewells over her shoulder.

After a few softly spoken words to Tom Benchley, Miss Culbertson followed Miss Mason and the dog. Miss Peabody had turned to Tom and was giving him crisply worded injunctions about how to handle the reporters.

Pleasantly in Susan's ear dropped the assistant district attorney's voice: "How about a drink?" Susan's level eyes met his equally level ones, and she became uncomfortably aware that she was not making her glance as coolly impersonal as was her custom with practical strangers. She heard herself saying with several shades too much enthusiasm:

"I'd love one!"

CHAPTER SEVEN

AFTER LEAVING Miss Vivian Peabody at the door of the jade and gold reception room, Thomas A. Benchley went up to the offices of the Tomorrow Club. There he spent a busy half-hour on the telephone. One by one, he called the offices of the city newspapers, and told them the sad story of the beautiful lady who had died at the Hotel Eden, apparently by her own hand. To the man on the last newspaper, however, he said merely: "Buck—I've got a story for you. I'm coming right over—stay put, will you?" Then he grabbed his hat, closed the office, and departed.

At the offices of the New York *Globe* he went directly to the City room. The person he sought was wearing his hat largely over his face; indeed, to all outward appearances, he was peacefully asleep. Mr. Benchley greeted him rudely. A hand came up slowly, pushed the hat far enough to disclose a mouth, nose and one eye. The mouth said, "Oh, it's you."

Mr. Benchley said: "Well, of course, if you don't care about the blonde that just passed out at the Eden . . ."

The chair descended with a plop and its occupant demanded: "Why the hell didn't you say so? Is she dead or only under a table?"

Mr. Benchley assured him that she was very dead, then, lowering his voice, began a prolonged conversation. Now and again the young man with the hat nodded, or made a note on copy paper. Several times he winked broadly, and after about ten minutes he got on the telephone and talked for some time. Hanging up the receiver, he disclosed that Howard Pierce had certainly consorted with the Frisorelli gang; but in what exact capacity his informant hadn't known. Mr. Benchley rose, saying: "Be seeing you, Buck," and loped out of the city room.

When he reached the street he paused, glanced at his watch, without halting, and walked rapidly for several blocks. Before an imposing office building, he came to a standstill, surveyed its immediate surroundings and entered it. He glanced first at the foyer directory and approached a bank of elevators marked "thirtieth floor first Stop." One of these presently deposited him on the forty-seventh floor in front of a double-door entrance bearing the announcement: Holden, Pierce, Crawford and Hamilton, Attorneys at Law. Mr. Benchley pushed open one of the two doors with a flourish and entered a square, elegantly furnished waiting room. The girl at the reception desk had red hair and very large blue eyes. She smiled.

Mr. Benchley cleared his throat and produced a credible Harvard accent. He requested an interview with Mr. Howard Pierce, announcing that he was Mr. Carrington Wells of Boston. The girl shook her red head and regretted that Mr. Pierce had gone for the day. Mr. Wells appeared disappointed, glanced at his watch, made tst-tst-ing sounds, and asked if Mr. Pierce's secretary was about. The girl said she would see, plugged in a line on her switchboard, and announced to him after a moment that Miss Hotchkiss, Mr. Pierce's secretary, would be right out. She eyed Mr. Wells some more, and Mr. Wells eyed her.

Speaking with an elegance only slightly impeded by her chewing gum, the young woman remarked that Boston must be a swell place. Mr. Wells dutifully assured her that it was a garden spot; and that coming to New York was lonely business. The redhead brightened perceptibly at this and said that it was an awful shame having to be lonely.

At this point, Mr. Pierce's secretary appeared. The red-haired young woman stopped chewing and began strictly minding her own business.

Miss Hotchkiss was very good looking, creamy skin, velvet-brown eyes, good brows—almost up to the standard set by the show committee of the Tomorrow Club, Tom thought. She was dressed for the street and quite faultlessly as far as Mr. Benchley could see. Around her shoulders were sables. Her Shetland blue wool suit and flat, round hat became her. She regarded the visitor coolly, explaining that Mr. Pierce's wife had died. He would not be in for several days; but if Mr. Wells's business was important— Mr. Wells assured her it could wait. He was, he explained, in New York about a piece of property and found he needed the advice of a local attorney. He would telephone early the next week. Might be going back to Boston in the interim. The secretary said she would put his name down tentatively, then, for the following Monday—if he would be so good as to phone about a definite appointment with Mr. Pierce. Mr. Wells said he would and bid her good-by. He took a little time reaching the door. When the secretary was out of sight, he turned back hastily to the redhead:

"About being lonely. Would it seem presumptuous, if I asked your help?"

"Depends."

"My intentions are strictly honorable, I assure you, Miss—"

The redhead giggled. "Holt," she confided. "Miss Ruby Holt."

"Ah, Miss Holt. I would like to ask you to dine with me but I have pressing—and annoying business appointments both today and tomorrow. But—er—ah—tomorrow could you join me for highballs, say about nine in the evening, at the San Horitz Hotel?"

Miss Holt, an ear cocked for the possible return of Miss Hotchkiss (as were Mr. Benchley's), said hastily it didn't sound like a bad idea. She wrote down the time and place and Mr. Wells's name. With a reasonably gallant bow, the gentleman from Boston made his exit.

When he reached the street, Tom ducked across it and stood in the protecting lee of a newsstand. After a few minutes, the trim and expensively clad figure of Mr. Pierce's Miss Hotchkiss emerged from the opposite building, arranging her furs. She walked quickly to the corner and summoned a taxi. Mr. Benchley did likewise.

"Missed the lady in that Yellow ahead," he told the driver. "Want to surprise her, buddy. Keep just behind and let me out back a bit of where she disembarks."

"O.K." agreed the taxi driver disinterestedly.

They sped uptown and were presently enmeshed in the late afternoon traffic of Park Avenue. Mr. Benchley's driver hugged the bumper of the Yellow cab which bore Miss Hotchkiss. When, above the Grand Central ramp, traffic thinned somewhat, Tom suggested that they fall a bit behind. At Fiftieth Street the other cab turned east, and stopped presently at a remodeled brownstone house near Lexington Avenue. Tom alighted a quarter of a block behind; paid his driver, and strolled up the block. At a florist's shop next to the building into which Miss Hotchkiss had disappeared, Tom stopped to gaze apparently enraptured at the window display. His hat was turned down, his coat collar was turned up.

He did not have long to wait. Three minutes later, another taxi drew up in front of the remodeled brownstone. A man got out, paid the driver, and walked quickly to the door. As he went down the three steps to the entrance, his hand tugged a key purse from his pocket. Tom left the florist's window and went slowly past the brownstone. In the vestibule Mr. Howard Pierce was opening the inner door with a key. Tom kept on walking. At the corner, he turned and retraced his steps. The vestibule of the remodeled brownstone was now empty. Tom went in and studied the names under the mailboxes. Second from the right said: Miss Olga Hotchkiss.

MEANWHILE SUSAN YATES and Lyle Curtis had descended to the blue-and-silver opulence of the Eden bar. Outside the weather had cleared and an afternoon cocktail-hour crowd had assembled. Curtis grimaced at the filled tables and buzz of voices.

"Shall we sit at the bar?" he asked, and swung out a stool without waiting for her answer. Susan sat obediently and smiled to herself, confident that had the room been entirely empty he would still have proposed the strategic position of the bar.

Lucien bowed before them. "Dry martini, Miss Yates?"

"Please." Glancing at the assistant district attorney with an air of mock intrigue, she added: "This is Lucien, the best martini mixer in Greater New York."

"Then I must certainly have one."

As Lucien turned to perform his rites, Curtis looked down at Miss Yates. "Smarty," he hissed. "Couldn't you think up anything else? I particularly dislike martinis."

Miss Yates smiled demurely. "What a pity. But introductions come so high this year."

"A bright girl, too. Well, what price an introduction to the waiter who served Mrs. Pierce?"

"That's free and can be accomplished on our way out." Then Lucien brought the martinis. Susan raised her glass. "Here's to crime," and she choked on the first swallow. "Goodness, how the clichés do betray one," she gasped.

Solicitously, Mr. Curtis patted her back. "Serves you right, of course," he said, ignoring his own glass.

Hands clasped before them, Lucien was saying sepulchrally: "Miss Yates, my so very sincere condolences about the young lady that have the accident upstairs."

Susan thanked him solemnly; said it had been shocking, and then inquired if Mrs. Pierce had not been at the bar shortly before her death.

"I think it is true, if it was the very blonde lady with the so very bright eyes. Yes? I noticed particularly because there was a little— comment dirai-je—a little trouble. Also, she was not easy not to see, hein?"

"A little trouble? What do you mean?" questioned Susan.

Lucien explained. "Madame—ah, bon, Mme. Pierce came in just after you go, Miss Yates. She sits with a man at that divan table there. The man is not in the good humor. Without paying his bill, he leaves. Madame is upset. She comes here to my bar. Then it is I am the upset. Pickups not permitted." Lucien rolled his Gallic eyes in thorough enjoyment of this post obitum morsel of gossip.

"Pickups?" repeated Susan.

Lucien nodded, explaining that he had not known the gentle- man—a person in tweed, who sniffed, but who had seemed, fortu- nately, to be the husband of one of Madame's friends, another member of their club. A whisky and soda at the other end of the bar called for Lucien's attention at this moment and excusing him-self he darted off.

"Nice work," commented Curtis. "Ought to have you on our staff."

"Thank you. Want more?"

"Infinitely more," he smiled and leaning over neatly replaced her empty glass with his full one. "Lucien," he called. "You make a magnificent martini. Another, please."

Bringing the order, Lucien once more took up his conversa-tional stance and Susan raised her eyes and inquired if Mrs. Pierce had remained at the bar long.

Lucien thought it must have been about ten minutes. She had described some sort of medicine to the gentleman; had gone and got a box of pills to show him.

Forgetting his role of disinterested spectator, Curtis leaned forward and asked if Mrs. Pierce had offered the gentleman one of her "pills."

The bartender shook his head. "No, she just show him—open the box, hold up a fat pill, put it back and close the box."

"After that?" persisted Curtis. "What did she do with the box?"

Lucien stared. "I do not understand," said he turning puzzled eyes to Miss Yates. A daiquiri down the line claimed his attention then.

Susan turned to her escort. "You've got him suspicious. If you want any more, you'll have to make it official now, I'm afraid."

"Not now," said the assistant district attorney and called for the check, his second order still untasted.

Susan leading the way, they headed for the Forty-eighth Street revolving door. Mike sprang forward, offering sympathies about the poor young lady's death upstairs. Susan, looking properly mo-rose, said she understood Mrs. Pierce had been in the bar shortly before her death.

"Sure," beamed Mike ghoulishly. "And wasn't she after being with a fine gentleman, now, leaving a lady with the check—and no tip."

"Dear me. Who was it, Mike?"

"Sure and I'll know next time I see him." Though dark in words, the little waiter's tone was philosophical. On sudden thought, he added: "It was the gentleman sitting by himself, Miss Yates; the brother of the older lady that stopped and talked to you at the bar. Excuse me, but I heard you say it was her brother."

"Really," and Susan restrained a smile. "Well, then you'll probably see him again. Perhaps he'll double his tip. Good night, Mike."

Curtis followed her trim back to the street. On the wet pavement he paused, raised an eyebrow and demanded: "Well?"

"You've got me feeling like a despoiler of confidences. The gent who left in a rage was, of course, Doctor Linwood Semmer, and the 'pickup,' Lucinda Mason's husband, Ethan Van Weck."

Mr. Thomas A. Benchley, leaving the remodeled brownstone, had turned to Fifth Avenue. Presently he reached his own rooms in West Fifty-second Street. The cocktail-hour rush of this famous café street was abating, and it was still too early for diners to be about. The rain had turned to snow, driven in windy gusts along the street. On the pavements it had turned to slush.

Mr. Benchley took the stairs three at a time and unlocked his door. He threw his hat on a chair, his overcoat on top of it, dashed across the room and settled himself before the telephone table. Then he became remotely thoughtful for a moment. At the end of this time he grunted with satisfaction, and grabbing the telephone book, began noting numbers on a pad. Presently he removed the receiver from its hook, consulted the pad, and dialed a number.

When the call was completed, he asked for Frisorelli. There was a pause. Someone at the other end of the line said, "Maybe he ain't here. I could look." Another pause, and an oily voice said: "Yeah, who are you?"

Mr. Benchley's tone became hearty and extremely vulgar. He appeared to be intent on renewing in Signor Frisorelli's memory a picture of a certain memorable occasion in the past, in which the name "The Little Jap" seemed involved. With great warmth, Mr. Benchley professed his close affection and undying friendship for the little Jap. The Italian apparently warmed to the subject after a

while, for his tone became less oily and more pleasantly bombas-
tic. After a few minutes of this social chitchat, Mr. Benchley said:

"Listen, Frisi, I gotta little stuff on the ice and I figure I maybe
need a good mouthpiece before I get through with it. What d'ya
know about Pierce? Didn't he get Zobinski off the heat a while
back?"

Frisorelli's tone became ecstatic. He warbled on for some moments about the capabilities of the person named Pierce. Tom, listening intently, made occasional notes on his pad. He asked a
couple of questions about Zobinski and needles, reassured his auditor of his practically undying affection and rang off, well pleased
with himself. To himself he said: "The trouble with you, my lad, is
you've missed a wonderful career on the stage."

Then, after glancing at his watch, he made a second call. Here
there was a little delay, but ultimately a suave voice came over the
wire. Tom introduced himself as the son of the late Dr. Franklin
Benchley, asked after the health of the speaker and his wife, then
inquired boyishly: "Can I ask a question of you, Dr. Whittacre?
Thanks. You see, I'm in the writing game these days. I've got a little
problem. Fictional angle. Mystery, You know. Is there any kind of
jellied capsule that would lie undigested in the stomach, say, eighteen hours before it exposed its content?"

The answer did not seem to be altogether to his liking. "Have
to change my plot, I guess." After repetitions of greetings to the
doctor and his wife, he said good-by, and returned the receiver to
its cradle, grabbed his coat and hat and dashed out.

CHAPTER EIGHT

ON THE STREET outside the Hotel Eden, Mr. Curtis seemed loath to part from Miss Yates. After consulting his watch, he suggested that they find some quiet place where they could have dinner and talk in peace.

"You know all these people and I don't," he said. "If you could tell me about them it would be a great help." He peered down at Susan, standing irresolute in the dusk. "I don't mean that I want you to incriminate your friends in any way," he persisted, seeing her still hesitating. "After all, we don't yet know that there's anything to incriminate them in. But if I'm to get anywhere with this case, whatever it turns out to be, I shall have to know more about Mrs. Pierce and how she impinged on the lives of all these people. I can dig it out for myself if I must—but that would take much longer."

"All right," said Susan. "What time is it? Five? I have an engagement for dinner, but there's plenty of time—why not come over to my apartment and have something that isn't a martini—we can talk there without being disturbed."

MR. CURTIS WAS GIVEN a brandy and soda and made comfortable on the sofa by the fire. Susan sat in the wing chair opposite him and said: "I don't know where to begin."

"Why not begin with Nancy Pierce. Know anything of her background?"

"Very little. I know she came from somewhere upstate—Binghamton or Buffalo. I have the impression that her family was

89

perhaps poor. And that didn't suit Nancy in the least. She was a determined young woman—determined to get the best in life. Howard Pierce was her second husband—I don't know anything about the first. He was apparently left behind in her past. When I first met Nancy she had been in New York about a year and had gained something of a reputation as a designer of jewel settings— not a usual profession for women, and one in which she could have gone on, I think, making a bigger and bigger reputation. But apparently it didn't provide enough limelight, and she was not what is known as a 'good organization person.' She's done a dozen things since, including acting in a stock company last summer on Long Island. I believe, she'd had earlier experience in the theater, but she did everything dramatically. Sort of a matter of second nature. And she had a gift—no doubt of it—for pulling wires and getting jobs whether she had training for them or not. She'd drop out of sight for a few months and then back she'd be in the fashion business with some post a dozen other better-trained people had been gunning for."

"You seemed amused," Curtis suggested, "over her 'picking up' Miss Mason's husband. Ethan Van Weck, isn't he?"

"Yes, but I wasn't exactly amused. I wondered if it wasn't the first step in a new campaign. Howard Pierce is wealthy, but not socially distinguished. At the luncheon table—when Nancy returned from her encounter with Ethan Van Weck—she was all a-twitter to know if he was Social Register. And his being Lucinda Mason's husband would not, I'm afraid, have deterred Nancy from attempting to appropriate him."

Curtis regarded Miss Yates with quiet, aware eyes. He said suddenly: "You don't believe she planned to kill herself? You don't believe she did kill herself?"

Slowly Susan shook her head. "It makes poor sense. Nancy was an opportunist, and the world was still full of things for her to snatch. If some plan of hers had miscarried, I believe she would have merely changed objectives and begun a fresh campaign. It seems to me, women like Nancy Pierce drive others to suicide. They don't commit it themselves."

"And the note?"

Susan frowned. "Very queer. Surely it makes no sense at all. If she were committing suicide because of a theft, why mention it? Why not hope her death would hush it up? Besides, I can't imagine Nancy stealing anything that would come under the legal definition of crime—husbands, jobs, yes; money, jewels—that sort of thing—no. Why should she? She had all the worldly goods she needed. She was after other things."

"Sounds reasonable. What about her record in the job-and-husband stealing game?"

"I sometimes wondered if she didn't start the rumors herself for personal publicity. There was always talk about her having nearly missed being named a correspondent in divorce cases. She never had been to my knowledge. I know, though, that she was after Hortense Culbertson's television opportunity. It was naturally appealing to her—to hope to be the first television star. Lucinda Mason said this noon that she was also up to some sort of intrigue with Vivian Peabody's publisher; but it's beyond credulity that Nancy hoped to replace Vivian who is the flesh, blood and spirit of *For Ladies* magazine. It's queer. She seemed very anxious—peculiarly so, for Nancy—to have Vivian read nothing into the Colonel Gamberson episode in the ballroom this morning. Asked me to tell Vivian so."

"Hu-ummm—" Curtis gazed into the fire. Then: "I'd like to know just what Mrs. Pierce's surface relations were with each of you at the luncheon this noon. Can you do that for me, briefly?"

Susan thought a moment, then said slowly: "Briefly a state of honeyed warfare—not always so honeyed. She wasn't capable of any other relationship with women who constituted any kind of competition for her widespread ambitions. It's a fact that none of us liked her. I frankly feared her inventive tongue. Of us all, I suppose only Caroline Semmer thought she was really glamorous; but then Caroline was scarcely a fitting subject for Nancy's envy, possessing little or nothing, I should imagine, that Nancy craved. Her demanding eyes seemed to give Tom Benchley the creeps, but I don't think they'd met before this noon."

"Is Miss Culbertson the girl Tom used to be in love with?"

"Why the past tense? They patched everything up today, I thought." Susan laughed a rippling laugh which seemed to spring from just under the surface of her thoughts, gay and unforced. Watching her, the assistant district attorney seemed to have a little difficulty composing his next question. He turned away from the smile born with her laugh and stared again at the fire. When he spoke his tone was again cool and even. "Aside from a boss here, a husband or fiancé there, what basic thing could Mrs. Pierce have stolen from any of you members of the Tomorrow Club?"

"Basic thing? Our reputations? Our unsullied places in the sun? That sort of thing, you mean?"

Abruptly Curtis changed his question: "What man did she try to take away from you, Miss Yates?"

Susan flushed, and suddenly realized that in helping to build a murder theory, she was probably becoming, in Curtis' eyes, "one of the suspects." Hadn't murderers sometimes cried "Murder," hoping to divert suspicion from themselves? She hesitated, then said lightly: "No man Nancy Pierce could have 'taken away' from me would have mattered much to me, and that would have re-moved—for her—the fun."

"Good!" exclaimed Mr. Curtis with somewhat surprising em-phasis, and Miss Yates found herself flushing again, but wonder-ing at the same time if the assistant district attorney weren't per-haps a particularly adroit interviewer—a shrewd and cagey young man despite his disarming tone, and suddenly flattering habit of seeming to pay personal compliments by the expression of his voice. He was speaking again, and she suspected his under-emphasis was deliberate, and designed to cover up that unexpected "Good!" of a minute before.

"This Colonel Gamberson—had Mrs. Pierce known him before their collision in the ballroom this morning? He didn't stay for lun-cheon with you, I understood."

"Oh no, he exited himself for good reasons, I should imagine, after the lights came on. It must have been a bit embarrassing with his fiancée staring down at them. Stanley Gamberson must be a

fool. But to answer your first question, I know they had met before. I happened to be present at the time. Vivian Peabody had
brought him to tea at the Eden before a committee meeting. It must
have been all of a year ago. Caroline Semmer was there with her
brother, Doctor Semmer, and I remember Caroline presenting her
brother; so it must have been before Nancy had pneumonia last
year, because she told me this noon that he doctored her through
it. Nancy came in and hesitated prettily between the two tables
where men she might meet were. Vivian didn't invite her to sit down
with them. Vivian rarely engages in misplaced astuteness—though
Nancy didn't think so. Well, the Semmers were at the next table,
so Nancy just moved on and attached herself to them. I heard
Caroline at that point presenting her brother."

Susan consulted her watch and stood up, smiling. "Now I'm
afraid I must throw you out. I have to dress for a seven-thirty dinner."

WHILE MISS SUSAN YATES lay in her bath, she reviewed her conversation with the assistant district attorney with a fine-tooth mental
comb. She disliked the position he had thrust her into, but she disliked murder even more. On the whole, she felt she hadn't done so
badly by those often opposed forces of good taste, friendship and
law and order. She hadn't mentioned the incident of Nancy Pierce
tête-a-têting with Ethan Van Weck while Lucinda paced the streets
outside the bar with her dog—and with the bar's doors to disclose
the incident. She had said nothing of the suave Vivian's sudden
panic the spring before over discovering she was thirty-nine years
old and still unmarried—a fact conveyed to Susan by what Miss
Peabody had not said in a curiously, starkly human conversation
they had had by chance. It had been then she had first realized
that Vivian was not immune to the essential impulses of feminin-
ity. And after all, the tight golden lid of a successful career had
come off before in the hands of self-sufficient women as they approached middle age. A fiancé once obtained might have been far
more important to the editor of *For Ladies* than the world imagined. Certainly, there had been something odd in Nancy's desire

to have Vivian reassured regarding her clinch with the colonel. Why had that mattered?

Susan squeezed her sponge reflectively, and thought she hadn't revealed, either, to the alert ears of Lyle Curtis, Hortense Culbertson's desperate eagerness for that television job. Hortense had a mother to support, and no wealthy husband or father. She must carve her own future. Even a reunion with Tom wouldn't solve her financial problems. Tom Benchley was a promising young publicity man, but he had won no monetary spurs, and he drank too much. Susan rubbed soap on her sponge and decided all of these things were, anyway, very nebulous—ridiculous when considered as motives for cold-blooded murder. Shivering suddenly at her own calm acceptance of the word "murder," she hastily ducked her shoulders under the warm water of the bath and tried to relax.

Drying herself five minutes later, she stared with unseeing eyes in the triple mirrors of the bathroom. It was a very pleasing, glistening figure reflected back; and above it was a finely molded face. But in her warm brown eyes a look of doubt and of something akin to horror was deepening. She thought: "The hardest thing in life isn't suffering. It's often glorified in curious, sublimated ways. But doubt is awful. Doubt of other peoples' and your own capacity for living; doubt of the motives behind familiar things quite as much as the strange actions and words of people you don't even pretend to understand. Yes, doubt of ordinary things like laughter, and expressions of pity and ridicule." She tried for a few moments to stop thinking altogether, but thoughts kept intruding into the effort to be a blank. "What is the contour of courage, or of fear or wickedness? Once you begin to doubt anything not understood, you are brought up against inherited and cultivated habits of thinking—viewpoints often as useless as they are a habit."

In a sudden excess of healthy refusal to accept this mood, Susan began rubbing her body so briskly that it glowed with the racing blood. She hurried into the fragrant serenity of her dressing room. But her rosy flesh was in happy contradiction to the thoughts persisting like a mechanical, nagging machine.

CHAPTER NINE

SUSAN YATES SAT UP in bed and yawned. It was eight o'clock the morning following Nancy Pierce's death. Yesterday's downpour had given place to a gusty snowstorm. She thought: "Was it only yesterday I met Lyle Curtis? I wonder what kind of boyhood he had, what kind of young man he really is? Perhaps if I concentrate very hard, I can be of some help to him. Why on earth did he ask me what man Nancy Pierce could have tried to take away from me?" With that her eyes fell on the late edition of a newspaper she had been reading the night before. It was still folded back to the paragraphs about Mrs. Howard Pierce. Scanning the story again, Susan noted that Tom Benchley had got emphasis laid on "Skirts"—the club's show, and the supposition that Nancy had taken her own life because of ill health. Howard Pierce, lawyer, was reported prostrate. A servant at the apartment on Beekman Place had said Mrs. Pierce had been under a doctor's care since her illness the year before. The physician was not named.

Susan dropped the paper and rang for her maid. When the maid appeared, she said: "Lillian, bring the morning papers before my breakfast tray."

"You wait till I git this room warm," warned the maid. She lowered the windows, brought a maribou jacket and finally the papers. Miss Yates turned to the obituary page finding nothing on page one. No murder theory in the mind of the press anyway. Her maid was lingering at the door. "Yes, Lillian?"

"There was a man here already this morning selling things—insect sprays and things. Hy-hypodermics, too, he said. What that, Miss Yates?"

Susan laughed. "Now that you ask me, I don't exactly know. Doctors inject medicine in your arm with them. People who take dope sometimes take it that way. I think you must have a doctor's prescription to own one."

"This man thought you might be wanting one. I told him no."

"That was right, Lillian. I haven't the slightest use for one. Coffee, please, now. I'm slowly dying for some."

The maid departed, but Susan continued to stare after her retreating figure for several contemplative minutes. Then she yawned again, shrugged and turned back to the papers. The morning editions all carried practically the same story of Mrs. Pierce's death as that given the night before.

With the breakfast tray the maid announced that she hadn't liked the man with the atomizers. She had her suspicions of him. Next thing they knew people would be peddling dope right to folks' doors. Miss Yates said they would have to tell the police if that happened, and displayed a disinterest in further conversation.

When the maid left the room, Susan reached for the telephone on the table beside her bed and rang up Thomas Benchley who answered in a cross, sleepy voice.

"You woke me, I have the honor to admit," he said, "out of a sound sleep."

Miss Yates expressed regret and asked if, should she depart from this globe, she could depend on as excellent service as he had given Mrs. Pierce in the great American press.

Inelegantly Mr. Benchley said: "Nuts! Besides, it was suicide most likely. Why shouldn't the press say so?"

"Yesterday you wanted an assistant district attorney called in. Remember?"

Tom explained that it was invariably impossible for him to recall what he had said the day before, and added that he had, by the way, told Lyle Curtis that the chances were all against Susan having murdered Nancy Pierce.

Susan rang off rudely.

She returned to the press accounts and read them all through a second time, letting her coffee get cold.

CHAPTER TEN

THE OUTER ROOM at the district attorney's office resembled a combination newspaper's city room and locomotive factory the morning following Nancy Pierce's death. The police department had persisted in viewing the lady's demise as suicide, and the case had been turned over to the D. A.'s office on its contention that further investigation was desirable. Most of the men looked as if they had gotten no sleep. Sergeant McQuire, who definitely had not weakened to the point of a single wink, was in and out on mysterious missions, his booming voice filling the air with double negatives which lingered behind him like mountain echos. Two other men—Sylvester and Drummond—in the sergeant's position of being "loans" from the police department, and Quintus, Sterling and Hapgood, regular district attorney's office investigators, were coming and going on assignments or dictating reports to the several stenographers placed at their disposal.

Inside, in Curtis' office, the telephone was ringing constantly. A very weary young chief assistant district attorney uncradled it regularly, said: "Hello" with determined crispness, and listened to reports from outside men. A male secretary sat at an extension line taking stenographic notes on each of these conversations, whisking them to waiting typists, who had been born not to complain that reading someone else's stenographic notes is a neat feat.

The outside men, so far as Curtis had been able to juggle present facts into line, had been unearthing all manner of extraneous data

97

about those who had been present at the Tomorrow Club's luncheon—enough, he thought with a wry grimace, to make everybody guilty of the murder—if it were a murder—and also enough to make nobody guilty.

A door opened unceremoniously, and District Attorney Randolph Scofield stuck his iron-gray head in, announcing with very thinly veiled vexation that the police commissioner thought they were cuckoo.

When the district attorney's head disappeared—as abruptly as it appeared—Lyle Curtis regarded the notes which the typists had been laying before him since the night before. Boiled down, the only definite data seemed to be that Medical Examiner Dr. Mordecai Dugan had ascertained the cause of Nancy Pierce's death to have been poisoning by potassium cyanide. It had been shot into the capsule which she had swallowed five minutes before her death. Every other capsule in the same row in her box had been spiked with the same poison. A hypodermic syringe must have been used to prepare the poisoned capsules, Dr. Dugan stated. Once a capsule had dissolved in the victim's stomach, death would have been practically instantaneous. It took at most five minutes for that kind of capsule to be digested. Why so many had been poisoned was anybody's guess.

Among the other questions Mr. Curtis very much wished to have answered was why, if it was suicide, the girl had poisoned so unnecessarily large a number of her capsules? Why, if it was murder, had anybody else planted that particular kind of suicide note?

Curtis had had four men on the trail of the ballroom waiter and stagehands since the previous evening, and there wasn't the vaguest suspicion of any of them being even slightly connected with the case. They apparently had neither heard of nor seen Nancy Pierce before the morning of her death.

Curtis sighed, clipped the typed notes together and telephoned Miss Vivian Peabody's office. Within an hour he was sitting beside the lavishly modern desk of the editor of *For Ladies*. Miss Peabody's long nails were even a brighter shade of red lacquer this morning. Curtis noticed she had done her hair a new way—higher.

Her eyes were bright and steady, but the assistant D. A. sensed a new rigidity about her lips. Otherwise, Miss Peabody seemed perfectly poised and determined to be both philosophical and psychological about the "frightfully sad happening" of the previous noon. When Curtis came adroitly to the subject of hypodermic needles, she raised her fine black brows and professed complete ignorance of them, their appearance, and their inclusion in his conversation. She praised the police department for its intelligent handling of the case; and either assumed or pretended to assume that Mr. Curtis had called on her solely to receive the club's thanks for his gentlemanly presence the afternoon before.

"How right Mr. Benchley was," she pointed out, "in suggesting that a man like you would help us through so unfamiliar an experience as a police questioning—although I quite understand that these things must be handled officially in the case of sudden death. We were obligated to do all we could to help. But the Tomorrow Club is very grateful to you, Mr. Curtis. Without you to speak to him, I'm afraid Howard Pierce's state of nerves might have raised—ah—what shall we call it?—a criminal issue of some sort. But naturally no one murders young women like Nancy Pierce. Their caprices are recognized as glandular disturbances. Alas, poor Nancy was obviously also a psychopathic case, or at least inordinately neurotic. I am not, of course, an expert in these matters, but every intelligent employer these days finds it useful to have as much lay knowledge as possible of the strange workings of the human mind. Thank heaven, there is less and less neuroticism among business-women than among so-called 'protected women.' I'm afraid," and she laughed, "we are far too busy with engrossing problems of the world to plot feminine retaliations and cultivate the despondencies of other eras. I may say to you quite frankly that Mrs. Pierce was an exception—a definite exception to the average business or professional woman. It is an extremely unfortunate case."

Curtis pretended to be impressed. But, as he let her silken gestures and careful words sink into his memory, it occurred to him that an almost perfect crime might be possible for a woman so self contained and conscious of details as Miss Peabody. And he became aware, also, that because of these two perfectly leashed capacities she was without that simple, unselfconscious quality of natural charm. The studied force of her luminous black eyes held him without attracting any emotion. The rhythm of her hands held no caress. Yet they were beautiful eyes, and her hands were almost poetical in their loveliness. He hurried on to his next question before she could again assume control of the interview; but he was conscious with a wry, inward smile that, if she had possessed enchantment, he would have been tempted to hear her lines and not to read between them with such ready suspicion.

He tried to speak conversationally. "Had your fiancé, Colonel Gamberson, a long acquaintance with the deceased?"

Miss Peabody's eyebrows rose a minute fraction. He felt his taste quickly weighed and discredited. "My fiancé?" she repeated as if he were a small boy guilty of asking an awkward sex question. But she had no sooner launched this hint of reprimand than, with a quick glance at his face, she abandoned the my-dear-Mr-Curtis-you-do-amaze-me tone, and changed smoothly to one of warm and friendly confidence. But naturally her fiancé had encountered Mrs. Pierce about New York as any man of the world does a gay young woman who goes here and there. Mr. Curtis knew that sometimes "men would be boys!" It was half their charm! Tolerance, almost motherliness, flowed into her voice, but left on her face no imprint of themselves.

Curtis cleared his throat. "And that episode in the darkened ballroom yesterday morning. You perhaps felt it was—"

"Silly? Yes, I did, Mr. Curtis. Definitely silly. Women like Nancy are always putting charming men in awkward positions. She may have had nymphomaniac tendencies, of course. Unfortunately, such women—unfortunately for their sakes—amuse men. It is a pity."

Lyle stirred uneasily. It was all too smooth, too perfect and theoretical. This woman was as flexible mentally as fine leather, but more, far more transparent, he thought.

Instantly, Miss Peabody seemed to sense his reaction. She looked at him quickly and then, to his amazement, made her first obvious mistake in strategy. She became kittenish. It was altogether the wrong role and served only to intensify the tension of her narrow lips under their sophisticated rouge. It brought into startling importance the thin lights that came and went unknown to her in her eyes. What he had not fully guessed before became, through her unpracticed coyness, all too apparent. Miss Vivian Peabody was frightened, badly frightened. Whether for herself, or her fiancé or out of a vast concern for career women in general remained to be seen, he decided grimly.

CHAPTER ELEVEN

10 A.M. Wednesday

SUSAN EMERGED from her shop and began scurrying around town as if pursued by forty minor devils. She drove her car through traffic at such speed that she escaped several summonses only by her engaging smile.

In front of Lucinda Mason's imposing business façade she parked several feet too near a fireplug, but without mishap, as Miss Mason was not at business, and Susan's visit lasted less than two minutes. Miss Mason's assistant murmured something about her employer being home with a headache, and, "What an awful day yesterday was, Miss Yates! Miss Mason felt a perfect rag when she got back here. Dreadful, wasn't it, about poor Mrs. Pierce?"

Susan said yes it was; then eyed the intelligent-looking girl, and remarked that she didn't suppose, however, Miss Mason had been really any fonder of Nancy Pierce than many other people had been.

The assistant decorator shrugged, laughed and said that, of course, they had thought she was awful—about men and everything; but it was terrible having her pass out that way, nevertheless.

At the Tomorrow Club, Susan found Miss Semmer quite recovered from her ordeal of the day before, but all of a-twitter over the reporters who continued to call for additional news. She said she just hadn't known *what* to say, but had found that reporters were very helpful—just asked questions, and all you had to do *actually* was say yes and no.

Susan asked: "Did you hear somebody near you laughing rather hysterically yesterday afternoon, just after Nancy gave you that capsule—just before and again just after the lights went out for the desert scene?"

Miss Semmer thought about it and decided she couldn't remember, but that that really didn't *mean* anything. Because of everything that had happened afterward, she simply hadn't remembered *anything*. This morning, of course, she felt almost herself again, but she would never be able to forget the horror of yesterday. Could Miss Yates put Nancy's face out of her mind?

Susan escaped finally, but not before Miss Semmer had said, "What an *attractive* young man Mr. Curtis is—an old friend of Linwood's." Had Susan known that? And he had seemed to like Susan. Susan admitted Mr. Curtis had taken her down to the bar for a drink, but that she was afraid it had been a business attention more than a social one.

In her speedy car once more, Miss Yates drove to the *For Ladies* Building. Miss Peabody's secretary said she was momentarily engaged. Susan sat down impatiently and turned the pages of the latest issue of *For Ladies*—brims down—well-spaced busts—eyes important—skirts shorter—some longer—period influence—shoes—gloves—lipsticks matching nail polish—"Fashion!" snorted Susan aloud. Miss Peabody's secretary looked up startled.

"Did you say something, Miss Yates?"

"I said 'Fashion!' Meaning headaches."

The secretary looked vaguely reproving, and thought Miss Yates was acting rather queer this morning—a designer with her reputation—almost as good as the Parisians—and talking about headaches!

Then Vivian's private office door opened and Lyle Curtis came out. Susan grinned.

"Oh, it's Miss Yates," said Curtis. "Will you be long? I'd like to see you a few moments. I could wait."

Susan saw Vivian inside at her desk, staring at it raptly. She hadn't heard their voices. To Curtis she said: "Please do. I shan't be more than a second," and went in, shutting Miss Peabody's door softly before the secretary could precede and announce her. Then she turned and tapped on it to attract the editor's attention.

Vivian Peabody looked up with surprise, and exclaimed: "Sue! You startled me! Do come in!"

"Just for a second. I'm next on the district attorney pan, I fancy. Gent is waiting for me outside. Try to remember something, Vi. Who let out a couple of hysterical laughs just before the lights went out yesterday? I know it wasn't you. You couldn't laugh that way if you tried."

Miss Peabody stared. "Hysterical laughs?" she asked. "What are you talking about? Before—before Nancy died, you mean?"

"Right after Caroline Semmer swallowed her capsule. Lucinda had pulled a silly line about 'vitamins are vital.' You'd been telling her to hush. It was when she was over there reading off Nancy's box. Tom Benchley had just said he hoped the capsules were soluble in the stomach. Somebody gave a definitely feverish laugh."

"Haven't the slightest idea." Vivian looked both incurious and a little impatient. "What of it, darling?" she requested.

"Nothing, if you didn't hear it. Just thought it might have been the murderer."

"Susan! You aren't going around starting a murder story?"

"You're the only person I've breathed it to. Got to run, my dear. Thanks just the same." She opened the door, went through it and closed it softly behind her. Curtis was sitting where she had been. He had opened *For Ladies*. She asked him what would happen if she told some big husky policeman she'd seen him absorbing fashion news.

Curtis dropped the magazine, grinned, stood up and held open the secretary's door to the hall. In the corridor he shot at Susan: "Did you ever own a hypodermic needle?"

"No," said Susan, "but bright and early this morning there was a man around asking us to buy one. My maid thinks they'll be peddling dope from door to door next."

The assistant district attorney sighed and placed a certain member of his staff cheerfully in a far warmer climate. *"Touché!"* he said.

"I take my hypo peddler to mean that your office has taken over the case," said Susan.

"We have indeed," murmured Curtis. Then, suddenly: "How well do you know Miss Peabody?"

"Well enough. I mean we call each other pet first names, and exchange dinner invitations now and again. Even if I didn't admire Vivian, I'd have to be polite. Fashion magazines can be devastating to a designer!"

"Ever hear any gossip about her fiancé? This is official—not male curiosity."

"Oh. I'm glad you explained," said Susan brightly. "Yes, I've heard he's a regular old Bedouin."

"Would you say Miss Peabody had anyone in particular to be annoyed about?"

"I would not. I could not. Miss Peabody is not the type to have confided such an item."

The elevator opened its maw to them and they descended.

The young man pondered a moment, then asked if she was certain Tom Benchley and Hortense Culbertson hadn't been on speaking terms for months until the previous noon, and Miss Yates said she was absolutely certain. The elevator disgorged them at the Street floor and Susan said: "I really must be on my way, if the forces of law and order have finished with me. I'm a busy woman."

Curtis held the street door open for her. They said good-by, and he watched her take her place behind the wheel of the roadster. Then he turned and sought the telephone booth in the lobby.

CHAPTER TWELVE

Later Wednesday Morning

CURTIS TALKED for some moments over a telephone in the lobby. Then he went out and grabbed a cab which deposited him presently in front of an important-looking apartment building. A doorman, resembling a Whitehall guard, conservatively wearing, however, a military cap, attended his descent from the taxi. Curtis walked across the pavement toward the entrance, beckoning.

"Want a word with you," he said to the doorman who expressed pained surprise at his tone, but followed.

"Yes sir?"

"Come inside a minute. Take a look at these." He shoved an official identification of himself and a really excellent photograph of Nancy Pierce into the man's hand.

The doorman stared first at one then at the other, cleared his throat, apparently did some rapid calculations on the futility of misleading the forces of law, and dropping his voice, asked: "What about the young lady, sir?"

"Ever see her around here?"

"Yes sir."

"When?"

"She calls sometimes—on one of the tenants, sir."

"Which tenant?"

"Well—er, that is—"

"Which tenant?"

"Colonel Stanley Gamberson, sir."

"You on the door just in the daytime?"

"Yes sir—6 A.M. to 6 P.M."

"You mean, she came to parties, or alone?" demanded Lyle, retrieving the paper and photograph from the other's hand.

"Alone, I guess you'd say."

"How often?"

"Once or twice a week. Sometimes oftener."

"You don't know about nights?"

"No sir." But Curtis could see that what he hadn't seen, he'd heard about. He said so. The doorman admitted that he had heard of her being there at night sometimes.

Curtis requested and received the address of the night doorman, and advised the Whitehall guardish person to keep his mouth strictly closed on the matter, advice obviously well understood. He then strode out to the curb, and was handed with infinite care into another taxi.

The night doorman lived a few blocks away on First Avenue. He was asleep, but Curtis' identification of himself prodded his wife into instantaneous efforts to arouse her husband. She stood around looking scared when Theodore Jones, sleep heavy in his eyes, appeared.

Curtis said pleasantly: "This has nothing to do with your husband personally, Mrs. Jones. Please forget I've been here. Don't talk about it to anyone." He asked a few questions which were confirmed identically in line with the answers the day doorman had given. Reiterating the advisability of silence, he left.

After that he returned to his office. Red, blue and white sheets of memoranda covered his desk like sparkling mosaics. Investigator Hapgood, his secretary informed him, was on the telephone. A moment later, Hapgood was saying he had not been able to uncover evidence of larceny at any of the business establishments connected with Nancy Pierce's late activities, or those of her sister members of the Tomorrow Club.

Curtis said: "All right. We'll put auditors on the job if we have to," and ringing off, turned to a message from Sergeant Sterling. Gamberson's Filipino had seen no such item as a hypodermic around the colonel's premises. The maids at Miss Mason's had not seen any among either Van Weck's or his wife's possessions. Same report from the maid and cook at the Howard Pierce apartment. The Pierce maid and cook apparently had had no trouble with their mistress. They seemed to have considered her glamorous and comfortably (from their standpoint) disinterested in housekeeping.

The assistant district attorney turned anxiously to his desk. He read carefully but impatiently through the great pile of stenographic reports. At last, he shoved them all back on his desk. The room had grown dark. Premature dusk was beginning to settle over the city. He remembered suddenly that he had had no luncheon and that it must be after three o'clock. Wearily, he asked his secretary to have something reasonably digestible sent in from a near-by restaurant. Then he settled down once more behind his desk, foolscap before him.

Lyle Curtis began then a report to the D. A. The clock on his desk reached four-thirty; part of his lunch still remained uneaten. Wind was rattling the big windows peremptorily, and the streets below the district attorney's building were deep in gray slush. Snow fell like wisps of smoke. The counterfeit dusk now hung tenaciously over the city. Curtis blinked and switched on his desk lamp.

Finally he rose and stretched his aching shoulders. He reached down and drank the remainder of an almost cold cup of coffee. Then he poured a fresh cup from the thermos pot, gulped it eagerly and rang for his secretary.

"See if the D. A. can see me."

Word came back in a few minutes that Mr. Scofield was engaged. He wanted to see Curtis in an hour—unless it was urgent.

The assistant D. A. shook his head, yawned and looked a long moment at the inviting couch in the corner. Then he took up his telephone receiver. He asked for the Tomorrow Club. Presently Caroline Semmer's apologetic voice came over the wire. She sounded pleased when she found it was Mr. Curtis.

"I've been interviewed by so many reporters," she laughed almost girlishly, "that I am getting to feel quite like an expert—a novelist or a politician or someone."

Curtis said: "I want to find out who sponsored Mrs. Pierce for membership in the Tomorrow Club."

"Oh, dear me," hesitated Miss Semmer, as if matters pertaining to the club were something she never discussed with nonmembers.

"Only a routine record," Curtis hastened to reassure her.

"I—I see," and Miss Semmer still hesitated; then, as if it were entirely against her will, she said: "Miss Mason sponsored Mrs. Pierce, Mr. Curtis. Mrs. Pierce was doing jewel settings then, and Miss Mason thought it would be so nice to have jewels represented in the club. We're classified, you know; one woman from each of the fashion fields."

The assistant district attorney remarked that that was fine. Then feeling Miss Semmer was still worried over having disclosed a club record, he added that of course it was very sad they had had to lose Mrs. Pierce; but, of course, she hadn't been in the jewelry business any more.

Miss Semmer seemed to think there was some reflection on the club's stability in this for she said quickly: "Oh, but she was about to go into something so *very* exciting—television! Of course, that *was* a secret. I'm probably the only person out of broadcasting who knew about it. You see, I spoke of television myself to dear Mrs. Pierce. She was so good looking; and television isn't like radio. People *see* you."

Curtis asked: "How did you happen to suggest that to Mrs. Pierce?" He heard the secretary-treasurer of the club catch her breath as if his words had reprimanded an indiscretion on her part. "Oh," she said, "you see I'm *supposed* to be a sort of *clearing* house for our members on new professional opportunities. Everything I hear about I report right back to members who want customers or new connections."

"Wasn't the television opportunity," Curtis asked conversationally, "a job which your other member Miss Culbertson would have liked?"

Miss Semmer gasped as if that possibility had struck her for the first time. "Oh dear," she almost moaned. "You know, I assumed that if they were thinking of dear Miss Culbertson they would already have made their selection—and I had *heard* the position was *open.* Oh, I do hope—that is, it would be dreadful if Mrs. Pierce being interested had embarrassed Miss Culbertson in any way. That was very careless of me, Mr. Curtis. I—I just thought Mrs. Pierce was so good looking and—not *doing* anything particularly—"

The assistant district attorney cut this self-recrimination short. "And who sponsored Miss Yates in the Tomorrow Club?" he asked.

"Oh," answered a relieved voice at the other end of the wire. "Miss Yates was a *charter* member. Such a *charming* girl, don't you think, Mr. Curtis?"

"Yes indeed. Very. Very astute, too. I imagine she always knows a bit more than she tells, eh?"

Miss Semmer did not seem altogether to follow him in this observation. She repeated primly: "Such a charming girl," and added, "I think it is splendid that American designers are coming into such *prominence.* They are doing such *able* and *inspired* work; and then, of course, American women simply have no use for all those very *fussy* afternoon dresses the Parisians design."

Curtis escaped thankfully and recradled his phone.

CHAPTER THIRTEEN

WHEN THE ASSISTANT district attorney entered the chief's office, he found Mr. Scofield's temper had not improved. The district attorney was worried still about the police commissioner's lightheartedness in the Pierce affair.

"No doubt about it, Curtis. He thinks we've robbed a mare's nest. Threatened to buy everybody champagne if we could find a murderer in the case. He may be right. This Pierce woman was hitting life pretty fast. Suppose she did go off the deep end? She left a note intimating that she'd had enough."

"That's what gets me. She didn't say she'd had enough. And we can't find a single proof of the larceny angle. If she imagined it all, why was she in such a high and fancy mood yesterday?"

"Maybe she wasn't. No, I don't mean that. If your Yates oracle is holding out on you it suggests murder. I've decided we don't want a murder."

Curtis glanced at his chief with tired amusement. No one who had known Randolph Scofield the eight years he had, had ever known him to leave a case until it was finished—thoroughly finished. The commissioner must have been very irritating indeed.

He looked out at the petulant way the snow was falling and asked if the D. A. wanted him to make a report on all data to date. Mr. Scofield nodded irritably.

Curtis began by saying that he had taken up separately each of the persons presumably connected with the case, in order to organize their motives, possible possession of a hypodermic, opportunity

to have planted the poisoned capsules, opportunity to have planted
the note, opportunity for knowledge of how many capsules Nancy
Pierce had left in her box, general traits of character and public
attitude toward the deceased.

"First, I've analyzed the suicide angle." He began reading from
his digest:

> *Digest of Evidence in Nancy Pierce Capsule Case*
> Possible but unlikely that there is no connection
> between Nancy Pierce's death and note found under
> her right foot. If she committed suicide, she must
> have dropped note unintentionally—probably having
> intended to hold it in her hand. Only one point of logic
> making note explain her death: it suggests way out of
> disgrace lay in taking her life—that theft would then
> not be discovered. But then why mention it?
>
> Nancy Pierce, of course, had every opportunity
> to poison her own capsules. Question: *Why poison
> so many* when *one* would have done job.
>
> A. Perhaps she did not know poison acted quickly
> and thought she would be poisoned slowly over a
> long period of time. This would account for her kill-
> ing herself *where* she did; but would not account for
> *suicide note*.
>
> According to her maid and cook, she had been
> under doctor's care. Dr. Linwood Semmer, her phy-
> sician, admits this but says it was only for periodic
> examinations after pneumonia.
>
> Her husband, Howard Pierce, seemed more an-
> gry than bereaved when seen soon after death. He
> insisted his wife would not have taken her own life.
> Insisted it was murder. Did he know she was having
> an affair with Colonel Stanley Gamberson, fiancé of
> Miss Vivian Peabody, president of the Tomorrow
> Club? Did he know she had some sort of alliance with
> Dr. Semmer? That she was seeking out the publisher

of *For Ladies*, and had general reputation of person who had narrowly escaped being correspondent in various divorce cases? Appears he must have known of some of these cases.

No evidence that Dr. Semmer's temper disturbed Mrs. Pierce, nor that she was afraid of losing him, or Gamberson or her husband.

Murder Possibilities

Method: There are three possibilities—1. that capsules, spiked with potassium cyanide, were substituted for some in Mrs. Pierce's box; 2. that Mrs. Pierce's box was stolen, doctored and returned; 3. that a poison-containing box was substituted for hers. Last supposition seems most likely. Quickest, easiest method. Fingerprints on box found in her handbag after death were her own (also Miss Semmer's—who had taken a capsule also at luncheon table. No others.) This points to box having been wiped clean prior to luncheon and prior to these two women handling it at table. Otherwise prints of packer, seller, probably deceased's maid and others would have been legitimately on it.

Suspects: A number of people openly dislike Nancy Pierce—some with substantial reason. Alphabetically, an itemization follows of possible case against each one of them:

Thomas Benchley—*Publicity Man*

No proof Benchley knew deceased personally before day of murder, but she was trying to get important job away from his former fiancée, Hortense Culbertson of Consolidated Broadcasting Company. Seems doubtful Benchley knew this until just before murder. Does not seem to have been on renewed speaking terms with Miss Culbertson until then.

Benchley arrived at ballroom after episode on stage which gave various persons opportunity to see how many capsules were in box—necessary information for murderer if another box was to be substituted without arousing deceased's suspicion. Benchley has famous collection hypodermics collected by his late father, a well-known physician. Would he then have used, for lethal purposes, such an instrument? Benchley had scant chance to plant suicide note—doesn't seem to have been very near body. Lively imagination, quick witted. Polite attitude to deceased proves nothing.

Hortense Culbertson—*Radio Commentator*
Knew deceased. Didn't like her. Takes radio work seriously. Knew Mrs. Pierce was trying to get television job. Is ambitious (record), conscientious (record), clever and pretty. Claims she didn't see capsule box on stage. (In Inspector Beller's examination of suspects, Miss Lucinda Mason said Miss Culbertson "must have seen it" because (quoting Miss Mason) she had remarked at time: "If Nancy ever drops all her chattel in a broadcast her name will be mud." She didn't, however, go near deceased at luncheon table. No evidence she was alone elsewhere with deceased. Couldn't have planted capsules on stage. Peabody and Mason say Mrs. Pierce kept bag "right under arm" except when looking for her capsules (and dropping her lipstick). Then bag in her hands. Confirmed by electricians, who distinctly recall hearing deceased say: "All stagehands are light fingered." They—(the stagehands)—appear not to have resented this, under the impression—now stronger—that Nancy Pierce "was batty." Miss Culbertson's chance for planting "suicide note," even more than Benchley's, very slight indeed.

Colonel Stanley Gamberson—*Miss Peabody's Fiancé*
Every reason to believe (evidence of two doormen)
Colonel Gamberson was having affair with deceased.
Is vigorous, retired army officer with generally accepted weakness for opposite sex. Marriage to Vivian
Peabody is scheduled to take place soon. No proof
Gamberson possessed hypodermic needle. Is ambitious, ruthless, canny. Forthcoming marriage desirable. Nancy Pierce may have become thorn in flesh.
(Embracing scene in darkened ballroom casts some
doubt on this if he knew his fiancée was on stage and
sudden illumination of room possible. Usual attitude
with women in public described by acquaintances as
"silly," however.) Had no known opportunity to
know, Tuesday morning, how many capsules were
left in Mrs. Pierce's box, so doubtful he could have
planted substitute box during petting scene. But we
do not yet know where Mrs. Pierce spent the evening
(Monday) preceding her death. If with Gamberson,
substitution or doctoring may have taken place then.
(Find out if Mrs. Pierce took a capsule after breakfast. See paragraphs relating to capsule box later.)

Lucinda Mason—*Interior Decorator*
Ethan Van Weck—*Her Husband*
Miss Mason was furious with deceased because of
scene with dog. This happened only a short while
before murder. Time to procure and plant poison?
No proof that she knew before murder that her husband had met Mrs. Pierce in bar. No evidence that
Van Weck had ever met Mrs. Pierce before. No evidence of possession of hypodermic by either of them.
Van Weck's opportunity to plant note seems nonex-
istent unless Miss Mason was a confederate and did
so when she read from capsule box over Mrs. Pierce's
shoulder. Opportunity, perhaps, for Van Weck to

have planted substitute capsule box in bar. (Check further with Waiter and Bartender.) But unless Van Weck met wife before coming to bar, he could not have known approximate number of capsules left in box. His attitude to deceased polite, somewhat flattered. His wife's attitude definitely unfriendly. Makes no secret of it. Scoffs at idea that she would have "taken time" to murder Nancy Pierce. Unusually murderous attitude for a murderer. Bear in mind: Mrs. Pierce may have told Van Weck something. Also, Miss Mason had been lunching with deceased frequently. She could easily have known about "Threes System."

Vivian Peabody—*Editor of "For Ladies," Pres. Tomorrow Club*

International reputation as fashion editor, suave, intelligent, power in business life. Used to ruling people. Cold but diplomatic attitude toward deceased, also firm. Pretends to believe suicide theory and has psychological reasons to bring forward—neurotic fixation, etc. Definitely worried about something, but fancies she's ably concealing it. Gives impression she thought Mrs. Pierce just a neurotic, trivial young woman, "not representative of businesswomen." (Indicates she likes businesswomen to be businesslike.) Admits her fiancé Colonel Gamberson knew deceased and "was amused by her." Skims over any suggestion of intimacy. My guess, she doesn't know about "affaire," but suspects it or only learned of it recently. Makes pose of broad-mindedness. No proof of possession of hypodermic. McQuire investigating further through cook. Is Miss Peabody unusually capable of a well-planned murder? Does she think Colonel Gamberson may have been murderer? Her opportunity excellent (as noted) to have planted suicide note. But would she have made it quite so excellent an opportunity if she had proposed to commit a murder? No proof of opportunity to plant capsules. Why, if she planted note, *That Kind of Note?*

Howard Pierce—*Lawyer—Husband of Deceased*
Probably knew wife was cheating. Perhaps she was growing to be an expensive, undesired luxury. Pretends to be convinced of murder. Said to be prostrate, and have not been able to interview since immediately after wife's death. Then, expressed anger over suicide theory. Legal career not too fragrant. Has been just inside law several times. Excellent opportunity to plant capsules, but (as noted) why plant so many? And would he not have wanted to be certain she would die away from home? Could he be by planting so many? Could easily have ascertained potency of poison. How could he have planted *Suicide Note?* Confederate? Who? *Why That Kind of Note?* Is canny, ruthless, intelligent. Public attitude to deceased was, of late, casually disinterested.

Michael Shawnessy—*Waiter—Eden Bar*
May have had opportunity to plant capsules in bar. No opportunity to plant note. Could he have been anyone's confederate? No evidence he knew deceased in any way except as a customer of Eden bar. Good record—hard working, honest, conscientious. Attitude to deceased respectful. Apparently doesn't like Dr. Semmer.

Dr. Linwood Semmer—*Deceased's Physician*
According to bartender and waiter, Semmer was extremely angry with deceased less than an hour before her death. Is high tempered, ambitious,

probably neurotic—at least, emotional and moody.
Could he have substituted poisoned capsules when
in bar with Mrs. Pierce? (Why not full box?) Why
poison whole row when effect of poison would be
familiar to him? Did he seek to draw suspicion from
himself by pretending lack of knowledge? Had easiest access of anyone but Benchley to hypodermics,
certainly easy access to poisons. Therefore, would
he have used poison, and so usual a one? Was this
also to indicate layman's work and divert suspicion?
As deceased's physician, could he not, however, have
poisoned her without any suspicion of foul play? He
could even have been present at her death and provided death certificate. Did he perhaps plan and
carry out murder on short notice in a fit of jealous
rage? Who could have been his accomplice in planting suicide note? *Why That Kind of Note?*

Caroline Semmer—*Secretary-Treasurer of Tomor-
    row Club*
Probably disapproved of brother's interest in deceased. Is extremely fond of him. An apologetic, prim
person. Excited about being interviewed by reporters. Badly frightened at thought that she might
also have taken a poisoned capsule. Evidence not
confirmed that she was present on stage when
deceased's capsule box was displayed to Miss Peabody. Tries to keep in well with employers in self-
effacing, reasonably tactful way. Doesn't gossip
about club business Told Mrs. Pierce about television opportunity. Now distressed that may have been
disadvantageous to Miss Culbertson. Was definitely
worried when brother's name was mentioned by
Inspector Beller during police inquiry. Does she
suspect Dr. Linwood Semmer?

Susan Yates—*Fashion Designer—Owner of Own Business*

Distinguished national and even international reputation as a designer of women's clothes. Does not seem to have disliked deceased excessively, but says she feared her "inventive tongue." Seemingly very helpful with information, but seems to have hesitancy in talking too much just the same. Is it good taste, respect for her fellow workers in the professional and business world—or *Does She Know Something Harmful to One of Possible Suspects?* She is "on" to hypodermic inquiry. From evidence to date could only have planted capsules when talking to deceased in public corridor. Second best chance—to Miss Peabody—to have planted suicide note. Could not have known how many capsules were left in box unless Miss Mason told her—was not present at time box was displayed on stage. Intelligent, observant, reputation of minding own business. Well liked. Has some theories about murder she isn't divulging yet— my guess. Can she be persuaded to talk? Attitude to deceased amused, but calm. Cool headed enough to plan and carry out difficult scheme.

Maid and Cook at Pierce Apartment
Excellent character references. No reason to suspect. No opportunity to plant suicide note. Could they have been—or could one of them have been confederate of person who did plant suicide note? No reason to suspect. No evidence of them ever having had access to a hypodermic. Looked upon late employer as a glamorous person, comfortably disinclined to interfere in housekeeping management.

The Box of Capsules as a Weapon

The box, when seen on stage and when viewed at luncheon table (later evidence, Miss Yates, Miss Mason, Miss Culbertson, Miss Peabody, Miss Semmer and Mr. Benchley) contained two capsules at the beginning of the first row. All other rows were full until Miss Semmer took her dose and Mrs. Pierce took hers. Medical examiner found first capsule in first row gone. By evidence of others this was one taken by Miss Semmer. Also, second capsule in second row gone. Evidence of others, this was third "in" from first remaining capsule, and one taken by Mrs. Pierce herself. According to analysis, remaining capsule in first row was free of poison. Other capsules in second row were filled with cyanide of potassium. Others in box (like capsule remaining in first row) were normal—that is, contained only pure Vitamin A and D units, physiologically standardized. (See diagrams.)

The Capsule Box

   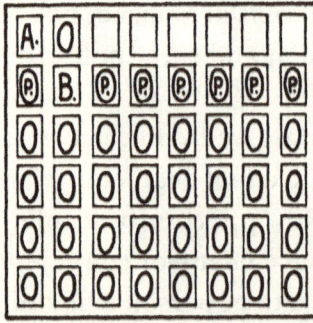

BOX AS IT APPEARED ON STAGE AND AT LUNCHEON.

BOX AS IT APPEARED AFTER DEATH. ALL CAPSULES MARKED "P" WERE POISONED. SPACE "A" CONTAINED THE CAPSULE MISS SEMMER TOOK, SPACE "B" CAPSULE MRS PIERCE TOOK.

Question

Were the first two capsules (all remaining in first
row when box was seen on stage) not poisoned because murderer knew Mrs. Pierce's habit of taking
every third capsule? If so, this would point, perhaps,
to Howard Pierce who had better opportunity than
anyone else to know of this habit of his wife's. (See
Howard Pierce above.) This fact might point also to
Colonel Gamberson and Dr. Semmer. Both on inti-
mate terms of some kind with deceased. All people
at luncheon table denied previous knowledge of
habit before exhibition of "system" at luncheon
table. May be concealing knowledge, of course.

Or does way of placing poisoned capsules point
to desire on part of murderer (if he did *not* know
about "system") to delay death of young woman until he was not present? If we accept premise that
people at luncheon did not know deceased's habit of
taking capsules, then attempted murder-postpone-
ment supposition definitely points to one of them.
This conclusion, of course, inconclusive without further evidence.

Note

Points immediately needing further clarification:
1. Where was Nancy Pierce the night before she died?
a. Could poisoned capsules have been planted then?
b. If so, it must have been someone who could have
   (or who had a confederate) planted suicide note.
2. Does Miss Hortense Culbertson's denial about
   seeing box on stage mean anything?
3. Could Colonel Gamberson have planted poisoned
   capsules during collision with deceased in ballroom Tuesday morning. Or night before if he saw
   her then? But then, how did he plant note? (Miss
   Peabody most obvious confederate.)

4. Which of persons connected with deceased had access to cyanide of potassium?

5. (See 3, above) Why is Miss Peabody apprehensive? Would she not be too smart to have sat directly beside deceased if murderer? Or did she expect suicide note to be accepted as such? (She pretended, at least, to be satisfied with it at police examination.)

6. What is real meaning of suicide note? (Did Nancy Pierce drop it, or was it deliberately planted? Or was its planting accidental? Seems too pat.)

7. Did Mrs. Pierce confide anything important to Ethan Van Weck? (Bartender's and waiter's impression seems very conclusive that they had never met before that noon. While not brilliant, Van Weck has reputation of caution regarding grasping women.)

8. If Dr. Linwood Semmer murdered woman, why did he choose so dramatic a way? Why did he poison so many capsules?

9. If her husband is murderer, why did he poison so many capsules? (With so many poisoned, she might at any time have taken one at home; and Howard Pierce must have known of "threes system.") Why that kind of note if Pierce did murder?

10. How could Howard Pierce have planted note? Confederate at luncheon? Who? No clue.

11. What does Susan Yates know—or suspect—she isn't telling? Could she have planted capsules when talking to Mrs. Pierce outside bar? She could have planted note. Why is she determined to help break down suicide theory if murderess?

12. What larceny, if any, did Nancy Pierce commit?

CHAPTER FOURTEEN

6 P.M. Wednesday

As Curtis finished reading his summary, the district attorney's secretary announced that Sergeant McQuire was waiting to make a report.

The bulky sergeant came in, his expression far from crestfallen. Miss Hortense Culbertson's maid (a part-time, afternoon girl) had told him right out, he said, that her employer had a hypo; that she took adrenalin with it under a doctor's orders. McQuire had gotten the name of the doctor, and the doctor had said, yes, that she did.

Quintus, a man on the staff, who had not been seen before by those under suspicion, had then visited Miss Culbertson at her office, posing as a salesman of atomizers, insect sprays and hypodermics.

Scofield tut-tutted. "I don't," he commented, "consider that to have been too brilliant a plan. It's a wonder they let him into an office in the first place; and in the second place, I fancy the commissioner will be downright shocked to hear that hypos are being sold from door to door in New York."

McQuire looked a little sheepish. "Well, Quintus and I worked it out together, Mr. District Attorney, and she swallowed the story line, hook and sinker." He became less unabashed. "'Course Quintus came around to hypos last—as a kind of piece of resistance, as they say."

Restlessly, the district attorney demanded what else McQuire had learned, and the sergeant explained that that afternoon, he had heard by telephone from Miss Peabody's cook. She had had to report that, while none of the staff had actually ever seen a hypodermic syringe around the apartment, Miss Peabody did have a big chest which she kept constantly under lock and key. The maids had long suspected that rejuvenating lotions of special value were cached in it; but it appeared to be the sergeant's secret conviction that, armed with a search warrant, he would take no time at all in discovering in Miss Peabody's chest the instrument which had monkeyed with Mrs. Pierce's capsules.

"And what have you discovered about the poison?" demanded the D. A. McQuire shrugged.

"We're checking with all the pharmacists in the city and in White Plains and Glen Cove," he said. "Routine—you don't have to walk into a drugstore and ask for it these days. You can buy it free as you like in weed killer. It's used in photography. It's used in jewelry work. It's used in electroplating."

"Weed killer, photography, jewelry," mused Curtis. "What leaps to the eye is, of course, the fact that Mrs. Pierce used to design jewel settings. Did you find out if she ever did any actual jewelry work herself, McQuire?"

"She had a regular workbench up at her apartment," said McQuire smugly, very proud of himself. "I looked it over careful. There was a jar of potassium cyanide, all right—a solution of it, I guess you'd call it. Anyway, it was marked potassium cyanide. I brought it in and gave it to the doc to examine."

"Why then," said the D. A., "that certainly makes the case against Howard Pierce much stronger. Looks to me as though you have a real lead there, Curtis." Lyle Curtis shook his head wearily.

"We might have," he said, "except that the poison is also found in weed killer, and Miss Semmer and Miss Mason both live in the country, and presumably have gardens complete with weeds. You'd better check on that, McQuire. And that one or another of our suspects is sure to turn out to be an amateur photographer. Wait and see. It lets everybody in. And if you want to get really involved, why doesn't it show that Nancy Pierce was the person who fiddled with the capsules, intending to poison someone else with them, and then forgot which ones she'd poisoned? Yes, I know that's idiotic—but the damn case is so confused, I'd believe anything."

The D. A. favored him with a cold stare and turned to McQuire.

"Check on that weed killer and on the photography," he said. "Did you try the jar of potassium cyanide from the Pierce apartment for fingerprints?"

McQuire nodded. "I handled it real careful," he said, "and had it dusted and photographed before I took it to the doc." The D. A. nodded.

"Get me both those reports as soon as they come in," he said. McQuire saluted and started out. At the door he turned and said:

"Oh—that Peabody dame lives in a penthouse, with lots of terrace and big flower boxes. Guess I better check her for weed killer too."

The D. A. nodded and said:

"Sure, that's all you have to report, McQuire?"

The sergeant scratched his head, and said he'd stopped at the Eden bar that afternoon, and had a chat with Lucien, the bartender, and Mike, the waiter who had served Dr. Semmer and later Dr. Semmer and Mrs. Pierce. But he'd learned nothing that Mr. Curtis had not already discovered. Neither of them remembered seeing anything suspicious in the behavior of Dr. Semmer, except getting mad and stalking off. They were confident he had not had the girl's box of capsules in his hands.

"Do you think, McQuire, they were giving you straight dope?" the D. A. demanded.

"Seemed like it; but then them fellows is part of the Eden system."

"What in the name of sweet heaven is that?"

"Aw, it's a system that says no wrong can be done inside the Hotel Eden. Poisoning people ain't allowed. Strictly forbidden, they was tellin' me."

After McQuire had retired, the district attorney said: "Of course, Semmer could be our man. He was worked up about the girl, had a fuss with her, perhaps exchanged capsule boxes and beat it."

"Popping off that way in anger wouldn't have been too diplomatic though," complained Curtis.

The district attorney admitted that he wasn't completely en-
amored of the doctor theory. Murderous medicos usually shied
away from any but the most obscure poisons. The whole case in
his opinion was screwy. Why the damn note at all?

Sighing, the assistant district attorney considered the possibilities of Dr. Semmer being their man. He explained that he and
the doctor had been college classmates. Semmer had been a good
student, but something of a sap; once he had raised a regular row
over what he considered an unjustified dismissal of a little wait-
ress. None of them had thought he'd despoiled the girl's virtue as
repayment, either. Romantic sort of chap at moments. Neurotic,
too, no doubt.

After they had wrangled over the doctor a bit more as a possible suspect, the D. A. said that husband Howard Pierce had shown
up that afternoon in the police commissioner's office playing the
big, brave and stricken role, and complaining once more that his
little darling had been snatched from his arms by a willful villain.
He had struck even the commissioner as a bit on the bilge-water
side, perhaps interested in gaining personal publicity in a celebrated case—or establishing by hocus-pocus his own innocence.
Friend husband had so failed to impress the commissioner as to
make him almost interested in the Nancy Pierce case.

"Of course," observed Mr. Scofield, "Pierce could have planted
both capsules and note in his wife's handbag, fixing it so she
wouldn't take a poisoned capsule until she was well away from
home, and counting on her sooner or later pawing around in her
bag and dropping the note. Women carry such a hell of a lot of
stuff around with them."

Curtis thought this was pulling rather too far the long arm of
possibility. It all seemed a little too neat and fortuitous. But Mr.
Scofield, pleased with the idea of encouraging the commissioner's
one suspicion of doubt, pointed out that it wasn't any neater than
the idea of Van Weck having picked the girl's pocketbook in a public bar, or the illustrious editor of *For Ladies* having knocked her
off to save her wandering colonel.

"Or," he continued, warming to the subject, "your trembly old secretary of the club expressing passionate brother love murderously, or that radio gal insuring herself a better job, or that publicity fellow helping her out, or the decorator thinking she was mean to dogs and disapproving of her Social Register husband buying her cocktails. I'll even break down and say *I* think Pierce more logical than your omniscient dress designer, with her nice philosophical attitude toward everybody."

"The note, sir. Still bothers me. Why would Howard Pierce—or anybody—have written *that* kind of a note?"

CHAPTER FIFTEEN

Nine O'Clock, Wednesday Evening

Miss Ruby Holt would have been shocked at the idea of engaging in what she termed "an ordinary pickup," but with customers of the firm of Holden, Pierce, Crawford and Hamilton, she felt a certain amount of hospitality was reasonable, and the elegant-voiced Mr. Carrington Wells of Boston seemed an eminently safe proposition.

Accordingly, at a few minutes before nine o'clock, the evening after Tom's sleuthing expedition, Miss Holt awaited her rendez-vous with him in the colossal lobby of the San Horitz Hotel. She stood, rather more on one foot than the other, a bright blue-gloved hand supporting one comely hip. She was engaged in attempting to maintain a casual interest in the ceiling.

Susan Yates, passing through the lobby from the restaurant to the lounge, accompanied by a client from Chicago, glanced at the blue-gloved young woman with amused approval of the inventiveness of her costume. As if the force of gravity ended at the top of her skull, Miss Holt had managed to place a halo-like hat at exactly that point. There it remained magically. A large, flat, red curl, vaguely resembling a dollar sign, was plastered conscientiously on her forehead. She had decorated an otherwise skimpy but docile little suit with a cheap bunch of artificial, blue cornflowers. Amazingly, Susan thought, the *tout ensemble* of the young woman's toilet possessed that tenuous quality known to her business as chic. She murmured as much to her woman companion, who sniffed audibly, after one glance at the redhead, and said: "Darling, if I didn't know all about your impeccable taste, I should say you'd lost your mind. Why the child looks like a floosie. Probably is."

Susan shook her head. "She has, my lamb, that thing you can improve upon but not endow—natural taste. One could make a knockout of her with a little time and trouble."

Miss Yates's companion remained unimpressed, and they passed on into the lounge where the waiters were busy serving brandies, highballs and coffee.

Meanwhile Ruby had not been unconscious of the passing of Susan Yates. She decided Susan must be a movie star—so swell and rich looking; personality, too. Anybody could see that.

Miss Yates and her guest had seated themselves with their backs to the lobby by the time Mr. Benchley put in an appearance. Unlike Miss Yates, he observed the redhead's costume from a distance and with considerable trepidation. The exquisite nuances of its chic were to be forever concealed from him, and he found himself regretting not having selected a more obscure rendezvous. Yet, so far as he knew, it was not the favorite of any of his intimates.

"Oh gee," the telephone operator greeted Mr. Benchley. "This is a swell place." She added more sedately, "I've been meaning to drop in here for some time now, Mr. Wells."

"Delighted you approve," replied Tom, adopting his Harvard accent. "Shall we have a spot to drink in the lounge?"

"Sure," agreed Ruby. "I'm so thirsty I'm about to die."

Mr. Benchley winced, and when they were seated, suggested the longest drink he could on the spur of the moment recall.

"A planter's punch," gurgled Miss Holt. "Gosh, that's one I've never had, although a friend of mine was telling me about going to Bermuda and drinking them all day long. Nights, too, I guess, knowing this person I was speaking of."

When the punches arrived, Mr. Wells grew gradually confidential. He supposed in the way of a theoretical discussion that it must be fascinating employment in a law firm—especially watching such a fast thinker as Howard Pierce at work.

Miss Holt was not one to toy with a drink. She had already consumed several handsome samples of the punch. She was beginning to feel rather witty, and remarked that inasmuch as Mr. Pierce had never taken her out, she had no firsthand information of how good he was at fast work, but she guessed he must be pretty good from the number of girls who were always calling him up—who had been—that was—until recently. Mr. Benchley picked up his ears.

"Why not recently?" he asked.

This reminded Miss Holt that she was talking more than was perhaps practical, and it took a little while to bring her back into gossipy form. By a good deal of side skirmishing, Tom finally elicited the information that the lawyer was at present very sweet indeed on his private secretary, Miss Hotchkiss, and that feminine calls for him had accordingly diminished at the offices of Holden, Pierce, Crawford and Hamilton. Ruby summed this up with the observation that "a fellow had to give girls some encouragement—even in New York."

With considerable perseverance, Mr. Benchley gained the information that it made Miss Holt really laugh the way Mr. Pierce was now carrying on about his wife's death. Having said as much, however, she clapped a hand over her mouth and looked worried.

"I guess," she cried, "I oughtn't to have said a thing like that—you being a client and all, Mr. Wells."

"Why not?" demanded the Harvard voice encouragingly. "Don't tell me you think we married men should have no pleasures? Surely, just because a poor man's married, you don't blame him for liking a pretty woman, and a bit of a fling, as the saying goes?"

Miss Holt agreed that that was O.K. with her, pointing out that she guessed it worked both ways.

"Look at me sitting with you, and you've just let out that you're married. Got kids, too, I bet."

"No. No children. Not one," Mr. Benchley hastily assured her.

"Well," said Ruby thoughtfully. "It don't make a lot of difference. I bet your wife wouldn't like to see you right now."

His little woman, her companion insisted, was very broad minded; very broad minded indeed. No doubt just like Mrs. Pierce had been.

But Ruby said Mrs. Pierce was different, she bet, from Mr. Wells 's wife. While she herself was not one to talk about the dead, Mrs. Pierce had, in her opinion, played around too much, Practically inviting Mr. Pierce's behavior.

Miss Holt expanded her theme and announced confidentially that just between them she bet Mrs. Pierce hadn't died laughing over Miss Hotchkiss, for Miss Hotchkiss was the boss's Waterloo, she guessed you might say.

"Waterloo?" questioned Tom, mystified.

"You know, Waterloo. That was the place that washed up a fellow named Napoleon—French he was. Mr. Pierce is just crazy about Hotchkiss. Anybody can see that. But you needn't worry about anything I've told you. They say he is a wonderful lawyer. Only it makes me laugh the way he's going on about her passing out. He's been at home mostly since. Hotchkiss was right about not being able to let you see him for a few days. He calls up on the phone, though, and sounds so sad. Gee, it's funny, you never know what a man's going to turn round and do."

Mr. Benchley had opened his mouth for a Wellsian retort when an all too familiar voice sickened the words on his lips.

"Why, Tom!" It was, of course, Susan Yates, grinning, he thought, like a Cheshire cat, and propelling an elegant companion toward the door. She stopped sweetly, casting Miss Holt a friendly glance. Turning to her client, she began in dulcet tones, "Mrs. Twimby, may I present—"

Tom got to his feet in record time. "Wells—Carrington Wells, of Boston," he announced emphatically, bowing to Mrs. Twimby. Casting Susan a beseeching look, he warbled on rapidly: "My dear Miss Yates. So pleasant to see you. My wife was only asking after you the other day. Ah, do excuse me, Miss Holt—Mrs. Twimby— Miss Yates—America's—ah—première designer."

Ruby got to her feet, her alert face flushed. Susan stood there still grinning like an idiot, he thought. She shook hands with Miss Holt, and Ruby said: "Oh gee, so you're *her*. I thought I'd seen your picture when you came through the lobby. I certainly think that's a beautiful costume you've got on. I suppose you must have designed it."

Mrs. Twimby appeared to be on the point of fainting, so Susan smiled again, thanked Ruby for her compliments, and raising her brows maddeningly at Tom, continued the progress of guiding her client to the lobby.

Miss Holt sat down, and returning to her drink, mused aloud:

"Gosh, isn't she wonderful! It's terribly exciting meeting her."

"An old friend of the family's—my wife's, you know," gabbled Tom somewhat incoherently.

"What's she call you Tom for? That's a funny short for Carrington," puzzled the girl.

"Oh, that!" Mr. Wells laughed with unwonted heartiness. "That? Amusing, isn't it? You—ah—see—my father's name was Carrington, too, and that made too many Carringtons around, so—well, when I was a boy they called me by my middle name—Thomas. And Tom for short."

"Uhhuh," murmured Miss Holt, losing interest. "Gee, she is wonderful. I suppose she gets her clothes for nothing—being in the business and all."

Infinitely relieved, Mr. Benchley permitted her speculations unimpeded progress. But presently he shoved in a question of his own, and contrary to Miss Holt's principle, awaited an answer.

"You think—you think Mrs. Pierce was rather onto the secretarial involvement of her husband?"

Miss Holt said my, didn't he have a way of putting things—secretarial involvement! And that, sure, Mrs. Pierce had been onto everything, being the kind of baby that didn't want to lose a good meal ticket.

"Not," she continued, "that I didn't suppose she would have gotten big alimony. Gee, the women that are getting alimony these days! But you can't always tell—can you?"

Tom called the waiter and ordered replenishment of his companion's glass. He managed to squeeze her knee and remarked, relapsing momentarily into a Benchlian phrase: "I think you're great, baby."

Miss Holt giggled profusely, and drew perceptibly nearer. "They *are* kind of strong, aren't they?" she reasoned.

Mr. Benchley gazed soulfully into the redhead's eyes, and asked: "You don't really think the Pierces were going to get a divorce?"

"Gee," complained the other. "You certainly are set on talking about the Pierces. I mean I happen to know he wanted one. But nothing doing. She wasn't having any." She eyed him quickly. "Oh, I get it! It's not the Pierces but divorce you're thinking about."

Tom neatly changed horses in midstream. "Brilliant deduction, Miss Holt. Very astute. You see, if I were—let us say—thinking of a divorce—I shouldn't like to go to a lawyer who wouldn't understand me; who might disapprove of the idea of it."

This struck Miss Holt as very funny indeed. She assured him that he'd be safe in her boss's hands on a point like that. "'Course he doesn't have to get one now—Mrs. Pierce having passed out; but listen, I heard him doing a lot of talking one evening about how good an idea he thought divorce was. He was talking to our Miss Hotchkiss, of course, and I wasn't exactly supposed to be listening. He said Mrs. Pierce wanted to have her cake and eat it, too. And Hotchkiss said: 'Darling, we're sunk. You can't cut a diamond with a diamond.' Elegant talker, she is. Say, listen, Mr. Wells, you wouldn't ever say I told you any of this? He'd fire me quick as a cork popping. You wouldn't, would you?"

Mr. Wells was very reassuring, magnificently so. He finished off with another squeeze of her knee and the devastating discovery that—crushing blow though it was—he must go to meet some men for a business appointment. She *did* understand? And could he ring her for luncheon soon?

Miss Holt said sure; he didn't think she was nuts, did he? Anybody could see he was the kind of guy that was a gentleman. Any time he wanted to call would be O.K.

"You are very sweet," said Mr. Wells and found to his surprise that he meant it. Rising, he led the redhead toward the lobby. At the same time an attractive woman in sables finished the purchase of a magazine at the cigar counter and followed them at a discreet distance to the street. Her brow was creased with a worried frown.

CHAPTER SIXTEEN

9:15 P.M. Wednesday

LYLE CURTIS FINISHED a solitary dinner and set out to meet his chief at the entrance to Gamberson's apartment house. The colonel's apartment, the district attorney and his chief assistant discovered, had been decorated in part by Lucinda Mason. But where the decorator had stopped, Gamberson had begun. He had lavishly added to the designer's gaunt, tubular ideas an extraordinary collection of war trophies, mounted sailfish, and souvenirs of big-game hunting. All of this was preserved between salmon-pink walls with burnished copper bindings.

The two men were required to wait for some little time in this amazing chamber. When the colonel finally put in an appearance, he greeted his guests with military punctiliousness, but no apologies. He had dined late, he stated, as if anything might well happen when a man did that. He did inquire, however, into their after-dinner drinking preferences. A Filipino houseboy arranged low tubular tables, brought filled glasses and vanished noiselessly. The colonel caressed his bristling mustache and commented on the inclemency of the weather. His own verdict, without waiting for theirs, was that it was "entirely unseasonable. Let the tropics," he commanded, "stay where they belong. And the North Pole too." The recent alternate mixture of both, they judged, had been far from his liking.

As Scofield chatted easily and aimlessly about the colonel's past military posts and weather indigenous to them, Curtis sized up

Gamberson as a man cut from Vivian Peabody's own metal—strong willed, probably ruthless, certainly passionate and thoroughly ambitious. But he doubted if Gamberson were the politician he had found Miss Peabody to be. The colonel's views, he suspected, were most likely based on predetermined form. Obviously, he was a confirmed hedonist, though, and the assistant district attorney wondered idly why such men chose military careers in their youth; or whether it were another question of which came first, the chicken or the egg.

After a good deal of light skirmishing with the D. A., their host finally faced the cause of their visit.

"I suppose," he suggested pompously, "you gentlemen wish to see me about something to do with our city's welfare. Mr—ah—Curtis, I'm afraid did not make it quite clear."

Mr. Scofield agreed that, in a broad sense, that was precisely what had brought them. The district attorney's office was investigating a matter in which they felt the colonel might be of certain aid.

Accepting his lead, Lyle asked abruptly if Colonel Gamberson knew whether Nancy Pierce had been in the habit of taking drugs.

Gamberson bristled. "What, gentlemen," he demanded, looking from Curtis to Scofield, "is the meaning of such an absurd question?"

Evenly, Mr. Scofield said: "We are men among men, Gamberson. That the late Mrs. Pierce was often a visitor in your delightful apartment should not offend any one of us. Now, she is mysteriously dead. Under the circumstances, we cannot follow the dictates of the etiquette books. If a man's personal knowledge may help us, we must call on him for it."

The colonel snorted, muttered something about an era of dictators and government interference in everything connected with a man's life. But his heightened color receded, and he managed an almost coy gesture of accepting their impudence with worldly tolerance. "Proceed, gentlemen. I won't say what I think of such an er—odd intrusion into private—ah—personal matters, because I hope that, first of all, I am a citizen cognizant of all my responsibilities, ready always to aid justice if that be in my power. Yes, I was acquainted with Mrs. Howard Pierce. But I warn you both, I shall tolerate no libelous—ah—er—imaginings regarding that fine little woman's morals. She—ah—came to see me as—ah—as she would have gone to her own father—ah—er—or brother. I took great pleasure in giving her the counsel of an older and perhaps wiser head."

"Exactly," agreed Scofield.

Lyle Curtis said amicably: "And as her friend and advisor, you would have known of any logical explanation for the presence in her body after death of a quantity of potassium cyanide?"

"Good lord," ejaculated their host, seemingly much taken by surprise. "Never heard of such a thing—ah—never heard of such a thing in all my life. Certainly Mrs. Pierce took nothing of the kind. She was a very healthy young woman; very—ah—active. Last thing in the world she would have done. Fine figure of a woman, as we used to say. Always anxious to keep fit. Liked her for it. Splendid idea keeping fit. I'd lay good money on it, she was no drug addict."

"Thank you," breathed Curtis softly, and made a gesture of rising.

Colonel Gamberson looked mildly astonished at the idea of the questions being finished, and Mr. Scofield said very softly also: "Those vitamin tablets you gave Mrs. Pierce—they wouldn't possibly have contained small quantities of the poison?"

Lyle Curtis was expecting another outburst. No such thing happened. He and Scofield were watching the man closely. He caressed his mustache slowly for a moment, apparently lost in thought, then he looked suddenly apprehensive. "Now, I wonder?" he exclaimed excitedly. "No, surely they couldn't have. Incredible. Best pharmaceutical house in the country. Reputation above reproach." He turned to the district attorney. "Of course, I didn't actually buy the capsules for Nancy Pierce—but I recommended them, told her exactly what to get, which brand. I did, indeed. She seemed to me to be always such a child of the sun. I felt she needed to benefit from it the whole year round as—ah—perhaps—ah—less vivid personalities do not. Yes, I definitely remember advising her to take Vitamins A and D. That was after she had pneumonia last year. Some pretty-pretty doctor she had pulled her through, but not my taste. Lah-de-dah sort of chap. Vitamins, I told her, would do more than a whole collection of Dr. Semmers. Pasty fellow himself. If *they* harmed her, I should never forgive myself. But good lord—gentlemen, you surely don't believe seriously that there could be potassium cyanide in products sold on the open market?"

"We wondered," Scofield said quietly.

"You wondered? Why the devil don't you ask a doctor? Haven't you got medical examiners or such in your department? Never encountered such inefficiency. In the army we should have found out like a shot."

"We have found out that potassium cyanide is not customarily found in Vitamin A and D capsules. This seems to have been a very special instance," Curtis explained coolly.

The colonel appeared to ponder this intelligence. Presently he said slowly: "Of course, I know relatively little about pharmacy. No reason to. But, by God, I doubt if a reputable house would dare make such a mistake. A modern drugstore yes, if the girl went out and bought some soda-book-and-alarm-clock purveying store's product; but I gave the name of a responsible house. And those capsules are a common, counter proposition; supposed to be full of cod-liver oil and nothing else, I'm led to understand. Might be killing people all over the place. Can't do a thing like that in a civilized country—" He abandoned his sentence with an irate gesture.

Scofield and Curtis exchanged quick glances. The district attorney said: "We shall, of course, look into the matter further."

"I shall investigate the matter myself," the colonel assured them, and Curtis pictured the military figure on a round of corner drugstores demanding a mending of their ways. It didn't quite ring true, and yet it did. He was worried.

"Perhaps," suggested the district attorney, "we can accomplish that adequately for you. We are far from dropping the matter."

Gamberson appeared to look relieved, but Lyle Curtis felt that perhaps he changed the subject just a whit too quickly, when he said in a moment: "H—er—by the way, gentlemen, speaking as we have been, as men of the world, there is—ah—no reason for this—ah—little distraction of mine—that is to say, this little habit I had of advising Mrs. Pierce—ah, that is to say, no need for it to be discussed outside this room?"

"We hope not, certainly," replied Mr. Scofield thoughtfully, and rose.

The colonel accompanied them to the door, reiterating his profound disbelief in any harm arising from the taking of ordinary vitamin tablets. Only at the door did another thought apparently occur to him.

A hand on the door, he cried, "Bless me, I believe you gentlemen are courting the idea of foul play."

"Or suicide," repeated Scofield evenly.

"Or suicide," repeated the assistant district attorney.

On this suggestive note, they bid Colonel Gamberson an immediate farewell and walked quickly down the hall.

IT HAD TURNED into a brisk night, with only fitful stabs of snow, and the two men, on quitting Colonel Gamberson's building, decided to walk.

"What do you make of him?" Curtis asked.

"Gaseous enough to carry a dirigible, but not a numskull. Overdid it, though; overdid the whole show, in my opinion. Tumbled to the notion of murder a damn sight too belatedly. After all, he must have heard from Miss Peabody that the possibility was being considered. I'm not abandoning Howard Pierce, not at all; but we must look into Gamberson. Nothing else for it."

Curtis nodded. "Smooth as castor oil, and about as palatable, to my way of thinking."

"We can't overlook the fact that he's got a very good marriage coming off. Peabody's not only an attractive woman, she evidently has plenty of money. Maybe she told Gamberson that unless he toed the line, everything was off. Now, I'd say Gamberson likes nice things. He's had money of his own, and according to my information, has been losing heavily in the stock market lately. Nancy Pierce was probably becoming an embarrassment—perhaps was turning out to have disturbingly unshakable qualities. Chances are she declined to take *finis* for an answer. So the colonel recommended cod-liver oil capsules, bided his time, and finally spiked them. How's that fit?"

"It makes an equation all right, sir," said Curtis politely.

"It does indeed. What did we find out about Gamberson's possession of a hypodermic?" asked the D. A.

"Nothing. But he would have been too smart, don't you think, to let his Filipino boy see it, if he had one?"

"Oh, entirely too smart. What about the poison?"

"No indications," Curtis said. "But if we find that Peabody has some weed killer, I suppose Gamberson would have easy access to it."

"Look here, Curtis, I don't fancy this case," said Scofield. "Now a number of people are beginning to look guilty, where they all looked merely irritated before. . . ."

"I was just thinking about the Howard Pierce angle. You're particularly interested in the husband?"

Mr. Scofield grrumped, filled his lungs with the fresh, sharp air and grrumped again. "Pierce is definitely not my choice in humanity—"

As he hesitated, Lyle remarked that as far as that went he wouldn't be inclined to put Gamberson at the head of a list of superior representatives of the human race. "But," he added slowly, "there's another catch. Gamberson couldn't have planted the note, and I can't see Vivian Peabody doing it for him. She'd be much more likely to choose another husband."

"Blast the catches. Whole case is full of padlocks and a hundred keys that don't fit. Ah, how fortunate the commissioner is to have had us stick our necks out. I must remember to give him full responsibility in the next little caramel nugget that comes along, *full* responsibility up to the moment I step into court. Yes, indeed, the commissioner shall have the rare privilege of practically preparing the brief. Excellent thought." Thus ruminating with projected pleasure, the district attorney strode on for another half a block.

Finally he said bombastically: "I want to know where Nancy Pierce spent the last evening of her life until one o'clock in the morning."

A little further along the district attorney added irrelevantly, "Gamberson was a regular buzzard in the trenches. Took his men into hellholes and didn't care how many he lost. Now he seems to be consuming the fruits of retirement in a blaze of modern decoration."

Curtis chuckled. "Never saw anything to equal that mounted sailfish nestling on the pea-green mantel beside the Matisse nude."

The district attorney laughed uproariously in recollection. "The colonel and his decorator," he remarked, "seem to have been at some odds. Can't think who really won. Anyway, my own choice of strange bedfellows was the trench helmet sharing a wall with the noseless, wooden saints. I'm afraid Gamberson didn't succeed in inducing his decorator to throw in a discount for the publicity her work would get—not if your Miss Lucinda Mason saw the place after the colonel had added his trophies."

They reached the Scofield house at this point. Lyle Curtis declined a nightcap, and they said good night at the doorstep. Deep in thought, the assistant district attorney walked on toward his own apartment house overlooking the East River.

CHAPTER SEVENTEEN

10:30 P.M. Wednesday

SUSAN WAS STILL SHAKING with laughter when she and her client reached the street outside the San Horitz Hotel. Mrs. Twimby was plainly disgusted. A nice-looking man like that! With a wife and all in Boston, and out with a common little huzzy. Susan admitted that it did look a little odd; but she did not put into words the thoughts coursing through her head.

At Mrs. Twimby's hotel, she said good-by, jumped into her roadster, and drove slowly home speculating on Tom's behavior. He was up to something. He wouldn't have pulled such a whopper merely because of an ordinary pickup. And why the married-man angle? Some sleuthing of his own, the poor benighted soul! In the morning, she would ring him up and drag the truth out of him.

Thus closing the matter for the time being, Susan reached her apartment and turned her car over to the doorman for the garage to pick up. Going up in the elevator, she recalled having given Lillian, her maid, the night off, and decided to fix herself some hot milk, find a thoroughly thrilling detective story and get into bed. The Nancy Pierce case was to be completely taboo for the rest of the evening.

At her floor, the elevator operator remembered something: "There was a colored boy here earlier in the evening, Miss Yates, with a letter for you. Your maid didn't answer so I shoved it under your door."

Miss Yates thanked him and proceeded on down the hall. She opened the door, switched on the hall light, and looked down. The envelope lay just inside the doorjamb. She picked it up casually, still thinking of Tom and the redhead, slit the envelope absent-mindedly and immediately forgot all about Mr. Benchley.

The letter was like no other she had ever received. It was neither written nor typewritten, but contrived out of single letters, parts of words, and whole words cut from newsprint and pasted together on a sheet of cheap paper. But it was very neatly done, the letters carefully chosen of approximately the same size, the lines of print straight. Susan held it toward the shaded light on the hall table:

> MISS YATES (it said) I NOTICE YOU ARE INTER-ESTED IN THE PIERCE DETH. IF YOU WANT SOME REEL INFORMASHUN FOLLOW THESE INSTRUCTIONS. DRIVE TONIGHT TO VAN CORTLANDT PARK. PARK YORE CAR ON BRIDGE CLOSE BY GOLF LINKS CLUBHOUSE. WALK TO FIRST TEE. I WILL MEET YOU THERE AT 1.30 IF YOU CUM ALONE. I WILL KNOW. DON'T TELL ANYONE IF YOU WANT TO SOLVE THE MISTRY OF NANCY PIERCE'S DETH. IF YOU DON'T THEN DON'T COME BUT I THINK YOU DO.

Shaking her head to clear her eyes, Susan read it through again—still the same words. She laughed. Someone was playing a practical joke, Surely. It was too silly and melodramatic to take seriously. She flung the note on the hall table and went on to her bedroom, trying to consider which of the new books on her night table she would read. But the queer note floated at the front of her mind. What if it weren't a joke? What if this was really the way to get information that would help Lyle Curtis—and stop the horror of suspicion among all of them in the club. She said aloud: "After all, my girl, this is your first murder case. You don't know the etiquette. Maybe this is quite *comme il faut*." She returned to the hall and read the letter through a third time. Then she walked to the telephone. She hesitated, then moved away again. But, as though stirred to life by her approach, the bell rang. She picked up the receiver. "Hello?"

For a moment, nothing at all happened. She repeated: "Hello?" There was a wisp of sound at the other end of the wire and then a voice laughed—the same queer laugh she had heard at the luncheon yesterday. After that a receiver clicked home. The line was dead.

That decided her, foolish reason or not. She was going to Van Cortlandt Park. Hurrying back to her bedroom, she put on rough tweeds and golf shoes—smiling wryly over the appropriateness inasmuch as she had been bidden to a middle-of-the-night rendezvous on golf links. Then, once more, she hesitated at the telephone. If the note were a joke, a pretty fool she'd look calling Assistant District Attorney Curtis. He'd think she was insane; that she'd probably murdered Nancy herself while having a fit. Thrusting the note in her pocket, she started determinedly for the door, but halfway there stopped short. She turned to her desk, drew the note from her pocket and copied it carefully word for word. She considered and finally put the copy in her pocket, the original in an envelope which she sealed. On the outside she wrote: "Found under my door when I got home at eleven-thirty this evening. Have gone to follow instructions." To this she clipped a sheet of paper and on it wrote: "Lillian: If I'm not home by 3 A.M. call Lyle Curtis at—" She stopped and found his number in the phone book—"RH-8-2756, and give him the message on outside of this envelope."

She propped the envelope up on the hall table, switched out the lights and left.

In the elevator going down, she asked the operator for a description of the boy who had brought the letter. Both elevator man—and a minute later, the doorman—described him indefinitely as a colored boy, perhaps fourteen years old, and in no way distinguishable from any other. He had asked if Miss Yates lived in the building, and had given the note to the doorman, who had in turn given it to the elevator operator, who had put it under Susan's door.

Susan's car had not yet been called for by the garage. She climbed in and pressed her foot on the starter, remembering suddenly that while the note had begun with her name, the envelope had borne no name or address. She thought: "But it would be like looking for a fearless opinion under a dictatorship for the police to apprehend one small colored boy in all of New York City to find out who had told him to deliver a note and where to deliver it."

However, someone had taken a long chance. She might have been home and inquired directly of the boy herself. Did that mean that the person who had sent the note had known she was not home? It seemed to Susan also that the laugher on the telephone had also taken a long chance. It was incredible she couldn't recognize that laugh. Obviously, then, it must be very unlike its owner— a laugh of hysterical bravura. Was it possible a man could make his voice sound that way; but, then, the only man at the luncheon had been Tom Benchley, and Susan had known him almost all her life. His father, the late Dr. Benchley, had brought her into the world. She had told Vivian that she couldn't laugh that way. But could she? Certainly, Hortense Culbertson's voice was known to millions of radio listeners. But unintentionally or intentionally it was possible to change one's voice; especially a trained voice. It hadn't sounded in the least like Caroline Semmer's timorous, apologetic tone, and not like Lucinda's forthrightness. The thing, she found, puzzling her chiefly, and which was, after all, not too reassuring was the synchronization of finding the note and the telephone call. With an attempt at calmness, she speculated carefully on whether the phone call had been a crazy dare for her to follow the note's directions, or an effort to frighten her away from doing that very thing. The latter suggested that the laugher had not written but knew about the note. Of course, she reasoned, it was possible—though absurd on the face of it—that there was actually no connection between the note and the telephone call. The telephoner might have known nothing of the note but have thought Susan knew too much and was asking too many questions.

As she swung the car from Fifth Avenue into One Hundred and Tenth Street, driving thoughtfully because there was plenty of time, Susan decided that like many happenings in life which seemed to be associated and were not, the note and the laugh probably had no connection. The note might be—indeed from its illiterate spelling, it might well be—from Mike, the waiter, or Lucien, the bartender. It might be from someone she had never heard of: someone who knew of her connection with the case and who felt impelled to talk to her under circumstances which would not involve himself. All of this, she admitted, assumed that the note was genuine, not a crank letter or a hoax planned for other and less reassuring purposes.

Turning into Riverside Drive, Susan was almost determined to go home and leave well enough alone; but she drove on, her heart pumping a little faster, her common sense pointing out that this trip was actually very foolish.

The more she thought about it the more she decided that the note's bad spelling did not necessarily mean it was from an illiterate person. The spelling was spotty and inconsistent. It looked more the result of trying to find the right printed letters and making the most of those which had come to hand. Probably both Lucien and Mike could spell better than that. If not one of them, could it have been the waiter who had served them in the ballroom? But would he have known her name? Miss Semmer always called her "Miss Yates"; the other girls called her "Susan." Presumably, he could have put one and two together. The stagehands hadn't heard her name. She hadn't been near the stage.

"If," she told herself, "I go on like this, I'll be a dithering idiot before I reach Van Cortlandt Park." Shaking herself impatiently, she drove on at accelerated speed, concentrating on the driving. In the upper reaches of Riverside Drive, there was still a steady stream of cars, but above One Hundred and Sixtieth Street, she turned toward Broadway and found the movie theaters out, the drugstores closed. An express train thundered over her head as she crossed under the elevated tracks.

The entrance to the park was deserted and shadowy. Susan slowed down, feeling a sudden acute reluctance. There was just enough light to see her watch. Ten minutes to one. Then she was very early. The note had stipulated one-thirty. She drove over the little bridge and out into the network of driveways beyond the park, then circled back, and coming to the bridge, consulted her watch once more by the bridge light. Only one o'clock. She brought the car to a standstill and read through her copy of the note again. Then she lit a cigarette and settled back trying to wait without thinking, but perfectly certain now that she was letting herself into a very queer if not actually foolhardy situation.

Surely, though, the whole thing was a joke. Then what was she—the successful, law-abiding Susan Yates—participating in it for?

She suddenly realized that prickles of excitement were actually raising the short hairs at the nape of her neck. So that really could happen, could it? She felt a tight, nervous spasm contracting her stomach and took several short puffs on her cigarette. This, she thought, was far worse than she had expected. It was far worse than cutting into a fifty-dollars-a-yard brocade. But that took courage, too; at least, it certainly had in the first year of her career when four yards of ruined brocade would have been a whole month's profit! Disgusted with herself, she threw her cigarette away, took the key from the ignition and got out of the car. She glanced again at her watch. Ten past one. She pulled her scarf more tightly about her throat and decided she might as well start. There might be some trouble about finding the spot. Shivering, she set out toward the golf course. Not a car had passed her while she had waited on the bridge.

CHAPTER EIGHTEEN

UNDERFOOT, THE GRASS was wet with melted snow. Here and there were patches of ice for the night had grown colder, and snow was in the air but not actually falling. In its place was a white mist. She made out the white frame clubhouse, specterlike, indefinite like a child's drawing in chalk. Stumbling on, she wondered why she hadn't brought a flashlight. But then, she charged herself rudely, of what practical thing had she thought in this mad expedition? She found presently that she had circled the clubhouse in her confusion. Then a few yards ahead, suddenly, minutely sharp, as the mist momentarily lifted was the outline of a small, square shape. "That," she thought, "is the sandbox at the first tee."

Less clearly, she made out masses of gray shapes—trees, she presumed, flanking the fairway. Perhaps, if she stood in their protection, she should be able to see whom she was meeting before he—or she—saw her; that was, if she had actually arrived first—if she was not already under observation. Anyway, she should have something solid at her back. "Not," she muttered under her breath, "that people always get attacked from the rear!"

Sliding over the patches of ice, Susan made her way to a big maple, unmistakable even in its mist-shrouded, winter nudity. She stood solidly against it and waited, her heart pounding so loudly, she felt it must be audible to anyone in the clubhouse—only the clubhouse was shuttered and dark. The weather had evidently put all thoughts of golf out of the minds of the municipal links' players, or at least out of the public play programs of the authorities.

The silence was positively noisy, she thought suddenly. But then it *must* be at least one-thirty by now—not exactly a convivial hour for the most active golf course.

Waiting in rigid attention for what seemed to her fully half an hour more, she whispered to herself "So this is what people call having your teeth chatter!" Why, in the name of heaven, had she come? But having come, she could, even so, depart. She put a foot out to start for the car but at the idea of leaving the solid protection of the tree trunk, she reconsidered.

Again she grew very still and watchful. Not a sight, not a sound which had not been there before. Yes, she decided, she had known this feeling before but in a far different circumstance. It had been the first time she had designed with scissors and pins—and no pattern—an evening gown, cutting with heart-pounding concentration into a material worth fifty dollars a yard. Halfway through a plan, no decent designer could turn back. But was she only halfway through—was there another side to this strange piece of cloth— another side with fine sharp selvage, or extermination as the finishing feature?

It had been insane not to have called Lyle Curtis. There should be a hefty detective hiding behind every other tree along the fairway, a dictograph under the tee's sandbox. Of course, the note she had left for her maid would send them ultimately in the right direction, but it might by then do her slight good. Or wasn't anybody coming at all? Should she have to crawl back to her car presently, slipping and sliding on the damp grass, the fine victim of an ill-timed practical joke? Again she shook her head in a characteristic gesture of self-impatience. Having cut into the evening's material this far, she would stay and see what the finished design was to be. She would stay if it killed her. Finding that thought none too consoling, she began telling herself that naturally there was nothing to fear, and that she was perfectly calm, that she had never been calmer. In the middle of this, she wished she could light a cigarette, but the match flaming in the darkness and the red glow of the burning tobacco would identify her location like a Broadway signboard. Then she remembered there was a lighter in her bag.

Crouching down, still backed against the tree, she fumbled for and found it, flicked the metal disk, shielding the brief flame with her other hand, and looked at her watch. One twenty-nine. She stood up.

It was then that she heard the first sound of something different from the hideously noisy silence around her. It seemed far away at first, nothing more than a denser form of silence. But her awareness grew that someone was approaching, haltingly, watchfully it seemed, but with unquestionable purposefulness. Black against the white clubhouse a shifting shadow became in a second a large dim shape. Whether a man or a woman her instinct did not help in determining, and suddenly she was quite sure that her intellect was not functioning at all.

The shape seemed to be coming straight toward her now, slipping as she had on patches of ice but coming on with less and less hesitancy. Why? How could it know where she stood? Then her intelligence took a jolt into activity. Fool that she was! A designer and color expert, too! Her tweed coat was flecked with white which would form a phantom outline of herself more sketchy than the solid sandbox and chalk-drawn clubhouse, but nonetheless detectable.

Then a voice, muffled in the mist, demanded in a queer tone. "Are you there? Is that you, Susan?"

Muffled as it was, it was unmistakable. That voice could belong to only one person. It was too familiar in tonal quality. "No, no, not that!" she muttered hysterically.

Susan's heart seemed all at once to be simultaneously pounding in her knees, her ears and her throat, to be careening through her body like an enormous globule of quicksilver. She was trying to scream. But curiously the scream seemed to be imprisoned inside her, held captive by an even stronger impulse to conceal her position. She tried to edge around the big maple tree. Its bark was rough and icy to her hands. Then, as she felt the nearness of the approaching shape, the scream forced its way up and out of her with the high, shrill note of wind whipping through a ripped sail.

A car coming over the bridge and along the road below the clubhouse swept her swiftly with its headlights, swept the approaching

figure, too, seemed to bring it forward more surely. The big shape
was like a giant in a childhood nightmare. She screamed again,
freely this time and in uncontrolled terror. Again the voice called:
"Susan," coaxingly now as if to reassure her into standing still, and
awaiting its will.

At her second scream, the car down on the road slowed abruptly, its brakes screeching. Susan closed her eyes. It was too late to
run, but surely the driver had heard. Better stand still behind the
tree. Then strong hands reached out and grabbed her arms. She
tried to beat them off and found her fist embedded in firm wool.

Close to her face, more coaxingly, but horribly, the voice in
lowered tone said: "Susan! Susan!" She opened her eyes. Huge
through the mist and with an iron grip now on both her wrists,
stood Thomas Benchley.

SUSAN FOUND AFTERWARD she could recall the next five minutes only
in terms of a newsreel seen around the nervous head of a very tall
man in front of her. She knew that the man driving the car which
had screeched to a standstill at her second scream was evidently a
citizen who investigated yells in lonely parks at night, and she
thanked God that some such citizens existed. He had come running toward them with quick curious eyes as she stumbled toward
the road, Tom's arm around her like an iron band. She had heard
Tom explaining fatuously to the other man that she had stepped on a
snake. Didn't the man know there weren't snakes at large this time of
year? Apparently he did, because he looked first incredulous, then
suspicious; and finally, as together the three of them returned to the
lighted road, a kind of apologetic leer had passed across his face. He
had actually patted her shoulder, and had said in a gruff though jocu-
lar voice: "O.K., sister, sorry if I barged in on your fun. Only you
certainly have a mighty fine screaming apparatus. Never heard a
better yell." He started to move off toward his own car. Her terror
taking second breath, Susan cried out hysterically: "Oh, I—I want
you to know Mr. Benchley—Mr. Thomas Benchley, Mr—"

"Jones," said the stranger with another bright leer. "Jones. Always at the service of ladies in distress." But he had stored away
Tom's name. She was certain of that. And Mr. Thomas Benchley

wouldn't dare proceed with any funny business that night for the man had got a very good look at her, too, in the road lights, and had undoubtedly stored away a picture of her features.

After the man had driven off, Tom had asked for the key to her car, had walked with her to the bridge and the parked car, jabbering about her being insane. A subterfuge because of the suspicious Mr. Jones? It was impossible for her to make up her mind. And yet Tom Benchley—almost her oldest friend!

Tom unlocked her car and held open the door on the right, saying, "I better drive. You've had a nasty shock."

But Susan shook her head. "I'll drive. How did you get here?"

"Subway, and then taxi to the other side of the clubhouse."

Miss Yates wanted to ask why, but she couldn't just then. Her teeth were still chattering, and surely, surely there was some explanation for Tom having been there, something he would tell simply and honestly of his own accord. She dropped into the driver's seat and he got in beside her.

"Sure you feel well enough to drive?"

She nodded mutely.

Tom exclaimed: "I'll never forgive myself for adding to your fright. I couldn't be sure it was you. All I could see was a crazy outline of somebody. I thought if I called you'd know who it was— and, well, that you'd know that you weren't alone if I yelled. Guess I was a dundering idiot. But I had to come."

Now she could ask it. "Why?"

"Why? Good lord, I dropped by your place to—well, never mind now—tell you later—and your maid had just got your note and was in a dither. Thought I was losing my mind when I insisted on tearing it open, read the enclosure, and realized you'd actually gone to follow its directions. You must be crazier than a whole flock of loons." He faced her with an outraged expression.

"But," thought Susan against her will, "Tom is a very clever boy. And it seems very funny he'd choose an hour like that to drop around at my apartment."

He was saying in a fresh rush of words that he had thereupon dashed after her in the fastest way he could think of. "*Any*body might have written that note. Why didn't you call the police? Did

you see anybody—that is, except the frightening spectacle of me?"
His words fell over one another.

They were heading straight down Broadway now, Susan driving as rapidly as she dared. She had not turned west at the beginning of Riverside Drive. Broadway seemed more brightly lighted.
She said now in a small voice, "Perhaps I did call the police," thinking that would give him practical food for thought at least. But it
couldn't be Tom who had written the note. And yet? Her thoughts
floundered once more.

"Did you see anybody but me?" persisted Mr. Benchley.

"I didn't *see* anybody else," Susan evaded still in the small,
scared voice, her eyes on the street ahead.

Mr. Benchley laughed rudely. "Don't try to pull the wool over
my eyes. You *didn't* call the police. Otherwise, why would you have
left that message for your Lillian, telling her to call Curtis if you
weren't back by three o'clock?"

"Maybe I left that particular message for inquiring murderers,"
Susan said ominously.

"Well, this business is no joke. This is a murder case you're
sticking your neck into."

"I know," said the small voice briefly.

Suddenly, Mr. Benchley turned again and peered at her face
with positive fierceness. "My God," he bellowed, "you haven't got
the cockeyed idea stored away in your head that *I* lured you up
there with that note and then appeared as per schedule? My God,"
he repeated.

Susan suddenly knew that she'd rather he thought anything but
that she thought that—no matter what he had or hadn't done. "No,
Tom," she said in a flat, queer voice that tried to sound confident
and natural.

Tom swore some more and repeated, like a small boy accused
of a crime of which he would not have dreamed, the circumstances
of his arrival at her apartment and subsequent reading of the rendezvous note. Then his wild dash to her aid. He was very red in the
face, and kept asking Susan over and over why in hell he'd want to

converse with her in the depth of Van Cortlandt Park when he could talk to her in the bosom of her own home?

Susan said: "Of course, of course," several times in the same queer, flat voice. Her heart still seemed to be beating in all the wrong places—all over her body. Finally, they reached her apartment. She firmly, but with greater poise, declined his offer to come up with her; and a very solemn-faced young Mr. Benchley went lumbering off up the street as she passed into the elevator.

Upstairs, Lillian's black anxious face awaited her, and Susan collapsed sobbing on the maid's ample breast.

"Let me send for a doctor, Miss Yates. You is tuckered out. Mr. Benchley he was awful scared. Here, I'll get you to bed." Presently Lillian brought hot milk and sat by the bedside soothing Miss Yates's throbbing temples. But Susan refused the ministrations of a doctor. What she needed, she thought, was to be alone to think everything over; to review in her mind just how Tom had come toward her, just how his voice had sounded. After awhile, she lay quiet pretending to sleep, and Lillian put the light out and tiptoed away.

But there was no sleep in Susan. Hour after hour she lay rigid in her bed, going over the events of the night. Over and over again, she heard Tom's voice: "My God, you haven't got the cockeyed idea that I lured you up there. . . ." Over and over again, those minutes on the misty golf course, the approaching figure, the voice calling coaxingly: "Is that you? Are you there, Susan?" If the car had not passed then? If the stranger had not heard her scream? If he had not come running, if he had not seen Tom—seen him well enough to remember his face? If she had not carefully, with what little control had remained in her, introduced Tom to the (thank heaven!) inquisitive "Mr. Jones"?

Of course, Lillian had confirmed Tom's story of coming to the apartment and tearing open the note. But what did that prove? If it was Tom who had sent it, what better cover up? She opened her eyes suddenly in the darkness. Where was the note now? She switched on the light by her bed, and instantly an anxious Lillian appeared in the doorway.

"Miss Yates! You not asleep yet?"

"Lillian, when Mr. Benchley left—after he'd read the note—what happened to the note?"

"Why, Mr. Benchley took it with him," replied the colored woman. "Now go to sleep, Miss Yates, do, poor child. You worn out, that's what you is."

"I will, Lillian," agreed Susan. The light was turned out again. Again she lay there in the dark. "My God, Susan, you don't think . . ." "And a taxi as far as the other side of the clubhouse." "Oh, it couldn't be Tom," she moaned. Tom whom she had known since childhood. Tom whose father had brought her through measles and mumps. Tom who had inherited from his father a passion for chemistry and a collection of surgical instruments and hypodermics— Tom, who would know better than most laymen, what the effects of poison might be.

CHAPTER NINETEEN

SERGEANT MCQUIRE was waiting for Lyle Curtis when he reached his office the following morning. The hot fever of enthusiasm glistened in the sergeant's eyes.

"Y'know," he began without preamble, "that Peabody dame has got weed killer for her roof garden. Only it's in powdered form. I took it over to the doc. He'll give you a report later today. You know, Peabody was on personally bad terms with the murdered woman. I kinda favor her as our woman."

Mr. Curtis pretended surprise. "Name a woman not to favor on any basis, McQuire, and I'll say you've got something."

McQuire methodically pondered this, then brightened and said: "Kind of a tramp, the corpse was; had that young Doc Semmer on the run. I stopped around at his place, like you said, to quiz him about hypos and whether the dame was a hop head and so on. He'd been cryin' like a baby. Told me he had a cold. I nearly busted out laughin'. Fine thing for a doc to have. 'Specially with the kind of million-dollar dames he's got for patients. I should have thought he'd have picked one of them for a sweety. Well, I guess that ain't here nor there. He says she wasn't no hop head; and he called me some full-house names—medical terms and others not so much so—for suggestin' it."

"Did you see anything suspicious?"

"He looks like a quack. His place ain't no office. It's a club. I could see for myself. Regular palace. Open fire burnin', ladies chattin'. I seen all that from cross the hall where his girl parked

me—while doc finished his cryin' spell, and he's got one of them anti-
septic cases too, with a dozen hypos in it along with some other stuff."

"What about Miss Peabody and the murdered woman?"

"Yeah. I was gettin' to that. I got to talkin' with an office boy
up at her magazine. Seems she and Pierce—Mrs. Pierce, I mean —
had a reg'lar row couple weeks ago. The blonde dame brought in
an article she'd put down on paper. Manuscripts they call them.
She wanted Peabody to print it. The kid I was jawin' with was in
and out of her office while they was talkin. Miss Peabody was tellin'
Mrs. Pierce as how everybody about thinks he or she can write,
and that everybody can't. See? I guess that's right except, at that,
some of the things I've seen in my life would kind of—well—" Sergeant McQuire paused, his eyes pensive. He rallied, and went on,
"Yeah, Miss Peabody told her off, it seems, from hell an' gone; said
there wasn't nothin' in what she'd written. Mrs. Pierce had a reg'lar
fit, sayin' she oughta known better than to bring her stuff to *For
Ladies* on account of it—the magazine—being 'stuffy.' This kid I
was talkin' to couldn't remember just what else she said—something French, I guess. Besides, though he was enjoyin' himself, he
had to go and leave the room on account of dooties elsewhere. But
he was telling me the Peabody woman is terr'bly good when she
wants to lay anybody out. Few minutes later he had to go into her
office again with some copy. Peabody was tellin' Pierce about how
it was a very busy day for her and she 'really couldn't go into the
matter further.' That line. Then she said: 'Nancy, there's really no
use your losin' your self-control over the matter.' Like ice she said
it. Then she added: 'Besides, my dear, I don't really think writin'
is your force.'"

"Forte, perhaps?" suggested the assistant district attorney.

"Yeah. Maybe it was that. Anyway, she said it 'bout the way a
fish would have, and rang for her secretary, gettin' up at the same
time as much as to say, 'Beat it kid,' to Mrs. Pierce."

"Huumm," said Curtis. "Dig up anything else at *For Ladies*?"

"That seems to have been the only time the Pierce dame was
ever there personally. But one of the telephone operators was goin'
out same time I was. (Cute little trick, she was.) I says to her in the

elevator, wasn't it awful 'bout one of them fashion gals killin' herself. She turns up her nose and wants to know if I mean Nancy Pierce and I says yeah. Then she kind of sniff'd and says you could have knocked her over with a soda straw when she heard it on account of her never havin' thought the ravishin' *Mrs. Pierce* would go and kill herself—such a great one for entertainin' and everything. I said: 'Entertainin'?' And she says, 'Sure she's called up the big boss (she meant the publisher of *For Ladies*) plenty lately askin' him for dinner and parties,' and that she'd seen her, too, at bars and places. (The way them little tricks get around these days! They make eighteen dollars a week and drink at the Ritz 'stead of eatin' proper.) I asked her, like it was just that there idle curiosity, was the publisher sweet on Mrs. Pierce, but that didn't set so well. We'd got downstairs by then and was walkin' along. She turns to me and says who'd I think I was talkin' to 'bout personal matters, because she didn't recall as how we were acquainted. Seem' I wasn't goin' to get no further, I says, 'O.K., toots, you're O.K. with me,' and went my own way. But I guess the Pierce woman went right up to the roof when she didn't get to base with that Miss Peabody."

As the sergeant was thus summing up his suspicions, the assistant district attorney's telephone rang. It was Heininger.

Curtis said: "What's the dope on Howard Pierce?"

"So sweet on his private secretary that he wanted a divorce," replied the operative, whose idea of reports was less fluent than the sergeant's.

"Anything else?"

"Was out with the secretary until 2 A.M. night before his wife passed out. She got in about an hour before he did. Servants don't know where she'd been. Haven't got any further line on her yet except that she wasn't with Gamberson. He was at a banquet at the Pierre until twelve forty-five, had a drink afterward with some other ex-officers at his club, and got home at 1:55 A.M."

"That all?"

"Yes sir."

"Very well. Report again early in the afternoon, or sooner, if you get any further lines."

The telephone rang again. It was Susan Yates.

"I've got something to tell you," she said hesitantly. "May I come over to your office?" Curtis consulted his watch. "Is it urgent?"

"No," she said doubtfully, "I don't have to tell it to you right away this minute."

"I have to go somewhere now with the D. A.," Curtis explained. "I don't know exactly how long it will take me—suppose we say five o'clock this afternoon—I'll surely be free then. Is that all right?"

"All right," Susan echoed, and hung up.

Curtis sat for a moment frowning at his desk. Then he got up, took his hat, and joined his chief on a trip to Glen Cove, Long Island.

CHAPTER TWENTY

LUCINDA MASON VAN WECK was in a garden off the driveway, combing a shaggy sheepdog. G. B. and a setter were disputing a bone nearby. She greeted Scofield and Curtis by rising from two knees to one and holding out a limp hand.

"*Chez vous*," the district attorney asked cheerfully, "are you Miss Mason or Mrs. Van Weck?"

Lucinda said coldly, "I am a modern woman, Mr. Scofield, and have never encountered difficulty in continuing to be known as Miss Mason, except once when some silly man greeted Ethan as Mr. Mason."

"That, I trust, we shan't be so misinformed as to do. You know Mr. Curtis, Miss Mason?"

Lucinda went on combing the dog, raised and lowered her big, green-cast eyes, and remarked more to the dog than to Lyle: "We met—if that is possibly the word—at a *soirée* the other afternoon. As I think of it now, there was no legality in that meeting. We were rushed into it and not told at all that it was a murder investigation."

"And you now feel it was?" Lyle asked conversationally.

"What *am* I to think? The papers have carried the most unconvincing reports of poor Nancy dying at a business luncheon with suicide the reason according to the police."

"And that leads you to suspect murder?" The young assistant D. A. prompted. "As I recall, Miss Mason, you felt the other afternoon that suicide was quite within the realm of probability."

"It's all very dreary. But what *am* I to think that *you* are thinking when you call up poor Ethan on the telephone and enrage him by suggesting that he gave Nancy a poisoned cocktail?" She raised stormy eyes. "Ethan is being quite unbearable. There has never been a scandal in his family—at least none ever came to light enough to be remembered. Besides, he has a very short memory."

The D. A. and his assistant exchanged quick glances which said: "Does she mean something or is she just being an abused wife?" Scofield said severely: "Mr. Curtis, am I to understand you directly accused Mr. Van Weck of poisoning Mrs. Pierce?" Lucinda, having returned her attention to the dog, did not see the wink which accompanied this question.

Mr. Curtis replied solemnly, "We have made no accusations as yet, Mr. District Attorney."

"In that case," announced Miss Mason, rising and heedlessly brushing her tweed skirt of some sheep dog hairs, "Ethan has been jumping to conclusions again. We will go inside." She led the way across a flagstone terrace, and through tall French windows into a library pleasantly filled with beautiful American Colonial furniture. A great peace graced this chamber. Books, distilling a glow of muted radiance, reached from floor to ceiling. On the hearth burned a fragrant log fire. There were hothouse flowers everywhere and ancestral portraits—Van Weck's, Lyle presumed.

Lounging, with lengthy legs extended to the fire, was another shaggy figure which got to its feet and grinned. Curtis blinked and exclaimed: "You here, Tom?"

"In behalf of the Tomorrow Club, Mrs. Van W— Miss Mason asked me to be present. So far the press has been very kind to— er—career women. We feel, however," and Mr. Benchley raised his eyes gravely to heaven, "that with the district attorney's office pushing this way and that"—he emphasized the words ever so slightly as if inserting quotation marks—"we are forced to take all reasonable steps toward protecting an organization of distinguished ladies."

"Yes," an irritable voice behind them stammered, "b-b-but in my opinion—which I-I-I a-am l-led to b-believe neg-negligible, there should be a l-lawyer here instead of this—this great Dane."

Mr. Ethan Van Weck, seated at a card table in a corner of the room, looked angrily from Thomas Benchley to the newcomers, then turned to the deck of cards in his hands and neatly finished a "four-ace change."

"My husband, gentlemen," Miss Mason explained evenly. "Ethan, this is Mr. Scofield, the district attorney, and Mr. Curtis, his assistant."

Mr. Van Weck dropped his cards and came toward them. "Sit down—sit down," he motioned reproachfully to the room at large, and pushing past Benchley, seated himself in the wing chair from which the publicity man had risen. From under heavy, irregular brows he watched the others arrange themselves in a semicircle around the fireplace. Curtis observed that their host appeared not to have been up long although it was close to eleven o'clock. Sleep still lingered in his eyes, and on the side of his small weak mouth was an unmistakable coffee stain. Toast crumbs decorated his tie and vest over which he wore an extravagantly plain, maroon silk dressing gown. Beneath its ampleness, small, slippered feet extended timorously. His right foot he tapped in an irritable toe-wriggling way on a bit of hardwood flooring which peeped out between Oriental rugs.

Miss Mason removed a gray hat she had been wearing in the garden and flung it onto a tip table. With equal signs of irritation, she flung herself onto a deep couch and regarded her husband for a fleeting second with her green eyes. Then she turned to Scofield, who was smiling pleasantly and acting quite as if he had dropped in from next door during a morning's stroll.

Mr. Benchley, having been successfully circumvented by his host in reclaiming the comfortable wing chair, resumed a seated posture in a discouragingly fragile little ladder-back affair next to Van Weck.

Curtis was observing the scene with a touch of amusement in his eyes. His words so far had been monosyllabic and purely perfunctory.

Pulling a fine linen handkerchief from one of the large pockets in his dressing gown, Van Weck blew his nose with trumpeting

abandon. The assistant D. A. saw Lucinda's glance return fleetingly to her husband. For a second, a sneering little smile crossed
her face and was gone, leaving her expression one of imperturb-
able serenity. "Is this," she questioned, "to be an official inquisi-
tion or shall we have something to drink?"

Ethan looked around the assemblage and scowled. "I have just
breakfasted m-my d-dear, b-but if you f-fancy such f-fantastic
n-notions b-by a-all m-means. Yes, quite," he finished and blew
his nose again resoundingly.

Lucinda motioned to Tom and indicated a bellpull. Mr.
Benchley unwound himself from the fragile chair, crossed the
hearth rug and jerked the handsomely embroidered rope. He then
looked about the room cautiously and selected a large, firmly built,
roundabout chair as far removed as possible from the red-nosed
Ethan.

A servant came almost immediately, and Miss Mason ordered
whisky and soda. Lyle asked suddenly if Mrs. Pierce had said anything about the capsules to Mr. Van Weck.

"T-t-the capsules?" Lucinda's husband blinked. "W-what kind
of damned nonsense is this?" He glared first at Curtis, then at his
wife.

The assistant D. A. elaborated, his eyes on Van Weck's face.
"You were so kind as to take pity on Mrs. Pierce when she was
stranded, so to speak, in the bar. Did she say anything to you about
having been given by anyone a fresh box of Vitamin A and D capsules?"

"T-there they go again," Ethan complained wildly to Lucinda,
including Tom disdainfully in his glance. "I want it understood,
gentlemen," and he snuffled vigorously, "that I did not give that
little lady a poisoned cocktail. Until m-my attorney arrives, I shall
s-say absolutely n-no m-more."

"Oh, Ethan," interrupted Lucinda angrily, "you can't have sent
for Vanderpoor? What an idiotic thing to do. You have been asked
a civil enough question. You probably were yesterday on the phone.
I might have known you were simply using that precious imagination of yours. Can't you understand that these gentlemen have not

accused you of being a murderer? In fact, you don't even look like a murderer, if I do say it myself," she added triumphantly.

Her husband appeared appeased by her last remark. He blew his nose more quietly, and said almost roguishly, "W-well n-no, to be entirely accurate—I-I haven't sent for Vanderpoor—yet. But I know certainly nothing about this poison n-nonsense." He continued brightly, "W-why I scarcely knew *her*, to put it directly. She was in distress because some glowering y-yokel walked out and left her alone in a p-public b-bar. Not that I consider b-b-bars at all the proper places for females. But, my dear," and his reddish eyes lingered speculatively on his wife, "you m-might as well g-get this straight. I-I p-picked her up. That's exactly wh-what I d-did. I picked her up as the saying goes. But I d-did not—most certainly I did not—inquire into her m-medication habits. So there you are. Quite." Mr. Van Weck put his fine linen handkerchief away and leered happily over having acquitted himself so well.

Mr. Curtis had watched alternately Lucinda's and her husband's faces. The only expression on Miss Mason's now seemed to be a definite effort to avoid laughing aloud. Curtis said pleasantly: "We are not inclined, sir, to attach any blame to you in this bad business."

"An excellent plan," approved Lucinda's husband as if, having had his say, he were no longer vitally interested in the conversation.

"But we did hope," the assistant district attorney continued, "that Mrs. Pierce might have confided something of importance to you—some little item which might forward our investigation of her death."

Their host considered this for a moment and brightened again. "She did," he assured them. "Yes, to be exact, she did confide in me."

Lucinda flushed and her green eyes narrowed minutely. "Dear me," she said unemotionally.

"Ah, and exactly what, Van Weck?" requested Mr. Scofield softly.

Silence for a moment filled the pleasant library. Ethan Van Weck appeared to be lost in the catacombs of memory. He snuffled once or twice, regarded the ceiling speculatively, wiggled his toes in his slippers once or twice, and finally turned his gaze upon his wife. With complete unexpectedness he said: "She accused you, my dear."

Lucinda's casualness evaporated instantly. She stiffened, and a dangerous look entered her green eyes. "Accused me, Ethan? I dare say you wouldn't mind saying of what."

"Yes, my sweet, she accused you."

"I asked you, of what?"

Ethan chuckled and produced another dramatic pause. "Of having m-married me for *my* money," he stated cheerfully.

Miss Mason's growing rage was checked in mid-air. She burst into uncontrolled laughter, in which Van Weck amiably joined her, while the other men glanced from one to the other in some consternation.

Finally Lucinda paused to say breathlessly, "How very like Nancy. She always had the most profound misinformation on every topic. Really delicious, Ethan. I'm afraid our guests can't quite appreciate our gaiety. No use trying to look tactful, Mr. Scofield. Everyone knows Ethan married me for *my* money, while I married him for *his* ancient lineage. Of course, I don't always make announcements about it this way, but really the occasion calls for the most utter frankness. I'm sure you see that." She went off again in a peal of laughter.

Curtis was trying to look unamazed. So was Mr. Benchley, with scant success. The district attorney had remained the most imperturbed. He asked coolly: "Inclined to snap judgments was Mrs. Pierce?"

At this moment, fortunately, the servant arrived with a decanter, syphon and glasses on a huge silver tray. These were deposited before their hostess, and, still in apparently highest good humor, Lucinda began to pour.

Searching for a momentarily tactful subject, Lyle Curtis requested of his host whether Miss Semmer had come into the bar while he had been talking with Mrs. Pierce.

Ethan looked at his wife with returning irritation. "Semmer? Semmer? Do I know any person of that name?"

Lucinda, who had controlled her laughter at this question, laughed again. "Ethan wouldn't know Carry Semmer, Mr. Curtis. He wouldn't remember her if he did. He rarely recognizes our nearest neighbors."

"T-that's h-hardly accurate, my dear. Most inaccurate, if you want it direct. I always remember faces. It's names I forget. They leave me quite cold. W-what's in a name, anyway, as the Bard of Avon p-put it? However," and Van Weck turned his reddish eyes on Lyle, "this Semmer person you speak of, Curtis, is not, I am c-confident, among my acquaintances. Never heard of her, to be exact. Quite."

Still a little at loss for a question, Curtis bullishly continued to concentrate on Caroline Semmer: "You don't recall a middle-aged, small, compact kind of woman coming into the bar? She'd dropped her gloves."

"No reason for me to have n-noticed. But perhaps I did. She picked up some f-female accessory or other. Might have been gloves. Yes, it was. She said to Mrs. Pierce the way women say ridiculous things to one another—'Lost my gloves, but found them,' and then Mrs. Pierce said—ah—something ridiculous about—ah—g-garters. Supposed to be amusing, I presume. Very unimportant. Does the district attorney's office, am I to understand, run a l-lost and f-found d-department?"

"She wore a hat like a flashlight camera," remarked Mr. Benchley irrelevantly.

Ethan Van Weck regarded the tall young man with a suspicious scowl. "I know nothing of such nonsense. What is this fellow talking about, Lucinda?"

"A figure of speech, Ethan dear. Mr. Benchley is a writer."

As they sipped the highballs, Curtis and the district attorney permitted conversation to become general. Meanwhile, Tom Benchley spoke softly to Lyle for a minute about having been instructed by Miss Peabody to do his best to keep the career women angle out of the story, while he himself, he confessed, was a bit drawn and quartered between the instructions and a realization

that "Skirts" would go with a great bang if built up from the publicity angle of Nancy Pierce's death. Everybody, Tom predicted,
would want to visit the ballroom and sit near, if not in, the chair in
which a woman had died.

"Unless," he lamented, "you go and arrest one of the members
for murder, and they decide to scrap the play as a matter of policy."

"Anything make you think they might do that?" Curtis asked.

"Well, Miss Mason was telling me how really conservative they
are about the club—how they would not for the world have any
blemish attached to its fair name, and how distressing it is for them
to go on working on rehearsals in the hotel ballroom around the
very spot where their dear Nancy died. But I think they won't drop
it, that the commercial aspects of ticket sales will be too persua-
sive. It's a natural, if they don't."

Curtis glanced around the room. The district attorney, he observed, had engaged Lucinda and her husband in casual talk concerned apparently with dogs and horses, grooms and hunting.
Lucinda seemed to be taking her husband with greater favor since
his little joke, and it seemed to Lyle that Mr. Scofield was getting
on very nicely with the red-nosed, red-eyed Ethan, who evidently
approved of the former's knowledge of good jumpers and the fine
points of hunting dogs.

Presently they rose to go, Tom accepting the district attorney's
invitation to drive back to town in the official car. Speeding toward New York, Mr. Scofield reviewed the case casually, asking
Tom several questions about episodes at the luncheon table: when
Mrs. Pierce had taken out the capsules; how she had offered them
around the table; and if he, too, had seen Mrs. Pierce select the
third capsule in from the left after Miss Semmer had removed hers.
Tom explained that, as it happened, he could definitely substantiate Miss Yates's recollection about this. He had seen Nancy Pierce
count off two capsules and take the third, had heard Susan Yates
ask her the reason, and Mrs. Pierce give her explanation of the old
Persian or Parisian custom, "Third from the end puts you on the
mend."

"You got the idea she meant it, that it was an invariable custom of hers?" the district attorney wanted to know.

"Yep. But she was a goofy kind of female. Sort of climbed at you with her eyes all the time. I think she would have mixed hummingbird's wings and bat's eyes for a gargle if somebody told her it would make a slave of every man she met."

"Yet," Curtis reminded him, "Miss Mason told us the other afternoon that Mrs. Pierce was a very shrewd young woman."

"Well, I still think she was goofy. Kind of female who takes your clothes right off with a look. Plenty of sex appeal all right; only I like 'em to sneak up on me a bit—first the fragrance and then the flower sort of thing, you know."

CHAPTER TWENTY-ONE

AFTER PHONING Curtis and being put off until five o'clock that afternoon, Susan had spent a busy morning at her salon and a hectic noon at a rehearsal of "Skirts." Everyone looked nervous as witches. No one suggested having luncheon in the ballroom. They descended to one of the crowded restaurants of the hotel and lunched there hastily among its throngs. Afterward, once more gathered in the ballroom, they continued to exhibit as much restraint as on Tuesday they had flaunted unrestraint. An edge of wariness was discernible in their slightest remarks.

Susan found herself not only susceptible to the general epidemic, which she recognized as a suspicion in each for the others; but, nerves strung taut, she found herself studying each face as a possible note sender, each voice as a possible hysterical laugher. Worn out from her sleepless night, she moved in a haze of formless apprehension.

Tom had called her at eight-thirty that morning, to ask solicitously after her health and if he might drop in to see her during the day.

"I'd quite forgotten, in last night's excitement," he had said, "to tell you why I came up to your apartment last night. It's a longish story—when may I come over and tell it to you?" Susan had put him off, protesting that she was busy all day and that he would have to wait.

"Tom—what did you do with the rendezvous note that you took from my apartment?"

"I guess it's in my pocket," he said.

"Well, better send it back to me," she said. "This morning. By messenger. Will you?" He had said he would, and she had rung off. So far no note had arrived.

She had almost been relieved when Curtis had put the appointment off until five o'clock, having called him on the feminine impulse of needing a shoulder, if only metaphorically. But once his pleasant voice came to her over the phone, she was panicked, not knowing what she would tell him when she saw him. By five this afternoon, she would have to make up her mind. Certainly he ought to know of last night's incident—but tell him about Tom? If Tom were not guilty—and how could it be Tom?—she would be landing him in an awful mess. But if it were Tom? Could she go on, today and the next day and as many more days as there might be before the case was solved, maneuvering not to be left alone with one of her oldest friends? Thinking terrible thoughts of a boy she had grown up with? Wondering when next some vicious hand, his or another's, would try again?

And why? Why pick on her? She must know something that was dangerous to the murderer. But what? What did she know that the others did not?

She sighed and shook her head and looked at her watch. It was two forty-five. Lucinda Mason dashed in at that moment, breathless and indignant. First the visit of Curtis and Scofield—which she did not mention—and then a welcoming parade on Fifth Avenue for a foreign celebrity had tied up traffic; it had taken her *hours* to get across town from the Long Island Station, she complained.

"Oh," said Susan. "I have a three-thirty appointment at the shop, and I have to go uptown on an errand first. I suppose I'll never make it in the car. I want to get to Broadway and Thirty-ninth."

Hortense suggested the Times Square shuttle or walking. Lucinda snorted and asked what good walking would do when Fifth Avenue was tied up. Caroline Semmer suggested timidly that perhaps driving up Madison to Sixtieth Street and then taking the B.M.T. subway downtown would be best. Susan sighed and said she supposed the shuttle to Times Square from Grand Central would be fastest. She looked at her watch again.

"I'll have to telephone the shop first and tell them I'll be late. They can keep my three-thirty appointment busy with the fitter and the new models till I get there. Bye—see you all later."

She dashed out and down. In the lobby she headed for the phone booths. No nickel, of course. Back to the cigar counter for change for a dollar; impossible to pick it up with gloves on. Impatient, she pawed at the change, and it went flying to the floor. The man behind the counter came crawling out, the elevator starter dashed over. Together, on their hands and knees, they collected her change while she stood tapping one foot in a frenzy of impatience. She was getting to that state of exasperated nervous hurry that is a special disease of all New Yorkers, and which attacked her most viciously when she was faced with using one of the underground means of transport. She hated the subway. It gave her the creeps.

Change all collected, a quick thank you, and back to the phone booth. Her watch showed five minutes to three. The number was busy. She dialed it twice more before getting her secretary, then cut short a long explanation of something or other; she didn't listen to what. Her instructions *re* the three-thirty appointment with Mrs. Archie Blankinsop given, she burst from the phone booth and out to the street. Then she remembered about her car parked outside the hotel, went back to the phone booth and instructed her garage to pick up the roadster and deliver it to her shop. She glanced at her watch. Three o'clock now. Perhaps she ought to give up the whole idea of her errand and go straight to the shop. But she wanted certain information before she saw Curtis. Mrs. Blankinsop would never let her go early enough to get it afterward, and before five. She would have to do it now.

Down two blocks, around the corner, into the Roosevelt and from its depths along the underground passage to Grand Central's lower level and thus into the Grand Central-Times Square shuttle station. It was crowded with humanity at a low ebb of politeness. Women with bundles. Men with bundles. Men and women and children shoved and hampered her progress. She could have screamed with impatience.

There—she had reached the shuttle platform at last. She stood, nerves on edge, gazing down the long tunnel with its double tracks leading to Times Square. What would Vivian think of her state of mind, she wondered—Vivian the calm and poised, who hated career women to show signs of feminine weakness? The train was coming, twin lights and muted roar that grew as the lights drew nearer. People jostled around Susan, pushing for the platform's edge. She gripped her handbag firmly. The roar suddenly expanded, released from the strictures of the tunnel to the open spaces of the platform. A shoulder brushed Susan's back and she put out her hand to steady herself on a pillar next to her. As her fingers closed on its edge, something pushed hard against the small of her back, a sharp, determined shove. In the confusion of subway sounds she heard, or fleetingly imagined she heard, a brief, queer laugh near at hand. Instinctively, her weight went back on her heels, her other hand went out to grab the nearest bulk. The first car of the train, grinding to a shuddering standstill, passed her.

Susan turned, eyes starting from her head. Nothing but strangers around her. Half sobbing, she pushed her way away from the slowing train, out through the pressing crowd, up the stairs through the station, into the air. She fell into a taxi, asked the driver to make the best time he could in the heavy traffic; and sat shivering in the corner. That had been no accidental shove; someone had tried deliberately to push her off the platform, onto the tracks in front of that oncoming shuttle train. She wished wildly now that she had insisted on seeing Curtis immediately that morning.

But at least it couldn't have been Tom on the platform—comforting thought in a welter of bewildered panic. He hadn't been at the hotel when she had spoken of taking the shuttle to Times Square to avoid the parade traffic. Tom couldn't have known she was going to take it, something she never did.

Relief flooding her, she paid off her taxi as it deposited her at last before the office building at 1441 Broadway. She dashed again for a phone booth. Getting the Eden Hotel, she asked for the ballroom. A man's voice answered—one of the stagehands. No, all the ladies had left. Or no, here was Miss Mason, who had just come back. Miss Mason was called to the phone.

"Lucinda—everyone else gone?"

"Susan! Why yes, my dear—they were all in a panic about the traffic and sure they'd never make their afternoon appointments, so the rehearsal broke up. They all left almost immediately after you."

"Thanks," Susan said. "I—I just wondered if they were all staying because in that case, I'd have made an effort to get back later. Thanks—I won't bother then."

She hung up, feeling weak in the knees. They had all left immediately after her—and where had Lucinda been? And why had she sounded so surprised to hear Susan's voice over the wire? The stagehand had said: "Miss Mason's just come back."

Very thoughtful, she took the elevator up to the fifteenth floor, and was horrified to find herself edging carefully to the rear of it so that her back rested firmly against the elevator wall.

Presently, Miss Yates was closeted with the manager of the merchants' credit association, asking various questions natural enough from the owner of a retail establishment. She jotted down the data provided, thanked the manager and took her departure, her brow puckered in thought. Great spenders they all were. Only Thomas Benchley seemed able to maintain himself without affluent use of credit accounts in New York stores and shops.

It was ten minutes to four when Susan reached her shop. Mrs. Blankinsop (the 3:30 appointment), her secretary told her, had arrived twenty minutes late, and was happily closeted with the fitter and Mme Laura, their best saleswoman.

"Think they can hold her for another five minutes?" Susan asked. "I haven't even looked at my mail today." The secretary went off to make sure of Blankinsop's equanimity, and Susan sat down to her mail. Advertisements, bills, statements, checks, complaints and praises. Nothing that could not wait. She shoved back her chair and stood up to go when her eye caught an envelope, at the bottom of the pile, which she had missed. It looked different, somehow, and she slit it open quickly. In it was a single sheet of paper:

Miss Yates about this death of Nancy Pierce think it might be important where she was night before she died. Since you're interested why not ask Dr. Semmer on Park Avenue?

Yours truly and respectfully.

There was no signature. She refolded the sheet carefully and replaced it in the envelope. This message was not pieced together from newspaper print, but printed roughly with a heavy crayon. She put the envelope in a clean envelope of her own, slipped the whole into her bag, and went to see Blankinsop.

CHAPTER TWENTY-TWO

AT JUST ABOUT the moment that Susan was gazing with a critical eye at Mrs. Blankinsop's portly figure, Lyle Curtis was receiving a summons to the district attorney's office.

"We have a visitor," Scofield greeted him grimly, "a voluntary visitor with something to tell us." He pushed a button on his desk, and said into the transmitter, "Send Mr. Pierce in."

Curtis raised his eyebrows, drew up a chair, and said:

"Am I turning psychic, or *is* Pierce going to lead us up an alley?"

Scofield grrumphed and spat. "Probably. A nice big forest fire would be more restful than this case. The commissioner has been on the phone again rubbing my hair with garlic. Pierce apparently has called on his Reverence again. After calling us in, he seems to prefer him to us. The old boy was chuckling all over the place, saying: 'So you thought it was murder! Wait until you hear what Pierce has unearthed—then call me back.' Well, I'm waiting."

Into this agitated atmosphere Howard Pierce walked. He was looking considerably less blustery than on Tuesday afternoon at the Hotel Eden, Curtis noted. Then, determined to yell "Murder" over the dead body of his wife, his expression had been more furious than shrouded with the incoherence of grief. Now his face showed astonishment and anxiety. The assistant D. A. stared at him in surprise. Pierce took a chair and lit a cigarette. Almost immediately he threw it away and lit another.

The D. A. watching said abruptly: "Who do you think really poisoned your wife, Pierce?"

174

Nancy Pierce's widower now turned confused and moved in his chair nervously. "Hasn't the commissioner told you? I thought it better not to talk over the phone."

Nettled by being placed in a false position of ignorance by the commissioner, Mr. Scofield belatedly took wily refuge in the Bard of Avon's philosophic remark, reminding Curtis later that they "are reputed wise for saying nothing." He assumed a ponderously grave expression, and surveyed the visitor with suspicious silence. Pierce stirred again, and mashed out his cigarette.

"It's true," he said at length, "that I was convinced Nancy had been murdered. No use beating about the bush. I had my suspicions. I thought there was nothing in her make-up to give the slightest verification to suicide. I would have sworn it. And I'd lived with her for eight years. I thought I knew her—well, pretty well." He straightened his shoulders, and turned his hawk nose toward the strong light of the windows, seeming to forget for the instant both Scofield and Curtis. After a long moment, he said: "I didn't even think it was one of those damn women. Of course, she was always rubbing their hair the wrong direction. I could see that. She had a way with her—got places—made pluses out of minuses all the time by shrewd means of her own. But, even so, I had reason to believe she'd been even more troublesome in another quarter. Now, with what I've discovered, I don't want to say where. No use. Needlessly libelous. But I thought she'd probably pulled a certain party's leg once too often. Even a worm turns— Well, there's no use in going into that. The carbon copy sends all murder theories to the dump heap as far as I can make out." He looked back at them quickly. "You gentlemen still don't hold, even so, to the murder angle, surely?" His tone was not one of criticism or complaint, but of sudden perplexity and incertitude.

Scofield moved with ponderous discomfiture in his chair. To save the D. A.'s face Curtis said briefly: "Mr. Scofield hasn't had time to tell me of what you've found. Would you mind going over the details for my benefit?"

Pierce turned to the assistant district attorney a blank glance as if he were seeing him for the first time since entering the room.

"Of course, of course," he said dully. "There's not much to the story. I was cleaning out Nancy's private desk in her sitting room last night." He said this apparently, Curtis thought, quite honestly—not in the tone of a deeply bereaved husband, but as one who had had an unpleasant job to perform and had performed it. "There were a lot of carbon copies of her business correspondence. A few personal notes, too, which evidently she had copied in longhand, as a matter of record. There was one folder marked 'X'—nothing more. In it I found a single carbon. It was of the letter they found under her foot after she died. I've brought it for you to compare," and he glanced at Scofield, "but I don't believe there's any doubt that it is a definite duplicate."

Mr. Pierce reached to the floor where he had placed a brief case, brought it up to his lap, opened the slide fastener and produced an ordinary, thin-paper carbon, passing it across the desk to the district attorney. The D. A. roused himself from deeply speculative observation of the lawyer, and reached for the paper. Curtis went around the big desk and stood looking over his shoulder. There seemed to him little doubt that this was indeed a carbon of the note found under Nancy Pierce's foot. The district attorney gave him a sharp look; and in a moment he went out of the room bearing Howard Pierce's exhibit in his hands. In his own safe was the original.

Presently he came back into Scofield's office and gave the chief a nod of confirmation. His own eyes and the eyes of a department expert had not taken long in ascertaining that the paper in his hand was the copy which had been made with carbon paper when Nancy Pierce's "suicide note" had been typed.

Howard Pierce was searching in his pockets again, and not finding what he sought.

"Cigarette?" inquired Lyle from behind him, and the widower nodded numbly. "Yes, thanks. I'm a little shot. Haven't got used to the idea that Nancy deliberately took her own life. It's like being told the Washington Monument is made of cellophane." He laughed grimly.

Curtis kept thinking: "All of this sounds authentic. And he *couldn't* have faked that carbon—unless he wrote the original himself. And that makes no sense. But something's screwy. The note still doesn't make sense. The note still doesn't ring true. Pierce's reaction which seems O.K. makes it ring even sourer." Then he thought that normally speaking he wouldn't be one to trust Howard Pierce and his like beyond the nearest lamppost.

The D. A. stirred, and his voice boomed out with more volume than was even usual. He asked: "What's the catch, Pierce? Why is it there's no evidence of this theft business the note indicates?"

The other shook his head and pulled on the cigarette Curtis had given him. "I don't understand it at all. What would Nancy steal for? I had all the money she needed. One thing can be said, I was never close with Nancy on money matters." He looked up with shrewdness suddenly etched in his eyes. "It reflects on me, too, if my wife was a thief. For my own reputation, I want to get to the bottom of this. And if there *was* a theft to make restitution."

"Certainly," muttered Scofield, watching him. Pierce's eyes had dropped. His hands were limp on the arms of his chair, the cigarette forgotten between two fingers. He was staring at the carbon copy Curtis had placed again before the D. A. on his desk.

Scofield pressed a button, and his private secretary came in. The chief dictated a brief record of what Pierce had told them, and presently the secretary came back with it typed. Pierce signed it. So did the secretary and an investigator called in from the outer office as a second witness. Scofield attached it to the carbon with a clip. The secretary and the investigator went away and silence filled the room.

"Well?" boomed Scofield, and added more mildly: "Anything occur to you, Pierce?"

"You don't suppose," the other asked, his expression detached and unfathomable, "that the carbon could have been planted?" Scofield and Curtis exchanged the briefest of glances. "Do you think it likely?" asked the D. A.

"I think it's more logical but probably most unlikely," Pierce replied with more asperity than he had yet shown. He rose then and bid them apparently the most absent-minded of adieus. Trailing his overcoat over one arm, he crossed the room and went out the door, still seemingly lost in thought.

"I'll be damned," ejaculated Mr. Scofield. "Can you beat it?" Curtis said: "You think it was a fine piece of acting?"

The district attorney grrumped and emitted one word: "Hell."

"Got those reports on the potassium cyanide found in the Pierce apartment?" Scofield asked after a moment. Curtis nodded.

"The solution was potassium cyanide, all right, but not a strong enough solution for so little to have killed her. But the doc says it can be reduced very easily—made stronger, I mean—and that you can find out how to do it in any elementary chemistry book."

"Fingerprints?" asked the D. A.

"Only what we would have expected. Mrs. Pierce's own and the maid's. No one else's. And the jar apparently hadn't been wiped clean—it was a mass of old prints."

"That gets us nowhere with Pierce, then, for the moment," Scofield said frowning. "Unless and until we can discover a good motive, and a definite opportunity, we've got nothing on him. But it's a damn funny picture. First he yells his wife has been murdered. Then when we agree with him, he about-faces. Wonder if he knows he's under suspicion? He must—he's a smart lawyer. And besides . . ."

"Hell," Curtis interrupted suddenly, "what a prize ass I've been. Of all the blundering idiots! My God, chief, the note—it's as simple as all hell."

"What are you talking about?" Scofield asked, looking at his young assistant as though he had suddenly gone mad.

"The damn note that made no sense—God, I'm an idiot—Nancy wrote it, but *not for herself*—you see what I mean? Then it makes perfect sense. If she wrote it for someone else to sign—it wasn't signed, remember . . ."

"Blackmail," Scofield said softly. "Of course. It fits. It fits everything. It fits what we know of Nancy Pierce's character—it gives us a motive for murder—and it lets Howard Pierce out."

"Why?"

"Because the person for whom Nancy had written the note must have been at the luncheon, to drop it by the body. And Pierce wasn't there."

Curtis' face fell.

"Except, of course," Scofield continued, "if your Susan Yates is lying. If she's lying and the note was there from the first, then Nancy Pierce may have had it in her bag after all—waiting to give it to her victim to sign."

"But if Susan Yates is lying about it," Curtis said quickly, "it still doesn't implicate Pierce. We have no evidence of any connection or collusion between Yates and Pierce."

"True," said Scofield, "we have no evidence. But we must keep an open mind on testimony as well as theories. It seems to me that you've been taking Miss Yates' testimony entirely too much for granted. Much of what you know about this case and its background, you've learned from her. She's very attractive, I'm sure—but that doesn't mean that she's incapable of deceit—or even of murder."

Curtis flushed. "I've not been as trusting as you seem to believe, sir. I have kept in mind that Miss Yates is also a suspect, and I have tried to corroborate as much of her evidence as possible by other testimony. But I haven't had time to corroborate it all—this case is only two days old, remember that, sir. However—Miss Yates is coming in this afternoon, at her own suggestion, to tell me something. I assure you that I shall get as much truth from her as possible."

The district attorney grrumphed. "Sure. See that you do, young man. From what I hear of that young lady, she's smart enough to outwit two assistant district attorneys. Have a check up made immediately on the bank accounts of all the suspects, and start an examination of the books of all the firms they worked for. We're getting somewhere now."

CHAPTER TWENTY-THREE

MRS. BLANKINSOP DEPARTED earlier than Susan had dared hope, and the designer went back to her office, giving orders that she was not to be disturbed for any reason whatsoever. Picking up her phone, she asked the switchboard operator for a direct wire, and instructed her not to put through any incoming calls until further notice. Then she opened her telephone book and ran her finger down a list of names. She called in turn Hortense Culbertson, Caroline Semmer, Vivian Peabody and last Lucinda Mason. To each she made the silliest possible remark. It was:

"Listen, darling, have you heard that Nancy was going to have a baby?" She listened with stretched ears to the series of replies, and her expression grew darker and darker.

"Susan! Not really!" had come Hortense Culbertson's liquid tone.

Caroline Semmer had replied in a shocked voice: "My dear, you don't *say!*"

"Susan!" Vivian exclaimed. "Who in the world told you?"

And Lucinda Mason remarked: "Good lord! Whose?"

To each in turn Susan then said: "Well, of course, I don't *know* that she was, but it just occurred to me."

Then each of them had gone on characteristically, Miss Culbertson saying: "Oh, Susan, such an idea! Whatever made you think of *that?*" Miss Semmer had remonstrated mildly that she *really* did not see how they could conclude *anything* so dreadfully sad, and that *really* there had not been any evidence, *had* there? Vivian Peabody was flatly annoyed. She told Susan that she should have thought she had more profitable employment for her time and brain. And why didn't she stop thinking about Nancy's death? She was growing morbid about it. Lucinda had laughed and said that Susan had given her quite a turn. "Such an idea, my lamb. But I'm sure *that* might have been enough to turn her thoughts to suicide. It's difficult to conjure up a picture of Nancy ever having been called Mamma by a little duckie."

Somewhat red of face, and a little exasperated at herself for having deliberately told such a whopper, Susan replaced the receiver after her last call and sat brooding. Someone, she kept repeating to herself, *had* laughed hysterically, not many seconds after Tom had remarked at the luncheon table that the capsules were presumably digestible in the stomach. Someone had laughed the same way over her telephone; and though it might be her imagination, she was all but sure that someone near her on the shuttle platform had emitted that selfsame, idiotic sound. It annoyed and no little chagrined her not to have been able to decoy a repeat performance out of one of them.

Angrily, Susan dialed Tom Benchley's number, but Mr. Benchley did not answer.

IT WAS FIVE-FIVE when Susan presented herself at the offices of the district attorney, her mind still unmade. The subway incident did prove that Tom had not been guilty of sending the note the night before—for certainly the two things were connected. And since he wasn't guilty, she would say nothing about it—it would only be getting Tom in trouble. But which of the people at the hotel that afternoon had it been? Susan had spent almost ten minutes telephoning, ten minutes of time for someone else to make preparations, between the time that she had announced her intention of taking the subway and her actual entry into it. Ample time for any or all of them upstairs to have made a not too hasty departure after her, or for anyone of them to telephone someone else from the phones upstairs. And she had announced that she would have to telephone first, so they had all known she would not be leaving immediately.

She was somewhat surprised when a secretary came to usher her into Curtis' office. She had expected him to come out himself. From his formal, "Good afternoon, Miss Yates," his bow instead of a handshake, she realized that something had happened. His polite smile as he greeted her was a mere grimace; above it his eyes remained grave and, Susan thought, a little sad.

She was disconcerted. Throughout the day she had been thinking that at five she would find reassurance and a human contact unspoiled by suspicion. Why had it not occurred to her that, although she could have no grounds for suspecting him of anything, he might very well be suspicious of her? The man who faced her across his desk was a tight-lipped stranger. What had happened? What had he discovered that seemed to implicate her in Nancy's death?

"What was it you wanted to tell me, Miss Yates?" he asked at last, and she realized that she had been staring at him like an idiot. Her mind thrust into confusion again, she stammered something unintelligible. Heavens, what would Vivian think of her? A fine show she was putting on for career women.

She pulled herself together and, opening her bag, produced the letter she had received that day.

"I don't know why this was addressed to me," she said, "but I thought you ought to have it right away."

Curtis nodded gravely and held out a hand for it. She presented it by one corner; he took it gingerly by another. He read it through twice, then laid it carefully on his desk.

"Thank you," he said, "it may be very important. You say you have no idea why it was sent to you. Have you any idea who may have sent it?"

"None," said Susan.

"Ah . . . what else did you want to tell me, Miss Yates?" She hesitated perceptibly for a moment, then said:

"Someone tried to push me off a subway platform this afternoon."

"Susan!" Curtis half rose from his chair, in evident agitation. Then he smoothed himself out, resumed his seat, and amended: "Miss Yates! Are you sure?"

"Quite sure," said Susan. She described leaving the ballroom, phoning, entering the subway, the push, looking around and seeing no one she knew.

"You say you were standing by a pillar—did you look behind it—on the other side from you?"

Susan confessed she had not. "I was so eager to get out at that point," she said, "that I couldn't have stopped for anything."

"Tell me again who was present when you decided to take the subway."

"Vivian Peabody, Hortense Culbertson, Caroline Semmer, Lucinda Mason—and the stagehands, though I think we were too far away from them for them to have heard."

"And you say that when you telephoned back, they had all left, with the exception of Miss Peabody?"

"With the exception of Miss Mason. Or rather, she had been out too, and had just come back.

Curtis studied her intently. "Any ideas?"

Susan shook her head.

"Why do you think you were chosen for attack, Miss Yates? What do you know that is dangerous to the killer?"

"I don't know!" Susan cried. "I've been racking my brains."

"Sure of that? If you know anything, it is your duty to tell it to me, Miss Yates."

"I don't know what it is I know that is dangerous to the killer," Susan repeated, and remained truthful by her parroting.

"If you feel that your life is in danger, Miss Yates, perhaps I had better provide you with a guard."

She shook her head again, but without conviction. "I'm going to be careful. Very careful. And no more subways."

"It won't necessarily be a subway next time," said Curtis. "I think I must insist on a guard for you, Miss Yates. He won't be conspicuous and he won't get in your way. You needn't have him quartered in your apartment—your maid sleeps in, doesn't she? She's reliable? Well, then, if the guard stays downstairs in the apartment lobby, that will be sufficient. And at the shop, I think the presence of your employees will be enough. Tell your maid and your secretary not to admit anyone to the apartment or to your office without first asking you. Have you a chain on the apartment door? Well, get one. And be careful what you eat. Have your maid prepare all your meals—no dining out—and take a shoe-box lunch to the shop. And don't take any candy from strangers."

He smiled, and leaning across the desk, laid his hand on hers. Then he remembered, apparently, and the hand was quickly withdrawn. The smile faded.

"Anything else to tell me, Miss Yates?"

"Nothing."

"You're sure of that?"

"Sure."

He waited a moment, as if giving her time to change her mind, then rose. "Well, then, if you'll wait a few minutes I'll go get your guard and introduce you."

He was gone twenty minutes. Twenty minutes in which Susan alternately fiddled and sat still, alternately resented his attitude and remembered the startled "Susan!" and the hand over hers. When he returned he was followed by a nondescript-looking man in dark serge. Susan, with a designer's eye, saw how the coat had been cut to conceal the broad shoulders, how the slight stoop deliberately gave the lie to a powerful chest.

"Miss Yates, this is Sergeant Withers. He will always be somewhere near you. If you need him, call. Sergeant, I'm depending on you to see that Miss Yates is not harmed."

Susan and her future protector bowed gravely.

"I'll try not to make it too difficult for you," she said.

"Indeed, Miss Yates," said the sergeant, "it's going to be a pleasure, I'm sure."

With which exchange of courtesies, they left, the sergeant six paces behind her. Susan felt as though she ought to be saying: "Company *march*," and giggled to herself all the way downstairs. She felt much better.

In the street she stopped at her car which she had had her garage call for at the Hotel Eden.

"Give you a lift, Sergeant?" she asked.

Withers shook his head. "Better not to be seen with you," he said. "I'll follow in a cab. Going home? Yes, I have the address." He opened the door of the car, surveyed the interior briefly, said: "No bombs," with a smile and helped her in. As she warmed the motor, she could see him in her mirror getting into the cab behind her. She started for home.

She was puzzled. If the presence of Sergeant Withers was for her protection, why shouldn't he be seen with her? What better warning to malefactors to keep away? Aha, she thought, that was it—Curtis didn't want them kept away. She was to be used as a decoy, was she? Or did it mean that Curtis hadn't believed her story, and had insisted on the guard so that he could keep an eye on her doings, not on her health? She frowned at Sergeant Withers' following cab in the mirror. "Your brain is being overworked these days, my girl," she said to herself. "Home to dinner in bed and a night of guarded sleep."

LEFT ALONE IN HIS OFFICE, Lyle Curtis sat unhappily at his desk. For perhaps five minutes he sat gazing into space. Then he picked up his phone and said:

"Get me the Eden ballroom, please." The operator reported back a minute later that the ballroom did not answer. Curtis looked at his watch—of course, it was after six, the stagehands would have left long since. He said: "Try the offices of the Tomorrow Club at the Hotel Eden." After a moment, a prim voice said:

"Tomorrow Club."

"This is Lyle Curtis," he said.

"Oh, Mr. Curtis, this is Caroline Semmer."

"Good evening, Miss Semmer. Working late, aren't you? May I ask you some more questions?"

"Why, of course, Mr. Curtis. . . ."

"Were all the members of the Tomorrow Club committee at the ballroom this afternoon?"

"This afternoon, Mr. Curtis?" Miss Semmer's voice was surprised. "Why, yes, early in the afternoon. They all left at about three—they had appointments, and I had work to do here in the office."

"Anyone else there beside the committee?"

"Why, no—the stagehands, of course—and oh yes, Mr. Benchley came in just as they were all going—but he only stayed a second, and left right away with Miss Culbertson."

"Thank you very much, Miss Semmer. They couldn't any of them have been up at One Hundred and Twenty-fifth Street at three-fifteen then, could they?"

"One Hundred and Twenty-fifth Street? No, I don't see how." Miss Semmer's voice was puzzled. "Except possibly Miss Yates, who left a little earlier than the others."

"I see," said Curtis gravely. "Well, thank you very much. You won't mention this little conversation to anyone, will you?" Miss Semmer said of course she wouldn't, sounding flustered and pleased.

Curtis hung up murmuring "Blessed are the red herrings," and made a mental note to remember this one when next he saw Miss Semmer, so that he would not look too blank if she mentioned One Hundred and Twenty-fifth Street. Then his face set again in its former grim and unhappy mold, and he said into the phone:

"Get me Miss Susan Yates at her apartment, please." Miss Yates herself answered; she had just got in.

"Miss Yates—why didn't you tell me that Thomas Benchley was also in the ballroom this afternoon?"

"Tom! In the ballroom!" Was he fancying it, or was there fear in her voice. "But he wasn't—not when I was there."

"Sure of that?"

"Of course."

"Very well then—good night, Miss Yates."

"Good night, Mr. Curtis." Susan's lips were trembling as she turned from the phone. Tom had been at the ballroom? Or was Curtis suspicious of something, and trying to trap her? She turned back to the phone again, and called Hortense Culbertson. Amenities exchanged, she said:

"Hortense, did you by any chance see Tom today? I've been try-ing to get him on the phone without success."

"Why, yes, Susan," said Hortense, "he came up to the ballroom just after you left—he must have come up in one elevator while you were going down in another. He asked where you were, so I guess he wants to talk to you, too. But I don't know where he is by now. I had to leave right away, and we went downstairs together, and then I left him at the door of the hotel."

"Thanks, Hortense—I'll just have to keep on trying his num-ber, then. Good-by." She hung up. Tom had been there and had asked where she was—and someone had undoubtedly told him. And he had left Hortense at the door of the hotel.

A very unhappy young woman once more, Miss Yates went in to prepare for her dinner.

LYLE CURTIS WAS no happier. After hanging up, he sat gazing at his desk, Scofield's warning about Susan ringing in his ears.

Miss Yates was frightened. He was sure of that. Was she fright-ened because of the subway attack—or had she invented the sub-way attack to explain her fright? And what had she wanted to tell him? The subway incident had taken place at three that afternoon. And the postmark on the anonymous letter read eleven o'clock. So what had Miss Yates wanted so urgently to tell him at *ten* that morning?

CHAPTER TWENTY-FOUR

Friday Morning

FRIDAY MORNING PRESENTED the kind of climatic change of which Colonel Gamberson had expressed definite disapproval. It had turned warm, but it was winter and should not have been warm. Warm as it was, it should have been bright and cheerful. It was gray and damp. Slush from yesterday's snow stood in pools on the pavements. People carried umbrellas because it looked so wet underfoot. The sky was obscured with smoke.

Lyle Curtis sat at his desk much as he had sat the night before, with the anonymous letter before him. It had been dusted for fingerprints, revealing, besides Susan's and his own, only a few unidentifiable smudges that did not check with any of the suspects' prints.

He uncradled the telephone receiver and asked for Dr. Semmer. When the physician's voice came over the wire Curtis asked a few questions. Dr. Semmer insisted that it would be quite impossible for him to come to the district attorney's office before evening. Hospital commitments and private patients, he explained peevishly, came first in a physician's curriculum.

Using the doctor's undergraduate nickname of Lin, Curtis inquired amiably when his office hours began.

"Four p.m.," icily.

"And you return to your office?"

"Naturally, just before then."

"Then, if I am at your office just before four—say at three-fifty—we could have a few minutes?"

The physician bristled. "Look here, Lyle, I've been outrageously drilled by a heavy-footed sergeant of yours, a human rhinoceros named McQuire. He seemed to have some damnable idea that Nancy Pierce was a dope addict. I say she wasn't. There's nothing more I can possibly enlighten your office about, and I don't mind saying outright that it's damned inconvenient having the police calling round here at all hours."

Curtis said that he thought there were certain ways in which Linwood Semmer could help, and pointed out further that, as a matter of fact, he himself did not resemble the public's idea of a copper.

Semmer wasn't amused at this effort at light-handedness. Half a minute of strained silence ensued. Then he demanded explosively: "Exactly what do you want?"

"I can go into that better face to face, I think."

"I want to know now. I've got no time to waste. Certainly I've got a right to know what I'm making appointments about. My God, haven't I the rights of an ordinary citizen?"

"I should think so. All of them."

"Then why don't you tell me what you want?"

"A suspicious man, Lin, might begin wondering what's eating you."

"Damn your impertinence!"

The receiver banged down at Semmer's end and the connection was broken.

The assistant district attorney replaced his leisurely, and sat studying the instrument. Two things in this world, he reflected, a man didn't have to listen to if he felt disinclined: radios and telephones. But what the devil was wrong with Semmer? Foolish thing to do.

As Curtis sat thinking, the telephone at his elbow jangled. He lifted the receiver again and heard a woman's voice asking, "Is that Mr. Lyle Curtis, please?"

"Right."

"Doctor Linwood Semmer's office calling. Doctor Semmer has asked me to say that the telephone connection he just had with you was broken. And very unfortunately he has had to hurry away to the hospital for an early morning operation, so he couldn't ring you back himself. He was very sorry, and will expect you here this afternoon at three-fifty, as you suggested."

ABOUT THE TIME Assistant District Attorney Lyle Curtis was telephoning Dr. Semmer, Mr. Thomas Benchley was also on the telephone. He was asking the gracious voice at the other end of the wire if it would be convenient to speak to Miss Yates. The voice said it would see, but returned presently to say it was very sorry, but Miss Yates was engaged. Mr. Benchley became importunate to an almost gaudy degree. The voice said: "I will tell Miss Yates if I find I can interrupt her," quite as if he were a father who had just ordered a ten-thousand-dollar trousseau. "Will you be so good as to wait once more?"

Susan came to the phone with mixed feelings.

"Listen, Susan. Remember I wanted to talk to you about something the other night? Remember that redhead you saw me with at the San Horitz?" Susan remembered. "Well, listen—she's in Pierce's office." He explained tersely what Ruby Holt had told him of Howard Pierce's affair with his secretary, his desire for a divorce and Nancy's unwillingness to give it to him. What he wanted Susan to do, he explained, was to give Ruby a job in her shop so they could keep her under their eyes as an ultimate prize witness. Susan at first refused, remembering Curtis' warnings and being none too happy at the thought of someone constantly in her shop sent by Tom. But Benchley was so insistent, that she had at last to promise to speak to Miss Holt—she could not refuse without making Tom suspicious.

"And, Tom—what about that note? I thought you were going to send it to me?"

"I was, Susan, but I can't find the damn thing. It must have fallen out of my pocket sometime during that wild night. Why? Does Curtis want it?"

"No," said Susan, "I haven't told Curtis anything about it," and hung up abruptly. She walked to her window. Oh blessed sight, across the street, having his shoes shined, sat the deceptive-looking Sergeant Withers.

ON HANGING UP the receiver, Tom immediately removed it again and dialed another number. Over the wire came the sweetly mushy tones of Miss Ruby Holt. For the moment, in his enthusiasm, Mr. Benchley almost forgot both the Harvard accent, and to announce himself as Mr. Carrington Wells. Recovering in time, he did so, then inquired of Miss Holt's health. She expressed herself as tickled to death to hear from him again, and so soon. She was even more enchanted by the idea of lunching with Mr. Wells. Of course she could. Where? Mr. Benchley named a far more obscure rendezvous than the Hotel San Horitz, mentioning twelve o'clock for the time, and was told that that was just the hour that Miss Holt was customarily relieved on the switchboard. Only, she would have to be back by one o'clock or get, it appeared, the devil. Mr. Wells assured her that such a program could be carried out. "Unless," he tempted, "something somebody has been on the telephone with me about gives you another idea."

"What!" screeched Miss Holt ecstatically. "Say, you wouldn't kid me, would you? Who'd call you up about me?"

"An admirer." And there, temptingly, Mr. Benchley left the conversation.

CHAPTER TWENTY-FIVE

Friday Noon

AFTER HIS TELEPHONE conversation with Dr. Semmer, Curtis began methodically clearing his desk of regular matters which had accumulated staggeringly during the past days. Later in the morning, he returned to the Pierce case and spent some minutes staring unseeingly into the strong north light of his windows. He wished desperately that the Pierce case could be settled with swift, iron-hand action, that it was settled, and the D. A.'s brief written. At the back of his thoughts hovered an unidentifiable dread.

Fear, Curtis told himself, was as vicious as gluttony—and very often its bedfellow; and fear, too, could become lethargy in its very perpetuation. People who lived day after day with fear developed an insensitiveness to its power, and generated within themselves an acceptance of it as a reality not to be conquered but to be followed blindly. Fear worshipers, he thought angrily, were the world's real troublemakers. Then he defined that more closely: fear was possessiveness—the fear of losing something. Running over the name of the personalities intimately connected with the Pierce case, he damned his incapacity to say which of them was most likely to be harboring this gnawing, gangrenous quality.

"If only," he thought irritably, "this were a mystery story and not life, the answer would be half as easy. It would be one of the people who seem to have no fears at all. But are there any?" Susan Yates? She had certainly been frightened when she came to see him the day before and afterward on the telephone. Hortense

Culbertson had seemed very nervous at the Monday afternoon investigation. Caroline Semmer was a fussy, apologetic old gal and had been upset at Inspector Beller's request for her brother's address. Lucinda Mason had appeared far from serene upon learning that her husband had been buying the deceased cocktails shortly before her death. At the Van Wecks' yesterday her behavior had been certainly extremely odd. Tom was fearful for Hortense—or was he? If current information was correct, he hadn't been near her in nearly a year until the past Monday. Howard Pierce was stirred with an emotion which might easily come in the fear category. Why had he switched from murder back to suicide so easily? Certainly Dr. Semmer was in a fine state of nerves. Fear did not seem entirely the word for Colonel Gamberson's attitude, but something was eating that personage. And if it had not been fear—closely guarded, held in check with tremendous poise—that he had seen in Vivian Peabody's eyes, Curtis was ready to abandon psychology as black magic and quackery.

He spent the next two hours reviewing again all the reports on the case. Then, thrusting his heavy chair back roughly, "Damn this case," he ejaculated, and pounded out of his office.

In the street, he ignored the line of official cars, discreetly parked along the curb, and hailed a taxi instructing the driver to deliver him to the Hotel Eden.

In the bar Curtis shocked Lucien by ordering black coffee. No one else was in the bar. He motioned to Lucien and said: "I want to talk to you and that dark waiter over there—Mike."

The Frenchman nodded, as if to say, "Very good, but what am I to do about it?"

"Call him."

"But certainly," Lucien responded gravely, and signaled the dark Mike who was hovering in the background waiting for the noon rush. "Mike," he spoke in a soft tone. "Come here. This gentleman will speak with you one moment."

Mike came looking prepared to receive criticism or praise with the same amiability. He waited for Curtis to begin.

But instead of speaking at once, the assistant D. A. took a card from his pocket and requested that Mike cast his eye upon it. Then he passed it to Lucien, and subsequently put it away again carefully.

"Now you know why it will be extremely wise not to gossip about what we are going to talk about. You remember a dark, rather sulky man the noon of the fifteenth—last Tuesday?"

"Sulky?" pondered Lucien, rolling his eyes.

"You know," translated Mike, "madlike." To Curtis he said: "You mean the guy I told Mrs. Yates about when you was in here with her the other afternoon? Sure I remember. Sat over in that corner. His sister come in and spoke to him. Then the girl that got murdered came in and had a drink with him. There's already been a cop in here asking did we see anybody give her poison."

Lucien nodded. "That is the truth. He was the man."

"The man who what?" asked Lyle.

"The man who left without paying his check."

"Or leaving a tip," appended Mike, without noticeable malevolence.

"Now listen carefully," directed the attorney. "What happened from beginning to end of his conversation with the Pierce girl? Tell me—both of you—everything you remember."

"You begin, Mike. You were nearest them."

"From the moment the murdered dame came in?" Mike said, obviously incapable of disassociating Nancy Pierce from her final violent demise.

"Right."

"Well, he was arguing like. She just sat listening and wriggling like out of her cape."

"Wait a minute, where did she put her cape?"

"Just let it drop back behind her. Why not?"

"No matter. Did she have a handbag?"

"Sure. Big as a tugboat. Them women carry trunks around nowadays."

"Where did she put it? Did he touch it?"

Mike pondered. At length he said with cheerful conviction: "No, he didn't touch it. She put it down on the other side of her. I remember because if other people had come in and been sitting next to her, it might have been dangerous leaving it there when she went to the bar. As it was, business was poor on Tuesday—count of the storm. Women do leave their purses around loose like. Just the other night some dame lost—" A solemn glance from Lucien stopped this gossip.

"You're sure she didn't put it next the man—between them?" insisted Curtis.

"No, other side of herself."

"All right. Go on. What happened next?"

"Well, he kept on talking. The girl was kinda laughing at him at first. Bored like. He was mad already. Sour kind of guy. Anyway, he went on talking about how she'd promised to tell him something; and how she didn't have no responsibility. He was getting madder and madder. Finally, the girl says: 'Say, you can't talk that way to me, skip it.' Something like that. Then up he jumps and says: 'Leave my profession out of it,' looking at her as if she was some bathtub gin left over from Prohibition. Then he beat it."

"Without paying his check," reiterated Lucien solemnly.

"Then what?"

Lucien picked up the story. "There was a gentleman—alone— here at my bar. Not an old customer. He resembles not the most customers. Clothes for the country on him. He has been looking around because of the noise that the man and the dead girl make. When the man—that doctor—leave, my customer here, he look at the young lady. I say to myself—a pickup."

"Then," broke in Mike, "the girl, she got up and walked over to the bar like."

"And," Lucien continued, "my customer said to her— What was it he say, Mike?"

"He didn't say anything. She laughed like and said the other gent had been kinda mad, hadn't he? Then she sits down saying, 'You're the husband of a friend of mine, aren't you?' and called him 'Mr. Van— something.' Don't remember exactly what she called him. She meant he was that Miss Mason's husband, I think. And he said 'yes.' Surprised him, I guess."

Lucien amplified. "He look a little as you say nervous, but quick he order her a drink. She was gay, the little one. Not at all *difficile* to talk with, I think."

Mike nodded.

"My customer," continued Lucien, "soon accommodates himself to the idea. They laugh very much. I remember, *très bien*, she say: 'But of course Lucinda she marry you for your money,' and he think that very funny."

"Sure, he laughed like anything," explained Mike. "I was around here you know—close like—on account of keeping an eye on pickups in a swell place like the Eden. You know, don't want no comebacks of people claiming they was doped."

"Ah, *mais oui*, that I was forgetting," Lucien interrupted. "That it was, is it not so, Mike, which worried us?"

"What?" demanded Lyle.

"The *pilule*."

"Pills, you know," translated the waiter.

"What about them?"

"Why," Mike continued, "just before she leaves, the girl runs back over to her purse and pulls out a box of pills, brings them back and shows Lucien's customer the box. But she only showed it to him; he didn't take any, and she didn't neither."

"That was why we did not worry longer," the bartender nodded.

"Why not? What do you mean?"

"Because no one take a *pilule*. That means no one get doped."

Curtis sighed, then turned to Mike. "Look here, you're sure the first man didn't mess around with that box of capsules, maybe changing one box for another. He's a doctor, you know," he added reasonably.

"Sure I know," said Mike, then stopped abruptly and began swabbing the bar with his napkin.

"Well?" demanded Curtis.

Mike considered, but shook his head positively after a moment's reflection. "How could he? The coat, the bag and the pills were all on the other side of the girl—clean across her for him to have reached them. I wasn't busy then. Most the time they was talking. I didn't have nothing else to do." He pondered again. "She'd have had to work awful fast handing him her bag or the box without my seeing her do it. Only had my back turned twice—walking up to

Lucien for her manhattan and later taking the red-nosed gent's coat."

"And you, Lucien," Curtis persisted. "You're sure that the man here at the bar didn't tamper with her box of *pilules*—exchange one box for another perhaps?"

"Exchange! Impossible. She bring the box here. She open it. She show it to my customer. Then she shut the box. *Voilà. Fini.*"

"But afterward. What did she do with the box after all that?"

"She hold it in her hand all the time until she say good-by. Then she get up and go back to the divan. There the good Mike help her with her coat. She smile at my customer. Wave, I think. Very gay, and out she go."

"She must have sat at the bar maybe five minutes with the box in her hand," confirmed the waiter.

"I still think," complained Curtis with a frown, "that the doctor *could* have gotten hold of the capsule box momentarily. Perhaps when he got up to go?"

Lucien and Mike exchanged glances of commiseration over such determined dullness. The bartender shrugged. Mike grinned slowly, and said: "Listen, Mr. D. A., I wouldn't lie about it. I'm telling you, the pillbox was in her bag on the *other* side of her, and I didn't have practically nothing else to do except keep an eye on the two of them. Oh, not obvious like. You know, sidewise. But I can see things that way good as any. When I can't see is, maybe, when I got my back turned. But nobody can then, I ever heard of, and I didn't have my back turned more 'n half a minute twice. See?"

Lyle gave up. He paid for his coffee, deposited an ample tip in each man's hand and departed.

CHAPTER TWENTY-SIX

MR. THOMAS A. BENCHLEY was seated in an obscure restaurant reaching the last stages of exasperation. The quiet rendezvous he had selected for his second conference with Miss Ruby Holt was not graced with her presence. She had definitely not shown up. Mr. Benchley had made intermittent telephone calls to Howard Pierce's office, and been told with maddening brevity that Miss Holt was busy and couldn't come to the phone. He had tried both the Carrington Wells accent and his own garden variety Benchlian. Neither had produced further information. The noon-hour operator, who evidently was having a large dose of overtime labor, grew as irritated as Mr. Benchley himself. There seemed to him to be three alternatives: either the young woman was simply mad because she was having to substitute so long for the redhead and not giving any personal messages for her out of spite; or Miss Holt had thought better of seeing Tom again, and was deliberately standing him up; or—and the final thought was giving him considerable pause—she was being detained deliberately from conversing with him. His own interest in her in that case had been observed. He must feel responsible for her safety. It was his duty to do so, he decided.

Finally, he made a last call to the lawyer's switchboard and was told with venomous irritability: "I told you a million times, she's busy and can't talk. Say, don't you understand English?"

Mr. Benchley paid his bill and departed from the restaurant.

At exactly three-thirty, Lyle Curtis entered the marble-lined foyer of the Park Avenue apartment house where Dr. Semmer's office was located. A highly discreet and elegant sign designated the location of the doctor's suite. A young nurse received him and indicated a small reception room, elaborately French. He decided it was probably the one in which McQuire had waited, inasmuch as across the hall he observed a larger and even more splendid chamber where an open wood fire burned, and chairs were strewn about with elegant casualness suggestive of an excellent club. Linwood, he thought, did himself well. Neither Hippocrates nor Aesculapius was unhonored by their representative. Evidently the De Morgans, overwhelmed with gratitude for his quick attention to their wounded offspring, had indeed introduced him to an extraordinarily good list of patients.

The nurse-receptionist was about to withdraw when Mr. Curtis said suavely: "You must be as shocked as Doctor Semmer over the untimely demise of Mrs. Howard Pierce."

The young woman raised her narrow eyebrows. "Oh, Doctor has felt dreadfully about it," she assured him. "He brought Mrs. Pierce through pneumonia so beautifully just last year; and then to have her die—like that."

Curtis was sympathetic. He suggested that it must have been a personal shock to all those who had known Mrs. Pierce well. Perhaps to the nurse, herself, too.

"It was. It certainly was," she said with dignity. "Mrs. Pierce was only here the night before. It just didn't seem possible that only a few hours later she was dead."

Curtis nodded, still sympathetically. "But, of course, one can't let the fact that she was under treatment reflect on Dr. Semmer's professional reputation."

The nurse was shocked. "Oh, goodness, no. And besides, she wasn't exactly under treatment. Doctor liked to keep her under periodic observation—especially during the winter months. But that night, she just dropped in—socially. Her husband was meeting her here. They and the doctor were going on somewhere. To a dinner, I think."

Curtis asked unexpectedly, "Do you find Mr. Pierce good look-ing?" The nurse glanced at him curiously, but he appeared to be giving this subject profound, if silly, attention. He had screwed up his eyes with naïve thoughtfulness. "You know," he rambled on, "I find women have such odd ideas about good looks in men. They always say a man's good looking if he's the exact opposite of the sort a man would fancy."

The white-clad young woman laughed, wrinkling her nose quite nicely, Curtis thought. "Oh," she said, "to tell you the truth, I've never actually seen Mr. Howard Pierce. When he's been here, it's always been after office hours—when I'd gone home. I believe he comes quite often though. Doctor has often spoken of his being here. But you see I wouldn't *know* whether my tastes would agree with a man's about Mr. Pierce. Why, don't you think he's good looking?"

"I don't quite know," Lyle pondered, puckering his forehead, "but I suppose a great many women would."

"Anything like you?"

"Not the least, I'm afraid."

"Well, now, that's a pity for him," the young woman averred artfully, and, flashing her brown eyes, retired.

Curtis settled back well satisfied, and stared at a black porce-lain horse supporting a gold-shaded lamp on a table across the little room. Not a bad start at all, he reflected, and decided the day was turning out better than he had hoped. He abandoned the black horse and lit a cigarette, which he puffed for a while before hear-ing an outer door open and Semmer's voice.

Save for the man's naturally petulant mouth, a casual observer would have said that Linwood Semmer had completely regained his poise. But Lyle sensed that he was only suppressing his morning's rage. His eyes looked unduly bright; his lips were com-pressed. He greeted his former classmate with marked formality. Then, more jovially, he went on: "Sorry, old man, about losing the temper this morning. Your Sergeant McQuire rather put my back up. I was very fond of Nancy Pierce. Her husband and I are close, and, altogether, I've been damned affected about her going that way. Only saw her that noon, too. Ran into her at the Eden. Had gone there to see my sister, Miss Semmer, who is secretary and treasurer of the Tomorrow Club. Bought Nancy a drink. By the by, I had rather a row with her, too—an insignificant matter—purely personal. Well, come along into my office, Lyle."

He led the way across the large room with the burning wood fire, past a small office in which the artful nurse-receptionist was quartered, and into his own big, private room. With a professional-courtesy gesture, he motioned to a deep chair by his desk. Settling himself behind it, he pushed a box of cigarettes to Lyle's elbow and placed his fingertips together, waiting watchfully.

"Don't give another thought to our jamboree over the phone," Curtis said carelessly. "Look here, Lin, I don't mind telling *you* we've given up all ideas of suicide. She was murdered!"

"Murdered! I know that's what Howard Pierce thought at first but, my God, it seems incredible. Incredible," he repeated. "Who could have done it?" His color was rising, and there was a growing expression of sheer wrath in his overbright eyes.

"We've not arrested anyone—yet."

"Yet? Then you think you know?" His tone was incredulous, but commanding.

"I've come to ask you a few questions, Lin. Mrs. Pierce spent her last night alive with you."

Dr. Semmer leaped to his feet, his face now furious. "Why you damned blackguard. How dare you—why, you can sizzle in hell for that, Lyle Curtis— Get out of my office."

"Sit down, Lin. And stop that talk. I amend my statement. She spent part of her last evening with you. You don't deny that, do you? And you two had really angry talk in the Eden bar the noon she died. The waiter heard everything you said, very nearly. He told me quite a number of things."

Semmer remained on his feet, hesitant, but his contorted face gradually calmed. After a few minutes, he had got control of himself. He sat down slowly, and a professional mask slid across his countenance.

"Sorry, old man. I seem to be doing nothing but losing my temper with you today. Nothing personal, and all that. But as I've told you, both Nancy and Howard Pierce were my friends. Howard still is. I couldn't let any man say Nancy spent the night with me. And I won't! But, yes, she was here in the early evening. We were—"

"Wait a minute, Lin, don't say anything you can't substantiate. You know that if you're going to tell me Howard Pierce came along here, and you three went out together, that Pierce, in his present mood—he's yelling murder and suicide to high heaven—will let you down if he *didn't* come here."

The doctor's face went white. He shut his lips with a quick motion, and sat staring straight ahead for a few moments, apparently in deep thought.

"All right," he said at last, "I suppose that was a damn friendly suggestion. I've been a fool—with your sergeant, with you—well, God knows, with my life. I was in love with Nancy Pierce. Her husband wasn't. But I wasn't having an affair with her. I respected her too much. Howard was willing for a divorce, but Nancy was old fashioned."

Curtis winced. La Nancy and old fashioned were a little difficult to associate. "Old fashioned," he repeated, waiting.

"Yes, she didn't like the idea of divorce. Thought the world was going divorce mad. While she was here that night—Monday night—we talked it all over again. I suppose—well, I suppose I was becoming overanxious. She was—perhaps always will be, now—the only woman in my life."

Dramatic, Curtis thought, but possibly true. McQuire had wondered why Dr. Semmer didn't take up with one of his millionaire patients. Perhaps what he had just said was the honest explanation of why he hadn't.

After another moment, the assistant D. A. prompted: "And Tuesday noon. Why did you quarrel?"

The doctor all at once scarcely seemed to be listening. He answered in an absent tone: "She hadn't come to a decision." There was a curious ingenuousness about the way he said it—or else, a masterful subtlety. It almost seemed, Curtis thought, that the idea had just occurred to Semmer that perhaps Nancy Pierce would never have come to a decision. From the look in his eyes, he seemed

to be undergoing a peculiar kind of mental torture. But the mood—
if such it was—passed, and he looked up abruptly. Using Lyle Curtis'
college nickname, he said quickly:

"Look here, Curt, I've been damned frank with you. Couldn't
have been more so. I don't say I would have if I hadn't seen it was
necessary. God knows, talking about all this isn't easy. Nobody but
my sister and Howard Pierce—and Nancy, naturally—knew how I
felt; how I hoped she felt. And I guess she did love me. She was
just young and—and a little irresponsible. Howard didn't object to
the divorce. It was just a quirk in Nancy's mind. She would have
overcome it in time. Howard has—well, a heart affair of his own, if
you want the truth. We—we had talked the whole thing over. Very
modern, you'll say. But we had. We had a gentleman's understand-
ing, so to put it. No hard feelings, that is. I loved her. He, as a
matter of fact, really didn't. They'd grown apart. The original bio-
logic situation that brought them together hadn't lasted. See here,
you've got to tell me whom you suspect. I'll—" He stopped abruptly.
"God, what am I saying?"

Semmer was behaving, Curtis thought uncomfortably, like an
actor who had suddenly in the second act of a play entangled lines
belonging in the first and third acts. It jumbled the sense of the
whole piece. He watched the doctor bleakly. What if he were being
handed a very subtle red herring by this seeming display of confused and tortured emotions? He stood up. In any case, there was
evidently nothing more to be learned at the moment from this apparently overwrought man.

"I'm going now, Lin," Curtis said briefly and started toward the
door. Turning round, he added: "Don't do anything foolish, but if
you get any ideas come to *me* with them." He realized the next
moment that he had said that almost involuntarily out of sheer
distrust of Linwood Semmer's state of nerves.

The other laughed a little queerly. "*Do* anything?" he demanded
angrily. "I suppose that if I leave cream out of my coffee from now
on your blasted department will know about it." He did not stand up
or even look up, but let his former classmate find his own way out.

CHAPTER TWENTY-SEVEN

MR. BENCHLEY'S ENTIRE DAY had been ruined. He was willing to give a moratorium to the conclusion that a redhead had deliberately stood him up on a luncheon date, but the alternative to that was even less reassuring.

After leaving the restaurant, he had returned to his office and accomplished heedlessly, and with doubtful skill, some pressing public relations matters of one of his clients. That done, he had sat in moody thought for a time. As a result of apparently deep reflection, he put on his coat and hat and disappeared from the premises.

Tom ducked into a subway at Grand Central and landed, shortly before five o'clock, near the Wall Street law offices of Holden, Pierce, Crawford and Hamilton. There he took up his old post in the lee of the newspaper vendor's stand, settling his vision ferociously on the exit to the building. Miss Ruby Holt would explain her actions, or he would know the reasons why not!

At five minutes before five o'clock, Tom's vigil was handsomely rewarded. Mr. Howard Pierce appeared in the doorway opposite, Miss Ruby Holt in tow. Mr. Pierce led his sprightly companion to a taxi. Tom, at record speed, leaped for the next one in the taxi rack. To the driver of his cab he said in a tone that would have done justice to a hard-pressed undertaker: "Keep directly behind that cab just ahead of us. There's a five in it for you if you don't lose it."

The driver slammed his car into gear, observing meanwhile that whatever the gent wanted was O.K. with him. His name was Streak

Zxhobijky, he confided, and he could trail the best G-man in the department.

The cab ahead had turned north, and was presently plunging in the direction of Brooklyn Bridge. They crossed the bridge, dived into near-river streets, bore south, turned east, and after several incredibly miraculous escapes from cross-street traffic, regained close pursuit. As Mr. Zxhobijky pointed out lucidly, the other cab appeared to have all the breaks. But Tom's driver had not been named in an irrational moment.

At last, the cab ahead whirled around a corner, zigzagged past some children playing in the street and drew up before a seedy-looking building. The curtains at its windows had all seen better days. Dirty children played on its doorstep. Despite the sleet, a woman leaned out one of the upper windows, apparently approving the evening. Miss Holt alighted and ran up the steps, scattering children in her wake. Mr. Pierce remained in the cab. From a quarter of a block away on the opposite side of the one-way street, where Mr. Benchley had directed his driver to come to a standstill, all of this could be seen as in a Whistler etching of the Thames through a fog. But visibility was improved, when, on Zxhobijky's logical suggestion that on a night like that they could go and sit in the gent's lap and he wouldn't see them, they drew a bit nearer.

Ruby remained in the ill-used building perhaps twenty minutes. Benchley's cab meter ticked merrily on, but he consoled himself with the thought that probably Howard Pierce's was doing likewise.

At last, Miss Holt bearing a suitcase in her hand put in an appearance. She looked, even through the sleet, far from downcast. Tom thought she even looked quite pleased with herself.

Once more, Streak Zxhobijky, not at all averse to the adventure, took up pursuit. They retraced their way and came again to Brooklyn Bridge, crossed it and followed Broadway, then Seventh Avenue uptown on the Manhattan side. Ultimately, they arrived at the Pennsylvania Station. The cab ahead turned in to the taxi tunnel, and deposited Miss Holt and her escort at the motor vehicle entrance. Mr. Benchley tossed a five-dollar bill in addition to the fare to the well-pleased Streak and disappeared in the wake of the couple. They went first to a Pullman window where Howard Pierce made a purchase. Meanwhile Tom lingered impatiently behind a fat woman who was surrounded by luggage and porters. Mr. Pierce then picked up Miss Holt's suitcase and made for the train entrance marked Pittsburgh. They went through it and down the steps. Tom rushed to a Pullman window and inquired somewhat wildly what the first stop was on the Pittsburgh seven-ten.

"Newark," said the ticket seller, "but you don't need a berth, sonny. That's only just under the river."

"What comes after Newark?" requested Mr. Benchley, not bothering to feel foolish.

The ticket vendor eyed him reprovingly. "Don't you know where you want to go?"

Thoroughly determined and fearful of the escape of Pierce and Ruby, Tom commanded sternly: "Where I said!"

"Philadelphia."

"How much?"

The ticket man said.

"Give me one chair. One."

Thus armed, the publicity man hastened to the Pittsburgh gate and down the iron steps to the platforms.

Miss Caroline Semmer was having dinner with her brother. Dr. Semmer was looking even more worn and haggard than when Lyle Curtis had left him a little after four o'clock. He had not followed his usual custom—since obtaining a Park Avenue practice—of dressing for dinner, nor had his sister. But though prim of face, and stocky of figure, Caroline had donned the earmarks of the fashion industry. She wore over her gray and wispy hair a hat made of ostrich feathers which was distinctly and definitely unbecoming. But she was trying to look, despite the dour expression of her brother, remarkably cheerful.

Caroline chattered along, looking with satisfaction around the smart little restaurant—for Linwood no longer permitted himself to patronize places that would be considered poky by his distinguished clientele.

Now and again a slight ripple of worry crossed her pinched face as she glanced at her moody relative.

Dr. Semmer was not paying the slightest attention to her small talk which she was conscientiously attempting to make smart and youthfully enchanting. She said: "That tonic you gave me, dear, is simply divine."

He grunted.

"If it hadn't been," she beamed, "for all the frightfully depressing troubles at the club this week, I should feel quite like sending myself orchids! It's really been a very exciting week for me, Brother—reporters and everything."

Linwood again grunted and looked, if possible, more determined in his depression.

It appeared not to occur to Miss Semmer that her efforts in the too too divine field of conversation held much the same effectiveness as a bomb made of matchsticks. She persisted.

Dr. Semmer regarded her briefly with brooding eyes and an expression which might have been either boredom or self-conscious embarrassment or both. His eyes, when he turned again from her feverish rush of chatter, wore a look of inadequately repressed exasperation.

Miss Semmer had to admit to herself that Linwood was deeply worried about something. But her past experience had been that direct questions were unavailing with him. She decided to hope that it was only some momentary professional problem, and not morbidity over the passing of that "horrible creature, Nancy Pierce," as she mentally characterized her.

As his sister seemed bent on continuing her idiotically bright chatter, Dr. Semmer said finally: "For God's sake, Sis, you sound as if they'd wound you up permanently."

Instantly, Miss Semmer was all apologies. She cooed and patted his hand.

Linwood looked unexpectedly sorry, conscious to a degree, for the first time during the meal, of her painful efforts to look fashionable, and the conscientious if ridiculous intensity behind her small talk. He mellowed suddenly and remarked: "Your hat is

pretty." And he did not add that she looked like a plump scarecrow
with it on her head.

Caroline gazed at him radiantly. "Oh, I'm so very pleased you
like it on me. I thought it rather nice." She continued in the Peacocks of the Tomorrow Club understatement fashion, "Just a little
thing."

"Don't mind me," Linwood went on. "I feel rotten tonight." He
looked at her closely for the first time that evening. "You look tired
yourself. You haven't got a fever, have you? Look here, how about
getting away to Bermuda or somewhere for a couple of weeks?"

Miss Semmer flushed more brightly. "Linwood! How *beautiful*
of you, how lovely and thoughtful. It makes me see how much you
really care for your chatterbox sister! But, dearest, I couldn't go
away just now—not with the club's show coming on and everything
so rushed. They'd think I had completely deserted the ship. Why, I
only just left the office when I came here to meet you. My work is
never done. So many details," she ended with a sigh of confusion.

Brushing aside this mixed flow of girlish excitement and apologetic explanation, Dr. Semmer exclaimed: "Forget it. You need a
rest. I see you need a rest."

"Linwood, my darling, I don't look nearly as seedy as you do as
a matter of fact. You look so—so gaunt. Tell me, Brother, you—you
are well, aren't you?"

With a return of his former irritation, Semmer snapped: "I'm
well enough. Overworked perhaps. My patients can get more
damned things the matter with them. I called you yesterday when I
saw how rushed I'd be today. Thought we could postpone dinner, but
not being able to get you, I managed to work it in. I'm going to pack
you off early, though, and get some sleep tonight. I am tired—and—
well, that damned Curtis is hounding me. That's what he's doing!"

"Hounding you?" repeated Miss Semmer with a gasp.

Semmer's color rose. "He and his flat-footed sleuths."

Caroline looked both startled and shocked. "But why? How can
they? I never heard of such a thing."

His vexation increased. "How can they? They can hound anyone, can't they? Anyone who could conceivably have had a motive

for Nancy's death." His tone turned from mental exasperation to one closely akin to pure emotion.

"A motive! But, dearest, you—that is—you had no such motive."

"Oh, hadn't I! Plenty of motive, the way they look at things. I had a row with her, for one thing, in the Eden bar an hour before she died. Good thing I admitted it, too. That damned waiter there had been talking—talking a hell of a lot from all I can make out."

"Talking?"

"Oh hell, Sis, talking, yes. That sort of fellow talks his blasted, ghoulish head off when there's anything like a murder afoot."

"Murder!"

"For the love of God. Yes, murder. Nancy died an unnatural death, didn't she? They think now she was murdered. The district attorney's office has taken over the case. Curtis was here this afternoon, prying and probing."

With deep, worried intensity, Caroline Semmer's eyes rested on her brother's distorted face. "But what, dear, could it possibly have to do with you—all of that? I—I don't understand."

Semmer shrugged impatiently. "I'm a physician, am I not? I know about poisons. Her death had something to do with a hypodermic needle, I gather. There was a police sergeant here eyeing my equipment case." He seemed to lose himself in momentary thought. Meanwhile, his sister's eyes remained on him, bright with fear. "Look here," he said presently. "I don't want to worry you, Sis, but at that I might be in a spot. She—Nancy—was here the night before her death—"

Miss Semmer gasped, then said quickly: "You were her physician."

"Nonsense. Doctors have fallen in love with their patients and murdered them before this. I was in love with Nancy Pierce. Desperately. No—you needn't turn up your nose. It only infuriates me. There's no accounting for love—or—or whatever it is. I was trying—the night before her death—to get her to promise to make up her mind by the next noon about a divorce. She swore she'd do it. That's why I was at the Eden. I know it was foolish rowing with her in public—but, well, she hadn't made up her mind. It was driving me distracted. In my position, it had to be marriage. It's even good for a doctor to have a wife—keeps the leeches and misunderstood away. Yes, I may be in a spot—" He finished on a flat note of contemplation more than speech.

Caroline tried to comfort him with her conviction that no one—not *anyone* could possibly think such *horrible* things about him. He was imagining it. That was all—just *imagining*. But her lips had formed a tight line, and fear had brought moisture to her nearsighted eyes. Linwood looked up at her with an expression of distaste.

"Now don't get overwrought." A muscle in his cheek twitched. "I should know better than to talk anything over with you. You get so emotional." Then in a tone manufactured of cold lightness: "Probably nothing will come of all this. Probably you're right; I'm just imagining things. Forget I mentioned it. What will you have for dessert?"

Miss Semmer's lips were still narrowly folded. "You aren't— you aren't—" she began. "That is, you don't feel in any actual danger, Linwood?"

"I said probably not, and what will you have for dessert?"

Absent-mindedly Miss Semmer said: "Just coffee, dear; a demitasse," and they finished their meal in silence.

When they were leaving the restaurant, Dr. Semmer said: "I'll drive you over to the station. What time is your train?"

Miss Semmer glanced at her watch and said there was one in half an hour. She followed him to his parked car with its green professional cross. As they approached the station, Caroline laid a hand on his arm. "Dearest," she murmured, "why don't you go and see some friends tonight? If you're tired and a little wo—that is, annoyed by these policemen, it will do you good to see some friends. Have a bit of a bender!" And she chirped girlishly.

He made no answer, parked the car in silence, and led her to the entrance to her train. There, two men passing by hailed him. He presented them to his sister. "You going back to your hotel?" one of them asked, and Linwood said he was and would drive them. Miss Semmer nodded approvingly, reached up and embraced her brother tenderly, nodded again to the two men and trotted on, hat bobbing, down the long platform.

WHEN TOM BENCHLEY reached the Pennsylvania Station track level, there was no sign of either Ruby Holt or Howard Pierce. He walked along the Pullmans of the Pittsburgh train, keeping outside the stream of passengers, porters and baggage carriers. At last, in a car bearing the euphonious name of Tallahassee, he discovered the girl sitting next a window. Opposite her sat Pierce, a timetable in hand, evidently explaining something to the decorative Ruby.

"How much less polished—and how much warmer than Miss Vivian Peabody's costly ruby," thought Tom, recklessly allowing his thoughts to wander to the question of why people named their offspring after jewels. He brought himself back to the matter at hand with a jerk and proceeded to station himself at the back of the Tallahassee with a view up the length of the train. The "all aboard" signal came and still Howard Pierce had not emerged. Mr. Benchley clambered up the steps on the third injunction of the conductor and the muttered supplications of the porter who wanted to take his stepping stool aboard.

Lingering first in the vestibule, Mr. Benchley finally ventured down the corridor sufficiently far to observe the interior of the Pullman car. Mr. Pierce and Miss Holt were still facing one another and were deep in conversation; or at least Pierce was. Ruby was listening. Tom dodged thoughtlessly into the Tallahassee's Ladies' Room, encountered the glare of a white-haired woman, and withdrew hastily to the men's smoker in the adjoining car.

At Newark, Tom alighted once more and took up guard. He peered along the train. The first person off at the front exit of the Tallahassee was Howard Pierce, square jawed and determined. He squared his shoulders and strode toward the street.

Mr. Benchley hastily remounted the steps of the Pullman to the delighted approval of the porter. As the train gained speed leaving the station, Tom approached Ruby.

"How completely unexpected," exclaimed Mr. Carrington Wells's voice.

"Well, gee," shrieked Miss Holt, "you could knock me over with a fly swatter."

CHAPTER TWENTY-EIGHT

THE LITTLE MAN PUSHED his way through the theater crowds in the Times Square subway with the absent-minded but determined aggressiveness of the habitual subway goer. He carried an early morning edition of the *News* in his right hand, but as he came to a stop at the downtown platform he did not open it. Instead, he stood gazing down at the tracks, a worried frown between his eyes. Around him milled a crowd of young people returning from a movie; stimulated by the film they had seen and by each other's company, they were shouting jokes at each other and laughing uproariously. The more middle-aged and sedate people on the platform regarded them with envious approval or stern displeasure, each according to his mold. The little man did not seem to notice them at all. With the worried frown still between his eyes, he sighed, and turned to look up the tracks. A distant thunder and two pin points of light announced the coming train.

A fresh burst of shrieks and laughter erupted from the young people. Two of them dashed to the foot of the stairs and called: "Hurry up, the train's coming." Feet pounded on the iron stairway, more young voices called, "Hold it, we're coming."

The little man sighed again, and stood waiting, the forgotten newspaper still clenched in his right hand. He stood with arms hanging at his sides, in the attitude of one who is used to standing so for long stretches of time.

The avalanche of young people on the stairs descended to the platform like a great wave, pushing, shoving and screaming. They were in time. The train was just entering the station. They made for the platform's edge, still voluble and excited. Someone was pushed against the little man. Suddenly, on the bare knuckle of the hand that held the newspaper, he felt a sharp and sudden stab. He turned his head, mouth open, as something pushed him from behind, and with a loud cry, he fell from the platform.

The train flashed past. For a moment, the gay young people were silent. Then the train brakes grated harshly and too late, and their voices rose once more. They were not laughing now.

THE NEXT MORNING Curtis was back on the job early. His first visitor was the maid of the late Nancy Pierce, a sniffly young person by the name of Brown. She had been called in to divulge her knowledge, if any, of an affair between her mistress and Dr. Semmer. The girl appeared to be telling the thorough truth that she had known of no such matter. Semmer had only been to the house at parties. She had considered Mrs. Pierce gorgeous enough to attract any man but was of the opinion that she had been invariably after bigger game than giving away her own charms. There had been that *For Ladies* magazine publisher, for instance. They'd had him for dinner. Mrs. Pierce had flirted with him "like everything to get him to publish something she'd written." But he had been "kind of skittish." She guessed "maybe lots of women tried to get things printed that way." There was a radio man, too, she'd been calling up a lot; but in Miss Brown's opinion it was all strictly business with "flirting just the icing on the cake as you might say." She confirmed the fact that Mrs. Pierce had always been taking vitamin tablets "until you would have thought her whole insides would have been sunburned, what with them being called liquid sunshine 'n everything." Nodding toward Sergeant McQuire, who was present, Miss Brown said that he hadn't been the only one interested in Mrs. Pierce's vitamin tablets; both Mr. Pierce and Dr. Semmer had interviewed her about whether the missus had taken one either the night before she died, or before she left home the next morning.

She'd told them all that Mrs. Pierce had taken one after breakfast. Curtis showed her the diagram of how the box was alleged to have looked on the Hotel Eden ballroom stage when Nancy Pierce had dropped it. The maid swore that that was exactly the way it had been after the breakfast capsule. It had been open on a bed-side table and she had happened to notice. Mrs. Pierce had taken the last capsule in the first row that morning. Usually she forgot to take one till after lunch. Miss Brown confirmed the trick system of capsule taking which she looked upon as a somewhat glamorous form of idiocy, and said yes, she was sure Mr. Pierce knew of it.

When Miss Brown was allowed to depart, a small, narrow-eyed man arrived to report that he had tested the typewriter in Mrs. Pierce's apartment, and found it to be the one that had written the "suicide note."

At that moment Mr. Scofield walked into the office. He looked tired and irascible. Sinking into one of Lyle's chairs, he listened while Curtis reported what he had just been told. "It proves, sir, that the poisoned box was substituted *after* breakfast." The type-writer expert was dismissed abruptly by Scofield.

"Seen the morning papers?" he asked his assistant.

"Not yet," said Curtis. "Why?"

Scofield unfolded a newspaper and read aloud:

"Man falls to death in subway—Waiter at Hotel Eden killed in-stantly by south-bound express."

Curtis looked worried. "We established beyond any doubt that none of the luncheon waiters up in the ballroom could have been involved. This is probably a coincidence. May I see it?"

Scofield passed the paper to him, and Curtis scanned the article.

"Michael Shawnessy, thirty-four, a waiter in the bar at the Ho-tel Eden . . ."

"Mike!" shouted Curtis. "Then maybe it does mean something. And it probably means that Miss Yates did not invent the story of the subway attack on her."

"Unless," Scofield suggested dryly, "it means that, knowing that Mike was going to die that way, she was making it seem as though she too had been a victim or intended victim."

"Yes," said Curtis heavily, "that's possible, of course. Anyway, I'd better go right over and see Mike's family. Maybe this hasn't

anything to do with the case—maybe he committed suicide for reasons of his own—but in any event, I'll go interview the family."

He reached for the phone, and said: "Get me the doctor who
examined the body of the waiter who was killed by a subway train
last night. Right away." He hung up, and finding the Shawnessy
address in the newspaper article, copied it carefully into his notebook. His phone rang. "Yes? All right—put him on." He held a rapid
and largely monosyllabic conversation and then hung up. Grim
satisfaction sat upon his face.

"Well, sir," he said, "we've got something. The man couldn't
possibly have committed suicide. The doctor found him full of
potassium cyanide—apparently from an injection on the hand. Even
if the train had managed to stop in time to avoid hitting him, he
would have died anyway."

MIKE HAD LIVED on a short, crooked street running at an angle into
the Bowery. It was cluttered with children, vegetable wagons and
the sounds of an organ grinder's tunes. The assistant district attorney and the sergeant pushed open a street door, and Curtis
nearly staggered under the impact of the mixed odors of food,
people and stove fumes which greeted them.

Mrs. Shawnessy's flat was on the fourth floor, and Mrs.
Shawnessy herself, in a large work apron, was weeping quietly in
the kitchen. Mike had been, she assured them, the apple of her
eye, a white-haired boy, but justly so. He had been kind, provi-
dent, good humored. No one could have questioned his morals. Of
course, she supposed he shouldn't have written "that letter" to Miss
Yates, but the lad had been afraid to say anything outright.

Lyle pricked up his ears. "The letter, ah. Why couldn't Mike
just come and tell me, Mrs. Shawnessy?"

"He was afraid; that's what he was. You never can be telling
what the police will do with information you give them. That Doctor Semmer was a customer, a regular customer of Mike's bar. The
Hotel Eden, they are that particular about the waiters talking. It
might have cost Mike his job. But I told him how the police were
so smart—the district attorney's office too, begging your pardon,

sir—and that they'd soon find out just the same how it was him that sent it. That's what brought you, sir, isn't it?"

Thinking rapidly, Curtis asked: "How did Mike know Mrs. Pierce spent her last evening with Doctor Semmer?"

"He heard him say so. It was when the doctor and the lady— God rest her soul—was in his bar. They was quarreling, Mike said. And the doctor said: 'After last night at my place, you promised to give me word today. And now you still haven't made up your mind.' Then the girl said, 'You sound old enough to be my grandfather.' Real unromantic she was."

There was little more to the story. Mike had closely observed Dr. Semmer and the Pierce girl, which Curtis already knew. He had heard the quarrel, seen the doctor depart, the girl go and talk to another man at the bar, the doctor's sister come and get her dropped gloves, the episode of the capsules shown to the man at the bar, and the fact that neither Nancy nor Van Weck had taken one. More than that he had not heard or seen, his mother thought.

"But he did think, sir, that you ought to know—after the murder and all—about the lady and the doctor having been together the night before, and he thought telling Miss Yates would be the same as telling you. Made for intimacy, he thought, she being a married lady. Then when you questioned him to his face, he was frightened, my poor Mike was. Thought you might be having him up on some charge for writing a letter without a signature on it. He was scared, he was, to tell you what he had said in the letter."

It being obvious that the police had not yet informed the mother of the full details of her son's death, and that she was still under the impression that he had merely fallen in front of a subway train, Curtis left her with condolences, and he and the sergeant made their way back to the office.

Reports were beginning to come in of the whereabouts of all people connected with the Pierce case at the time of Mike's death. The hour supplied by the subway guards had been eleven fifty-five P.M.

Miss Yates, on the testimony of Sergeant Withers, had not left the house all evening.

Miss Peabody had, on the statement of herself and Colonel Gamberson, been with him in a mid-town supper club in full evening dress. That, Sergeant McQuire pointed out, would have made her pretty conspicuous on a subway platform, even if the headwaiter at the club hadn't vouched for her presence there, and for Colonel Gamberson's, from eleven-fifteen o'clock until one. The colonel, true, had gone out to the gentlemen's room for ten minutes somewhere around midnight, but the headwaiter seemed fairly certain he had not left the building. There was, at least, no witness to say he had.

Miss Culbertson had been at home, according to the testimony of her mother. Their maid was a part-time one and did not sleep in, but the doorman of the apartment house swore Miss Culbertson had not gone out all evening. At the broadcasting station they said she had left at six-thirty after her last time on the air for the day.

Caroline Semmer, reached at the office of the Tomorrow Club, said she had dined with her brother and that he had taken her to the station for a nine-twenty train. She had been home and in bed by ten-thirty, she said. Her maid did not sleep in, so she hadn't known how she could *prove* it, but had told Sergeant McQuire her brother could tell him about the train.

Dr. Semmer had confirmed her statement. He had seen his sister go down the stairs to the nine-twenty, and had then returned to his hotel with two friends who had left him at his floor. He hadn't gone out again that evening, he said. The doorman at Semmer's hotel had said that if he "was to remember and watch everybody that went in and out a hotel like the Bristol-Plaza, he'd go blotto in a big way," but he hadn't seen Dr. Semmer that he could remember. At the desk, they said the doctor had called for his key at nine thirty-seven. It hadn't been turned in again, but sometimes the doctor took it with him.

Howard Pierce had dined out. The maid didn't know when he had come in. She had been instructed not to wait up for Mr. Pierce, but she thought he must have returned fairly late, as she herself had gone to bed at midnight, and Mr. Pierce had not then returned. Asked for his whereabouts that evening, Mr. Pierce had firmly declined to tell them, and had said that he had arrived home at about two-thirty.

Mr. Benchley had admitted arriving home at a quarter to two. He said that he had had a drink at Tony's before going home, and the barkeeper at Tony's remembered seeing him there, but not earlier than a quarter to one. Asked where he had been earlier in the evening, Mr. Benchley had replied that they would learn in good time, and had refused to say anything further.

Ethan Van Weck had spent the evening at home, listening to the radio, on the testimony of two servants. Mrs. Van Weck—Miss Mason—had spent the night in town; had, on the testimony of Osborne Devonshire ("that polo player you read about," McQuire interpolated. "He's a client of hers."), attended the opening of *Albert the Good* and been returned to the Sussex Hotel at eleven-fifteen. The doorman was sure that Miss Mason had not gone out again, but was not prepared to swear to it.

Curtis groaned. "Of all the alibis—every one of them watertight with pleasant loopholes—Gamberson was in the men's room around twelve—had been in a club two minutes from Times Square. He could have made it. Pierce won't say where he was—he could have done it. Benchley ditto. Miss Mason's alibi not sworn to. Miss Culbertson's dependent on a mother and a doorman who was only watching the front entrance—service entrance unguarded. Dr. Semmer's alibi dependent on not turning in his keys—and why would he, if he were bent on murder? Miss Semmer was seen to walk down the steps to a train—how do we know she got on the train? Miss Peabody seems to be in the clear—apparently she didn't move from her table in the club from eleven-fifteen until one o'clock."

"Aw," said Sergeant McQuire helpfully, "that don't prove nothing either. If Gamberson could have got out and done it, maybe they was in cahoots."

Curtis moaned. "Did you ask Gamberson what he was doing for ten whole minutes in the men's room?"

Surprisingly, the sergeant blushed a bright brick color. "Yeah," he admitted, "I did. He told me to go to hell—if a man couldn't go to the can without having an official investigation of his movements . . ." The sergeant stopped in distress, and amended hastily: "Motives, I guess he said—then what was this country coming to, and he thought he'd better move to Canada."

Curtis waved him away. "All right—go on, find out anything else you can." The sergeant mopped his face and departed. Left alone, Curtis should have been despondent. The damn case wasn't getting anywhere. But he wasn't—he was, in fact, curiously happy. Maybe he couldn't find a wholly suspicious alibi, nor eliminate all but one—but one alibi was watertight and rock ribbed and firm as Gibraltar. He trusted Withers, absolutely, and if he said Susan Yates hadn't left the building, she hadn't. Humming off key "I took one look at you," Curtis picked up his phone and said: "Get me Miss Yates."

CHAPTER TWENTY-NINE

WHEN HE SAT DOWN with Ruby Holt on the Pittsburgh train Tom had straightway proceeded to divulge Mr. Carrington Wells's real identity and the full nature of the investigation upon which he was engaged. Ruby was thrilled by the whole situation although somewhat disappointed to find Mr. Wells and his broad-minded wife a miserable myth. However, the glamour of train travel and the even more glamorous event of being thrust into a murder case were satisfactory appeasements, and served to loosen Ruby's tongue at once on the details of the secret mission she had been dispatched upon by Howard Pierce. It did not take Tom long to draw from her the fact that, the afternoon of the murder, she had listened in on an indiscreet telephone conversation between Pierce and his private secretary. In it, they had divulged that both of them had been in the Hotel Eden the noon of the murder. Tom pointed out that this undoubtedly accounted for Mr. Pierce's anxiety to get Ruby out of town. After due consideration, Ruby was won to the idea, and easily persuaded that instead of continuing on to Pittsburgh on her employer's mysterious business she should return to New York and be ready to testify if she could be of help in revealing the murderer. Accordingly, at Philadelphia, they had changed trains and shortly after midnight Tom was telephoning Susan. He explained why he had been unable to bring Ruby Holt to Susan's salon that noon, and, briefly, what had happened since.

"May I bring her over to you for the night, Susan? She ought to tell Curtis what she knows in the morning, and I'd like to know that she's safe from Pierce's clutches till then."

"I'm sorry, Tom," said Susan. "I can't have her here. Not possibly."

"But, Susan—what will I do with her?"

"Take her to a Y," suggested Miss Yates. "Pierce will never get her there."

Susan had spent the first hour of the next morning at her office, catching up with her mail and the week's sales. But her mind refused to stay on her work. It kept reverting to Nancy and her death, to all the events subsequent and to Lyle Curtis. When the phone rang, and a voice said: "Mr. Curtis calling, just a moment please," she found herself blushing as though he had, in person, caught her gazing at his photograph.

"Susan," his voice came to her. "Susan, I called to apologize."

"For what?" she asked.

"For suspecting you of deception—for not quite believing your subway story—for behaving as though you were a liar."

"Heavens," said Susan, "what's happened to persuade you that I'm not?"

"Something happened last night—and the murderer must have made it happen. And Sergeant Withers says you didn't stir out of the house all evening. So you're in the clear, from now on and forever, and will you have dinner with me tonight?"

"I'd love to," Susan laughed. "I have to go to a cocktail party, but I won't be there later than seven. But what happened last night—or mayn't I know?"

"I'll tell you if you promise not to repeat it," said Curtis. "Part of it is common knowledge—in the paper this morning. You probably missed it. Poor Mike of the Eden bar was killed last night— fell in front of a subway train on his way home."

"Oh no!" cried Susan. "Not little Mike! That's dreadful."

"It is," said Curtis. "But that's not all, although it's all that the papers carry. You see, he didn't fall just by accident. I'm not sure he 'fell' at all—I think, from your story of the attempted attack on you, that he must have been pushed. But the murderer was taking no chances of failing this time as he failed with you. Mike got an injection of potassium cyanide just before he was pushed."

"How horrible, how *horrible*," said Susan. "But why? Why Mike?"

"He wrote the anonymous letter you received," said Curtis. "The murderer couldn't have known about that. But apparently the murderer was afraid that he had seen or heard something dangerous to the killer. Probably everyone in the case knows that I interviewed him. And so he was killed—in vain, apparently. Or rather, for nothing. According to his mother, he didn't know any more than he wrote in the note."

"Poor little Mike," Susan said again. "You didn't find the hypodermic you were looking for then?"

"No," Curtis said. "But we have plenty of cause now for search warrants for the houses and persons of everyone involved. Tonight, by God, we'll find that hypo or know the reason why."

"I hope you do," Susan said fervently.

"I have work to do," said Curtis, "so I'll have to cut this short. I'll pick you up tonight at seven-thirty—all right? And for heaven's sake, stick close to Sergeant Withers."

MR. BENCHLEY CAME into the office of the assistant district attorney with a proprietary hand under the elbow of a redheaded young woman Lyle Curtis had never seen before.

"Morning, Curtis," Tom said cheerfully. "This is Miss Holt—Miss Ruby Holt—who has some things to tell you you might like to hear."

Mr. Curtis made suitable sounds of greeting, and then turned an interrogative eye on Benchley.

"Miss Holt," Tom Benchley explained, "works in Howard Pierce's office. I think she can supply you with a motive for Howard Pierce wanting his wife to die."

Curtis leaned forward, and Miss Holt, feeling very much in the limelight, needed no encouragement to pour out her story of the Hotchkiss-Pierce entanglement.

"You say Mr. Pierce had asked Mrs. Pierce for a divorce, and she had refused to give it to him?" Curtis asked.

"Well, I don't *know* that for sure," Miss Holt said brightly, "but I did hear him tell Miss Hotchkiss that Nancy—Mrs. Pierce—wouldn't consent to a divorce. And Miss Hotchkiss said they'd just

have to wait till Mrs. Pierce had found someone to marry her after
a divorce; that she never would unless she had a sure thing! Someone who could give her more than Mr. Pierce. Gee, was Hotchkiss
burned up. She was almost crying, she was so mad. And Mr. Pierce
was very gloomy, and he said he had hoped that maybe Mrs. Pierce
would want to marry her doctor, 'cause her doctor wanted to marry
her, but he—Mr. Pierce, that is—guessed the doctor wasn't swell
enough for her." Curtis nodded, and let Miss Holt's voice trickle on.

"That's all very interesting, Miss Holt," said Curtis, when at
last her flow of reminiscences was exhausted. "I had suspected
something of the sort, but I had no confirmation of it. But what I
really wish I knew is where Pierce was the noon that his wife died."

"I can tell you that," Miss Holt said.

Unimpressed Mr. Curtis said: "Oh, so you can, can you?"

Mr. Benchley's air was one of a supreme court judge. "Damned
if she can't. Go on, Ruby, my girl."

Enjoying what she appeared to consider the sensational triumph of her life, Miss Holt's voice crescendoed: "In the bar at the
Hotel Eden!"

Her triumph fell flat. Mr. Curtis' expression remained unimpressed although she might have discovered a faint flicker of surprised interest in his eyes. "Go on," he said crisply. "Go on—tell
me all about it."

"Well, see, it was this way," gurgled Ruby. "Miss Hotchkiss was
out a long time for lunch that noon—not that she isn't often
enough—"

"Stick to the point," begged Tom.

"I *am* sticking to the point," pouted Miss Holt. "Mr. Pierce was
out, too. They went out together! But the Hotchkiss—our Miss
Hotchkiss—came back alone. About the middle of the afternoon, I
guess it was, somebody with a stiff-shirt voice called up from the
Eden and said he had to speak to Mr. Pierce quick. How was I to
know it was the police or somebody? I said he couldn't speak to
Mr. Pierce because Mr. Pierce wasn't in. That burned him up. He
said to step on it and give him somebody in authority. Well, the
Hotchkiss certainly is that, so I plugged her in. Then, I didn't see

the harm in listening in, it being so easy, and I heard this guy say Mrs. Pierce had died. Miss Hotchkiss kind of gasped, but she went right on and got all the details this fellow could give. Then she said she'd reach Mr. Pierce at once. She signaled me as soon as he'd hung up and gave me a number. When I got it, I was to ask for Mr. Pierce. He came on the wire and I connected him with Miss Hotchkiss. Then, of course, I listened in, being interested in how he'd take it about his wife being dead." Miss Holt turned to Mr. Benchley. "I *told* you about all that. It was just that one thing Hotchkiss said that I forgot."

"Stop beating about. What was it?" Curtis snapped.

Miss Holt looked pained. "Well, I was just going to. Miss Hotchkiss said: 'Oh, Howard, you don't suppose anyone noticed us being at the Eden, do you? It won't look queer, will it?'"

She went on, "That meant they were in the bar. Wouldn't have been any point in them having a rendezvous in a room, with him being up at Miss Hotchkiss' apartment about half the time as I know, and Mr. Wells—Mr. Benchley, I mean—has seen."

"Ah, so Mr. Benchley has seen, has he?" Curtis cast him a suspicious look and asked how and when. Tom explained rapidly about his suspicions of Pierce, his meeting with Miss Holt and Miss Hotchkiss under, he admitted, an assumed name; his observation of Pierce arriving at Miss Hotchkiss' house complete with key.

When he finished his account of his Thursday evening vigil, ending in the trip to Brooklyn and the boarding of the Pennsylvania train, Curtis' attention was definitely alert.

"After Pierce got off at Newark," Tom narrated, "I went along the car to Miss Holt and came out frankly with what I was doing and everything. Then it came to light that Pierce must have been getting suspicious of Ruby having overheard something. Of course, I thought it was just her knowing too much about his secretarial romance; but now it was obviously the Hotel Eden conversation. So he had held her up about meeting anybody for luncheon and planned to get her out of town. She was to sit in a hotel room in Pittsburgh and wait for a cockeyed telephone call. It might, he told her, be a week before it came. She was to go home before train time, pack a bag, tell her folks simply that she was going on a business trip and would write them in 'due time'; but actually she wasn't to let anybody know where she was. That noon he set her to writing in longhand about fifty pages of some manuscript. That, of course, was just a stall."

Miss Holt nodded confirmation.

"Is that the whole story?" barked the assistant D. A.

"No," said Tom, and described the data he had gotten from the Italian, Fisorreli, who knew that although Pierce was supposed to be a corporation lawyer solely, he had been privately advising a group of cocaine importers, and could easily have laid hold of a poison that would have killed his wife.

And, Tom continued, wasn't Curtis interested in hypodermics? "Well, Miss Holt knows Pierce had one. She saw it on his desk once."

"Yes, that was when that Zobinski, Mr. W—Benchley found out about, was coming in every once in a while. After hours, you know. Only I don't always leave right on the dot. You see, I have my hair, and face and everything to do—"

Tom stopped this tangent. "Now, saying Mrs. Pierce was killed with potassium cyanide (I have an informant who says she was), I've discovered from a specialist in the field that she *could not* have been fed a capsule that wouldn't have melted for hours—twelve to eighteen. But that didn't change the possibility of Pierce's having spiked her *box* the night before. Of course, with what Miss Holt's recalled about his being in the hotel, too, that noon, he might have done it right then and there."

Curtis was watching Benchley closely. He said suddenly: "What's the name of this informant of yours, Tom? I'm sorry, but I'll have to know."

Mr. Benchley demurred, saying he'd given his word not to say. He couldn't afford, even if he wanted to, to get anyone in wrong.

"You refuse to say?"

"I've got to, Lyle."

"Very well. Stay in town, both of you. I'll get in touch with you when I want you. That's all now. Good-by, Miss Holt."

Miss Holt was looking extravagantly disappointed that their statements had raised so little of a stir; but she said good-by with a lavish smile, as lavishly ignored by Curtis.

They rose, and Lyle touched a button. His secretary appeared, and he made a quick motion interpreted by the other as "tails for these two."

Mr. Benchley and Miss Holt were thus well chaperoned when they left the building.

CHAPTER THIRTY

WHEN MR. BENCHLEY and his prize package of information had gone, Curtis took out his reports once more, and with a pencil made a rapid listing:

Pierce: Motive established—wanted a divorce which his wife refused. Poison and hypo—he had access to both.

Opportunity—he was in the bar that noon—could he have reached his wife's purse? If he planted the poisoned capsules the night before, why didn't Mrs. Pierce get a poisoned one after breakfast? Blackmail—? When could he have planted the "suicide note"? Mike's death—no alibi. May have been with Hotchkiss.

Hortense Culbertson: Motive—Nancy Pierce was trying to get her job. Weak without supporting blackmail. What could it have been? Hypo—has one.

Poison—is enthusiastic amateur photographer—has supply of potassium cyanide in crystal form, which she could easily have made into a solution.

Opporunity—to plant capsules? "suicide note"—only if Benchley was her confederate and dropped it for her.

Mike's death—alibi not watertight.

Vivian Peabody: Motive—Her fiancé was having an affair with Nancy.

Opportunity—excellent for "suicide note"—she was sitting next to deceased at the lunch table.

Hypo—none established. Poison—possesses supply of weed killer. Blackmail? Has it anything to do with Nancy's friendship with Vivian's employer?

Mike's death—alibi perfect—see Gamberson.

Gamberson: Motive—to get rid of Nancy before marriage to Vivian. Opportunity—could he have planted capsules when ran into Nancy in the dark? Could not have planted note.

Hypo—none established. Had access to Peabody's weed killer. Blackmail—only possibility so far—if Nancy threatened to tell Vivian of the affair.

Mike's death—could just have managed it.

Semmer: Motive—was in love with Nancy Pierce, angry over something.

Hypo and poison—access to both, as a doctor.

Note—and capsules? Mike says he could not have planted them in her bag that noon. If he did it the night before? Then why wasn't she poisoned after breakfast?

Blackmail—?

Mike's death—unsubstantiated alibi.

Caroline Semmer: Motive?

Opportunity—could have planted note—but when could she have planted poisoned capsules?

Hypo and poison—access to brother's hypos? (Wouldn't he know if one was missing?) Has weed killer for garden.

Blackmail?

Mike's death—pretty strong alibi.

Tom Benchley: Motive: Hortense Culbertson.

Hypo—yes. Poison? From Hortense?

Opportunity—could have planted note. Capsules? When? Blackmail?

Mike's death—with Ruby Holt.

Susan Yates: Perfect alibi for murder of Mike, therefore clear on all counts.

SUSAN SUSPECTED that the calls she was about to make might only end in adding to the growing conviction among her acquaintances that she was losing her wits over the Nancy Pierce case. It was not altogether consoling to one of her temperament to be called morbid by Vivian Peabody. She stepped on the starter of her car with unnecessary vigor, and glowered.

Her first call was made on Miss Hortense Culbertson. It being Saturday, she anticipated finding her at home, and was not disappointed. Refusing a glass of sherry, she came to the purpose of her visit, and asked Hortense if she had known that Nancy Pierce had kept a diary of "simply *everything* that had happened to her?"

Miss Culbertson's eyes widened and she smiled. "I can't rise to the heights of longing to read it. I'm afraid Nancy wasn't one of our more modest citizens."

"I was wondering if it wouldn't have named her murderer," Susan mused.

"It might give a lead—if she *was* murdered," Hortense said without much enthusiasm. She glanced at Susan with a little frown. "The police think it was suicide, don't they?"

Miss Yates nodded thoughtfully, and Miss Culbertson's pretty mouth opened and then closed as if a word had hesitated and died on her dainty lips. She glanced away and after a moment said: "Only your friend, Mr. Curtis, seems to have a murder theory."

"*My* friend?"

"Well, a little bird told me you two were cocktailing in the Eden bar last Tuesday after the informal investigation at the hotel. Quite a good-looking gent, you know."

"Quite passable, but it doesn't seem particularly pertinent. Anyway, if you don't know anything about Nancy having kept a diary, just don't mention it to anyone, will you?"

Hortense shook her head emphatically. It was the first emphatic gesture she had made, thought Susan, when, after a suitable interval, she departed.

ON HER WAY to the Tomorrow Club, Miss Yates breathed deeply, and told herself it was too magnificent a day for murder investigations. But what a week! Rain and snow and slush for four days— and then the weather decides to be good. The whole world looks scrubbed clean this morning. She hoped it meant the case would get cleaned up with equal unexpectedness; and her expression was less tense as she approached the Hotel Eden.

Both Madison Avenue and Forty-eighth Street were packed with parked cars in the fifteen-and-thirty-minute parking zones. Susan drove into the chauffeurs' parking space which bisected the hotel. At this hour, there were only a handful of cars, their drivers either dozing or intent on newspapers. She parked and hurried through the little side entrance which gave on a hall leading to the north-wing foyer, forgetful that this might tax Sergeant Wither's "tailing" capacities. Once she had discovered fire stairs there leading to within a few doors of the Tomorrow Club rooms on the mezzanine floor. Locating them she climbed hastily, arriving somewhat breathlessly in the club offices.

Miss Semmer shoved shut her desk drawer and began adding figures in a ledger. She greeted Susan with tired eyes and a murmur about how shocked she had been over her telephone message that Nancy Pierce had been going to have a baby. "So very dreadful that two lives were taken." Blotting the page, Miss Semmer closed the book and turned her chair to face Miss Yates who had bounced down on a deep couch.

"Wait till I get my breath," Susan laughed. "I ducked up the fire stairs. Too many cigarettes and stuffy ballroom atmosphere this week apparently. Or else my wind just isn't what it should be."

Miss Semmer asked solicitously if she would like a glass of water, but Susan shook her head, determined that no one, not even the most unlikely persons, were going to handle her food or drink until the Pierce case was settled.

Miss Semmer got off on her pet subject of so-much-to-do. "People laugh at the hours I keep. When I dined with my brother last night, the darling tried to make me promise to go over to Bermuda for a little holiday!" She laughed stoically. "But naturally, it's the last thing in the world I could do with the show coming on and everything."

"Perhaps we can fix it for you to get away right after the show," Miss Yates promised, noting the other woman's pinched features and tired eyes. "You do have your hands full when we decide the world should hear from the Tomorrow Club, don't you, Miss Semmer?"

But Caroline hastened to explain meticulously that actually it was her own fault because she couldn't bring herself to allow any threads to hang loose, and because, as she always said, a business-woman's organization should be an *outstanding* example of efficiency—such important women as the members were, and all. Regretting not for the first time having given Miss Semmer's conversational mouthings a lead, Susan hastened to recount her diary tale with some doubt as to whether she wouldn't soon be believing it herself.

Miss Semmer flushed slightly when Susan had finished the story and said: "I suppose it *will* be embarrassing for her husband. Poor man. I know they say she was a little—well, *giddy* is the word we used to use. I hope it won't be embarrassing for dear Miss Peabody, too." She clapped a hand over her mouth and blushed. "Oh dear," she cried. "I shouldn't have said that." She paused, then asked: "I suppose you mean the district attorney's office has found her diary. You didn't mean *you* have, dear?"

Watching, Susan suspected that Miss Semmer might not be above interest in the details of an enchantress's history.

"No, I haven't found it!" she replied. "But I dare say when a diary is found they have to use it officially, so to speak, in cases under investigation."

Miss Semmer tut-tutted, and sighed again, remarking that it was, she supposed, very foolish to mention names and details even in a very *personal* record. One never *knew* into whose hands it might fall. Wasn't that the way so many biographers got practically *all* their information?

Susan said yes, she supposed it was, and Miss Semmer proceeded to prove her guess right: their "drab bird" had a strong taste for the private history of people who had been in the news. Miss Semmer chattered on with a subdeb's enthusiasm about the intrigues in European courts disclosed in a biography of World War personalities which she had just been reading. A little apologetically—as if she feared she shouldn't, despite Susan's flattering attention, be displaying intellectual capacities before one of the stars of the club—she exclaimed: "It's so exciting and so really *dreadful* how so many people—even in papers written only for *posthumous* publication—never told the truth about their activities. You know, I really think that if one had done something—well, even an intrigue—with distinction and perfection, he'd *want* people to know about it after he was dead." She bit her lip and looked down at her desk, fiddling with various small objects on it. "I was just thinking perhaps that's what tempted Mrs. Pierce to write that queer note. Do you think it's possible?"

Susan shook her head. "Perhaps we'll never know," she said, and thought: "Lost within Caroline Semmer's rambling intelligence, there could be a lead—a lead so clear it would take the murderer of Nancy Pierce and Mike straight to the electric chair."

Miss Semmer had picked up her still open fountain pen. With prim efficiency, but with a look in her eyes which suggested her thoughts were still in European intrigues, she began screwing on its cap.

Susan turned her eyes from Caroline's plump fingers and happened to drop them to the secretary-treasurer's unexpectedly pretty legs. "Oh!" she cried. "What a pity. You've spilled some ink on your stocking." The older woman made a mooing sound of distress and glanced down, but Susan leaning over said: "My mistake. Only a bit of mud." They both laughed, and Miss Semmer started on the tireless feminine subject of what a luxury silk stockings were, and why didn't somebody make them so they wouldn't run.

"I really do think, Miss Yates, that a member of the Tomorrow Club should do that for women of the world. It would be a wonderful monument to the club's usefulness."

Finding a hesitant Semmer period on which to interrupt, Susan said she really must go.

In her car she remembered about Sergeant Withers. He came bursting out of the side entrance as she put her foot on the starter, alarm written in every line of his rugged face. Susan waved and turned the car thoughtfully in the direction of Park Avenue and Vivian Peabody's duplex apartment.

CHAPTER THIRTY-ONE

HE WOULD SEE if Miss Peabody were at home, Vivian's butler informed Miss Yates. Presently, he returned and escorted her to a sunny room on the second floor. Its mistress came sweeping in by another door, attired in a *moyen âge* negligee with a long train. She looked, Susan thought, like a cover from her own magazine.

"Susan!" cried Miss Peabody. "You do pop up at odd moments these days. But I'm delighted to see you, of course, though I can't say I thought too well of your silly telephone call the other night. Now tell me, how on earth could you possibly suspect Nancy had been going to have a baby?"

Susan felt that, if she did not wait to open her mouth, she should say the wrong thing. She felt, too, that her expression must be a cross between a simpering chambermaid's and a comic-strip detective's. She pointed, instead of speaking, at a great silver breakfast tray a maid was bringing into the room. "Me too?" she begged. "I'd love some coffee."

Thus diverted from her chosen role of critic and mentor, Miss Peabody swept gracefully into the role of a lady pouring coffee in a perfectly appointed room from a perfectly appointed tray. She passed Susan a cup and smiled, momentarily content, over her own. Susan, suddenly remembering Curtis' warning, set her cup down untasted. Miss Peabody did not appear to notice.

"Such a satisfactory morning, Saturday—beauty sleep, leisurely breakfast. I never make appointments on Saturday morning. But," she added hastily, "I adore having friends drop in informally.

234

Besides," and her tone became once more dictatorial, "I've been wanting a comfortable chat with you, darling. I have a little impression, my dear, that you're letting women down the least bit by the— shall we say agitated way you keep harping on Nancy Pierce's death. As businesswomen, we simply *must* avoid ever being morbid, or—excuse me, my dear—being gossipy. No, wait!" and she held up one of her handsome long-fingered hands. "Perhaps you feel I've no right to talk to you this way. But I frankly feel you've been acting a bit silly."

Susan was so concentrated on Vivian's expression, on the subtle tones in her voice, that she suddenly became aware she was gaping idiotically. She relaxed and purred reassuringly, "I entirely agree with you. I have become a veritable sewing-circle gossip the past few days. I can't understand myself! Really, I'm terribly pleased you've brought me up short. Women must," she added with wily ponderousness, "stand together."

Miss Peabody, who was nibbling Swedish biscuits, had turned her big eyes to the perfectly appointed coffee service. She smiled faintly, and Susan guessed to what extent it had grown necessary for Vivian Peabody to rule other people and to guide the course of life around her in an ever-widening circle. It occurred to Susan also that to spring her diary myth at this moment, would, after all, be good staging. She sprang it; and Vivian, a moment before convinced that she had attacked the citadel of Miss Yates's childishness, and drawn her to higher and more rarefied heights, looked shocked beyond measure. She looked baffled, too, and gave Susan a searching glare. But watching, Susan grew convinced that her hostess was more than shocked and baffled. She was startled and somehow fearful. Her vivid eyes closed for a split second. She raised them quickly and exclaimed: "Susan, this seems more of the same sort of thing! The sort of thing I've taken the liberty of criticizing you for. But I'm very disturbed to hear it. The newspapers may end by getting hold of such a document and publicizing it to the filth-craving public as an example of a businesswoman's private life. It's—it's really too disgusting. I think we must do something!" Again there slid over her face for a fleeting second that look of fear which Susan had caught.

Susan felt unbearably excited all at once. Hortense Culbertson and even poor old Caroline Semmer had taken her diary story much as under normal circumstances they might have taken it. Vivian was reacting, and, she thought with falling heart, badly.

After a moment, the designer forced herself to ask: "Do you suppose Nancy 'd have written much about us—about the Tomorrow Club members, I mean?"

Miss Peabody, regaining complete self-control, expressed herself with a ladylike snort, and added: "You said yourself, it's supposed to contain her innermost observations—and—so forth. I dare say, she knew things about us all—oh yes, about us *all*—which, in print, would not look too flattering. Good heavens. There must be some way we can suppress this ridiculous thing. One has certain power."

Susan felt suddenly still more disquieted. "Oh no!" she cried. "For goodness sakes, Vivian. I'm not supposed to know a thing about a diary. Anyone stepping out and trying to suppress one would just be tying a rope around—his neck."

At this Vivian did not look relieved. She asked slowly: "Have you any idea whether there was much—ah—amorous material in the diary?"

Susan told herself: "Susan Yates, if you ever tell another lie as long as you live, it will serve you right if it hangs you!" Aloud she said, with false glibness, that she had only been able to conclude that any Nancy Pierce diary would have had to contain *ses amours* or—it wouldn't have been a Nancy Pierce diary.

Coldly, Miss Peabody admitted she could well understand that and poured herself another cup of coffee. But her hostess, Susan found, did not have her mind on the remainder of their conversation. She rallied, however, as Susan rose to go and said: "Don't forget, my dear, you're coming here with the committee for cocktails this afternoon. My fiancé will be here, too, and Lucinda's bringing Ethan Van Weck. One or two other men are coming—and, oh yes, I asked Mr. Benchley. He's an old friend of yours, isn't he?"

Susan nodded, her own eyes vague now. A little abruptly, she took her departure.

UNUSUALLY FOR SATURDAY, Miss Mason was at her business establishment. She was surrounded by yards of damask and a good-looking but apparently anxiety-ridden young man was in conference with her. Susan recognized him as the famous polo-playing son of a client of her own. He had, it developed, decided to renovate his New York apartment and had gone slightly berserk in the effort. Susan's arrival—fortuitously for Lucinda—brought the young man to a sudden decision to leave everything to Mason Interiors, Inc. Miss Mason assured him that, in the long run, it would be the best plan; and the client took himself off with obvious relief. Turning to Susan, Lucinda said: "Thank God you came, darling. He was reaching the indecisive stage. Such a bore, for in the end they always do what I suggest. How are you?"

Susan tabulated her health as excellent and asked if Miss Mason had had any idea that Nancy Pierce had left a diary with simply everything in it.

"Heaven save us!" screeched Lucinda. "What a juicy morsel of literature that must be! I must get a copy and show it to Ethan as an Object Lesson. No doubt he would have been in it if she had lived a day longer. Wasn't it too ridiculous him letting her pick him up practically! Men *are* such fools."

Lucinda then explained with embellishments Ethan's big joke sprung on the district attorney and Lyle Curtis—about Nancy's having thought that *she* had married Ethan for *his* money.

Presently Susan went away, her brow puckered and her morning's calls milling about in her brain like a dog on an indoor exerciser. But as she started the motor in her car, a sudden and very definite point out of the morning's meetings came to a zooming halt at the very front of her consciousness. She drove a block, endangering the safety of everybody in the street by the utter concentration of her mind on this one point. At the next corner, she startled the traffic policeman by shouting to herself: "Of course! That's it! She was the only one who did!"

The traffic officer grumbled to himself: "Not a bit of sense these good-looking girls with sporty cars. Go about yelling and shrieking without a thought in their blasted heads."

CHAPTER THIRTY-TWO

SUSAN DROVE ON thoughtfully to her office. Her secretary had letters for her to sign, there were details of a fitting to be gone over, a debutante turned night-club singer to advise on her costume. . . . At last Miss Yates had cleared her desk, and was alone in her work-manlike office, her secretary dismissed for the rest of the day.

Susan made a telephone call, then sat for nearly half an hour gazing at her desk with profound abstraction. In her mind she went over and over again trivial words and phrases, a way of laughing, emotional habits and attachments—everything she knew of the people involved in the case that was not part and parcel of their self-conscious, outward behavior. At last, she drew a pad of paper to her, and made two columns. One was headed: "What Mike Could Have Known?' The other was headed: "What I Could Have Known."

At the bottom of the pad she made another computation: Why were these things, self-evident and in no case, so far as she could see, dangerous to the murderer, cause for the attempts on her life and for the death of Mike? On the face of it, nothing she had seen was in itself proof of a criminal action. Yet . . . yet . . . added to-gether, some of these straws in the wind made a damaging picture.

Half an hour later, her eyes worried, her lovely mouth tight, she had finished her notes. Hands trembling, she folded the sheets of paper carefully and locked them in the office safe. Then she went to refurbish her complexion.

In the street, five minutes later, she glanced at her watch. It was still too early to go to Vivian's party, and she had had no luncheon.

Under the disapproving eye of Sergeant Withers, she turned into a nearby restaurant, ordered luncheon, then went to the phone booth in the corner. Through the glass door, as she closed herself in, she saw Sergeant Withers change his table so that he might keep her under his eye.

She had Lyle Curtis on the phone almost immediately.

"You spoke of a search of people and their homes today," Susan reminded him. "When you search people, you like to search them all at the same time, don't you, and their houses and offices too? Well, all the still living members of the Tomorrow Club's annual show committee, plus Miss Peabody's fiancé, Lucinda Mason's husband and Tom Benchley, will be at that cocktail party I'm going to this afternoon—at Miss Peabody's. The party was planned before Nancy's death. I think, under the circumstances, the murderer won't dare not appear."

"Thanks," said Curtis. "That's fine. What time is the party?"

"Four o'clock," Susan answered. "Everyone ought to be there by five."

"You say everyone connected with the case will be there?"

"Everyone is invited—except Howard Pierce and Doctor Semmer. Do you need them?"

"Ought to have everyone. And between you and me, they're both important. Did you know Pierce was in the Eden bar the noon of the murder? Yes. And I don't like Semmer's alibi for the time of Mike's murder. Very thin. I'll see that those two are on hand."

When Susan had left the phone, she returned to her lunch, and ate under Sergeant Withers' still disapproving eye. He had been gambling his way through a French menu and wore a frustrated, unfed look.

CURTIS, AFTER THE CONVERSATION, had called Dr. Semmer. "Lin—this is Lyle Curtis. You said you wanted to help us find the murderer of Nancy Pierce."

"By God," the other declared, "just tell me what to do, Curtis— I'll do anything, I swear, I'll . . ."

"All right," Curtis interrupted him. "I want you to go to a cocktail party at Vivian Peabody's apartment this afternoon. Your sister's going. She can take you with her. Obviously, I can't be there and not look official, but you can. I want you to observe everyone closely and report back to me at the office around six. I want your opinion as a doctor on the state of nerves of all those people—you ought to be able to tell if one of them is undergoing a particularly severe strain, shouldn't you? Good. You'll do it then? Fine."

Curtis needed five minutes' thought before he put in a call to Howard Pierce. Ingenuity failing him, he said merely: "Pierce— can you be in my office at twenty minutes to five? Something has come up in connection with your wife's death—no, I can't discuss it over the phone."

And, hanging up, Curtis went out to see that his warrants were obtained and his plans laid.

SUSAN, MEANWHILE, had reached her coffee, and the sergeant had reached something he had ambitiously hoped would be apple pie. Miss Yates signaled the headwaiter.

"Louis," she said, "I am about to have a brandy. A very good brandy, please, one guaranteed to inspire me with both courage and wisdom."

Louis bowed and lost himself in thought. In a moment he had it.

"Not too old, for then the taste goes too; not too new, certainly, for Mademoiselle. It shall be something of the same that was served at the marriage of the Duke of Orleans—later Henry II—to Catherine de Medici."

"If that was an occasion for both courage and wisdom, then it will be all right," smiled Susan. She sat waiting, trying for a few moments to wash from her mind the horror of the decision she had made. It was simple enough to decide to force a murderer into the open; but it was altogether another thing to plan how to do it. "Almost," she thought ironically, "in the same dish with planning a murder itself."

Louis approached, bearing the brandy reverently. Susan sipped it, and approved.

"A pity," she remarked, "that I am not marrying a future Henry II."

"Ah, no, mademoiselle, it would mean your death."

She shivered and finished the brandy at a gulp. Then she rose, paid her check, and to the evident relief of Sergeant Withers, departed.

IT WAS JUST HALF-PAST FOUR, and, though growing dark, the day was still fine. The dry, clear air would do her good, Susan decided, and set out at a brisk pace to walk to Vivian's.

She felt better by the time she had reached the duplex penthouse, and smiled almost happily at the butler. From the drawing room came the sound of feminine voices, underlaid with deeper masculine tones. Susan went directly to the small powder room which, it occurred to her, could have been photographed just as it was, and used in Vivian's magazine to illustrate: "The New Coats and Handbags for Formal Afternoon Wear."

Susan took off her glossy Persian lamb, and decided to keep her handbag so that—horrifying thought—it would not even be necessary to smoke anyone else's cigarettes. She was still trembling a little over the indisputable fact that she herself was about to be in danger, as she passed through the door that led from the powder room to the drawing room.

Vivian came up to her, looking particularly glamorous in a golden flame-shot Yates hostess gown, trailing behind her the kind of regal train Miss Peabody fancied. Her hostess lowered her voice for a second:

"You haven't—that is, nothing more about that diary came to light?"

Susan shook her head, and Miss Peabody became once more the grande dame receiving her guests. An unusual brightness in her eyes was the only thing about her that in any way disturbed her customary, irreproachable poise.

While they chatted, Susan glanced around the room. Colonel Gamberson was holding court at a portable bar, with Lucinda Mason, Caroline Semmer and Dr. Semmer attending his dextrous motions with bottles and ice cubes. He was designing a new cocktail in honor of the presence of stars from the designing world,

Vivian explained in a voice that would have passed anywhere as gay. Seeing Dr. Semmer, Susan looked about for Howard Pierce. But he was nowhere in sight. Ethan Van Weck, not to be outdone by the colonel, was holding an attentive audience spellbound—an audience composed of Hortense Culbertson and Tom Benchley. Ethan was demonstrating his sleight-of-hand card tricks. It occurred to Susan that lightning speed with the hands was an unusually satisfactory compensation for a stammerer.

There was such an air of relaxed good humor in the room that, for a second, Susan bit her lip and felt a traitor. Any moment now, Curtis and his men would descend upon this smart little gathering. What a surprise it would be for the two personable young men from the advertising department of *For Ladies* whom Lucinda was presenting at that moment. Feeling, however, a fresh security in their innocent presence, Susan moved on with them. They circled the room, chatting and praising the colonel's cocktail, her sample of which Susan managed to set down, untouched, on the nearest table. Vivian, Hortense and Tom were applauding Ethan's "Neatest Trick of the Week"—a title which Susan felt to be all too apposite.

Beaming like a child who has received a report card full of *A*'s, Ethan announced, almost without a stammer, that he knew an even better trick, but he needed a larger table for it. Vivian led them into the library off the drawing room. There, she established Ethan at the head of the large library table. Colonel Gamberson and his cocktail admirers joined the group, and soon Vivian's guests were crowded into the little room. They watched Ethan's rapid fingers, peering over each other's shoulders, calling gay encouragements or disparagements to him. Miss Semmer, too modest to push her plump and withered figure into the crowd, was standing on tiptoe at its edge, her head in its fashionable and ridiculous hat stretched forward on her plump neck, her too smart handbag clutched awkwardly. Dr. Semmer, Susan suddenly did not see. But she assumed it was because she also had remained on the outside of the crowd, ill content to be embedded in the midst of the guests. Dr. Semmer must be standing near the sleight-of-hand act.

Ethan went through a considerable conjurer's preamble and was finally proposing (with a stammer) to change a deck of cards into twelve bright silk handkerchiefs, when Susan heard the doorbell ring faintly. She listened intently and—as the other guests laughingly defied Ethan to do it—she heard from the hall a gruff rumble of voices. Ethan turned his palms outward to show them that the cards were gone, then down with a rapid motion, and with successive flips produced the promised twelve handkerchiefs. In the moment of awed silence that greeted this minor miracle, a protesting voice could be heard plainly from the hall:

"But, gentlemen, Miss Peabody has guests . . ."

A gruff voice interrupted him:

"I can't help that. Here's the warrant—read it if you like—gives us legal right to enter and examine this house and the persons in it. So stand aside."

Vivian, her face puzzled and outraged, moved to the door of the library, and her guests moved after her. Now they could hear the suaver tones of Lyle Curtis, saying apparently to the butler:

"Please go into the pantry and stay there. One of my men will go with you and another answer the door, if necessary."

CHAPTER THIRTY-THREE

FROM THE DRAWING ROOM, above the startled exclamations in the library, Susan heard Lucinda Mason's Pomeranian, G. B., give a short but disapproving bark. They were all automatically stalking back into the drawing room, eyes turned to the hall door in direction of the official voices. Susan's eyes went in direction of G. B. and his bark. The dog was standing by the powder-room door. She started. Then, trying to make herself inconspicuous, backed up against the wall just outside the library door and remained there wondering if the final moment for an attack on herself had come. But for the time being nothing happened. Everyone stood rigid. Next, Lyle Curtis appeared in the hall doorway, bowing briefly. In equally brief, bare but polite words, he explained the purpose of his intrusion. Would they all please be seated. They sat, each in the chair nearest him, and with the look of people suddenly folding up with astonishment.

The young assistant district attorney's eyes traveled slowly from face to face. Behind him stood Sergeant Withers, Sergeant McQuire and a young man whom Susan recognized as Curtis' secretary. She could hear other men moving about the apartment, their footsteps pounding on the second floor of the duplex above their heads.

No one had said a word since the invitation—practically a command—to sit down. Now Curtis stopped his survey of the inhabitants of the room, and looking at Susan, said:

"I understood that Doctor Semmer was to have been here. Where is he?" With a start, Susan gazed around the room and noticed that Linwood Semmer was still nowhere in sight.

244

"Doctor Semmer was here," said Vivian Peabody. "He received a call from the hospital just a few minutes ago and had to leave immediately."

"Check on that call with the butler," Curtis instructed Sergeant Withers. Vivian flushed. Sergeant Withers was back in an instant. "That's right, sir," he reported. "The butler took the call from Physicians' Hospital and gave the message to the doctor four or five minutes ago."

Curtis bit his lip, then shrugged his shoulders and said: "Very well. Check back on that call to the hospital. And ask Mr. Pierce to come in."

"Mr. Pierce?" questioned Vivian, her eyebrows raised.

"I took the liberty, Miss Peabody," Curtis answered, "of inviting Mr. Pierce to your party. I hope you'll forgive me."

"My apologies, Miss Peabody," said Howard Pierce from the doorway. "I didn't even know where we were going." Curtis motioned him to a chair. He sat down heavily, and throughout the rest of that strange afternoon made only one statement in eleven emphatic words. Susan, watching him from time to time, could not tell whether it was the immobility of shock or a curious kind of relief. He looked like a man who has gone through much, and doesn't particularly care what happens next.

Curtis, meanwhile, had signaled McQuire, who went to the door of the powder room, opened it and motioned. From it emerged two sturdy police matrons, one with an armful of handbags, the other carrying coats.

"Will each of you," Curtis said, "identify your own possessions, and hold them in your lap?"

Sergeant McQuire, meanwhile, had disappeared into the hall, and Susan could hear him opening a door. In a moment he was back with the men's coats, gloves, mufflers, hats and sticks. With baffled remonstrances, they claimed their property. Cutting short the mystified and resentful murmurs of the guests, Curtis said:

"Does any one of you see any discrepancy in the wearing apparel or *accessories*—claimed by the others?" He used the fashion term with a bleak smile. They all regarded the objects in their laps, and in each other's, and shook their heads. "I mean, has everyone all his own possessions, and only his own?" They nodded in unison, like a class of astonished children.

Then Colonel Gamberson, purple in the face, burst out with:

"It's a blasted outrage. I suppose we may at least know what it is you are looking for?" Curtis only shook his head. Ethan Van Weck broke into agonized stammering, from which the word "attorney" at last appeared as intelligible. Curtis paid no attention to him. The two personable young men from *For Ladies* looked as though they had strayed into wildest Africa. Until Vivian spoke the women had been, Susan thought, unusually silent and submissive—a new characteristic at once surprising and possibly, to Curtis, suspicious.

Then Vivian's hand with its magnificent ruby fluttered. Her voice, though level, had a queer new ring to it. She said:

"You are a lawyer, Mr. Pierce. I assume you will tell me if I must submit my guests to this outrage?"

Pierce stirred in his chair, and Curtis motioned to McQuire. The sergeant drew the warrants from his pocket and handed them to Pierce. He glanced at them and handed them back.

"The warrants are quite in order and perfectly legal, Miss Peabody," he said.

Curtis added: "There aren't many issued in New York in a year's time, but today we have taken the precaution of having them. I am afraid you must submit."

Vivian as perhaps never before in her long years of domination, Susan suspected, was trying to hide a look of bright fear in her eyes. She alone, of course, held no wraps in her lap.

"Very well, then," she said, and rose. "If we are to be searched, let me be submitted first to this embarrassment."

Curtis nodded and pointed to the door to the powder room, where the two stocky policewomen stood.

"As you like, Miss Peabody," he said, and Vivian, her head high, her magnificent gold and flame train sweeping behind her, disappeared into the adjoining room. Then Tom Benchley, at a nod from Curtis, rose and went into the library, followed by two men summoned from the hall.

For the next ten minutes they waited, the tension in the room crackling like static. Susan could hear the search of the rest of the apartment continuing; and assumed that similar searches were taking place simultaneously at each of their homes and offices—perhaps even her own. She bit her lip and thought of the sheets of paper she had locked away in her safe.

Benchley was released from the library first, looking sheepish, but not amused. Then, an expression of utter disgust on her face, Miss Peabody swept from the powder room. One of the matrons appeared at the open door, and shook her head at Curtis, who turned and, to her amazement, motioned to Susan to go next.

Inside the powder room, Susan found herself wondering whether she was still suspected, in spite of all Curtis had said, or if she were being examined merely as a blind for the others. Certainly, if the latter, the police matrons had not been informed. Being one of those citizens who had heard of "frisking" and search, but who had never experienced it, Susan was amazed at the thoroughness of the two husky women. They left no possible hiding place uninvestigated. Nude before them, Susan discovered herself capable of humiliation which walking naked in the street could hardly have deepened. One of the women gave particular attention to her handbag and coat—pockets and lining—and to the smart, wide soles of her shoes. While she dressed again, the other woman's eyes never left her.

Coming back into the drawing room, Susan found that the two young men from *For Ladies* had been searched and allowed to depart. Gamberson, still hotly remonstrating about his rights as a citizen and retired army officer, was entering the library with excessive military bearing, and Caroline Semmer, flurried, but for once not looking apologetic, but maidenly outraged, followed Susan into the powder room. From then on traffic to and from the powder room and library became routine. Everyone else, who had been or was yet to be examined, sat stiffly on chairs and couches with an air of modern plebiscite voters.

Curtis remained standing through the whole procedure. His face was drawn. "He's horribly tired," Susan thought.

Hortense followed Caroline Semmer into the powder room, and Van Weck followed the colonel into the library. Then Hortense was returned to them, and Lucinda Mason, her strong, tweed-covered shoulders erect, her curiously green eyes watchful, disappeared with the matrons. Howard Pierce took Van Weck's place in the library.

The door had scarcely closed behind Lucinda, when it opened abruptly again, and one of the policewomen held something out to Curtis. It was Lucinda's pin-seal handbag, open and innocent looking enough.

Curtis took it and peered inside. Then there flashed momentarily across his face a look of sheer surprise as he glanced over the matron's shoulder at Lucinda Mason's white face.

Lucinda's acquired culture trembled for only a moment; then she stepped past the matron, and faced Curtis, her expression under control. Her words, though clipped and exasperated, maintained the sophistication she had learned. She was no longer the playboy of Tuesday's luncheon table, nor the forthright young woman of Tuesday's police questioning. She said: "I never saw that thing before in my life. I've never had one in my hands. I wouldn't know what to do with one. You won't find my fingerprints on it . . ."

"We'll soon find out, Miss Mason," Curtis said, and wrapping his handkerchief around his fingers, put a cautious hand inside Lucinda's handbag. With an equally cautious gesture, he drew it out again. In his handkerchief-wrapped fingers was a steel and glass hypodermic.

Ethan Van Weck was on his feet, incoherent in his rage, straining against the two firm hands with which McQuire held his arms. Curtis seemed not even to see him. He passed a hand over his weary face and said:

"Miss Mason, this is certainly very damaging evidence. You will have to come down to headquarters with me. And I must warn you that anything you say may be used against you."

"But I couldn't have killed Nancy," Lucinda said firmly. "I was never within grabbing distance of her handbag and capsules—except before them all at the luncheon table, with all the lights on."

"The district attorney's office is well aware, Miss Mason," said Curtis, "that you couldn't have managed Mrs. Pierce's murder alone—but there is such a thing in this world as a confederate." For one fleeting second his eyes went to the still spluttering Van Weck, struggling in McQuire's grasp.

"He's right, McQuire," he said, "he should telephone his attorney. Take him out to the phone."

There was a moment's pause while the two, almost locked in an unwilling embrace, made their clumsy way to the door. Susan, turning her head, saw Howard Pierce standing in the doorway of the library, coatless and collarless, his suspenders hanging, his hands gripping the door frame. He seemed unconscious of the state of undress in which the interrupted search had left him.

Curtis turned to Lucinda again and said:

"Do you wish to make a statement here?"

"I have no statement to make," Lucinda replied, "except that I did not kill Nancy Pierce, and I never saw that hypodermic before. I never even touched it."

"It will be dusted for fingerprints as soon as we get back to headquarters," Curtis said and looked down again at the little thing in his hand. Then, very carefully, he placed it, handkerchief and all, on the low coffee table by a couch. At his gesture, one of the men from the door came over to stand guard over it. Lyle Curtis backed away from it and said:

"Will you all come here—but no nearer the table than three feet—I want you to look at this." They closed in on the table, reminded to keep their distance by the determined arms of Sergeant Withers and Curtis' secretary. They stood gazing down on the almost pretty thing of steel and glass, still partly filled with colorless liquid, that had killed two people. "Any of you ever see this hypodermic before?" Silence answered him. "No one? Well, then, Miss Mason."

"Just a moment, Mr. Curtis." Susan's voice seemed to echo back at her from the ceiling and from the wall of blank and curious faces that turned to her. "I . . . you . . . that is, I have a statement to make," she said. Her voice was low pitched, but it seemed to fill the room. "Mr. Curtis," she repeated, "I cannot let you make this mistake. I know who killed Nancy Pierce and Mike Shawnessy. It wasn't Lucinda Mason." She paused, and took a deep breath. "Find Doctor Linwood Semmer," she said.

CHAPTER THIRTY-FOUR

THERE WAS A SNAP of movement in the room as though a bass viol string had broken. The mass gasp of astonishment reverberated like a spinning wire. Into the silence that succeeded it broke a shrill and agonized voice.

"It's a lie. You can't prove it. You know it's a lie." Caroline Semmer's hands were clasped before her, raised toward Curtis as though beseeching him. "Not Linwood. It's not true. It's not true," she repeated.

A profound silence answered her. Everyone was staring at Caroline Semmer's white and agonized face. Then Susan said softly, enunciating each syllable as though she were speaking to a child:

"Listen to me, Caroline—I say your brother, Linwood Semmer, is responsible for these murders. He was in love with Nancy Pierce. He is blind . . . and careless." Quickly Susan faced Curtis again, deliberately turning her back on the others.

"Can you prove what you are saying?" Curtis asked her.

"Yes," she said. "Why did the murderer try to kill me? Why was Mike killed? What could we have seen that no one else saw? We saw Doctor Semmer beside Nancy Pierce's handbag—the handbag in which poisoned capsules were put by her murderer. Only one person had access to that bag that noon, Mike and I both knew that. What we knew was of grave danger to the murderer. So attacks were made on us both—and poor Mike was killed. And the suicide note? I know who planted that, and how it was done. And that hypodermic . . ." She turned and pointed to the coffee table where the shining thing still lay. Across it, Caroline Semmer's face stared into hers. Susan paused, then turned again to Curtis and continued: "That was planted in Lucinda's bag. Who is more likely to own a hypodermic than a physician? Linwood Semmer is a doctor—a careless doctor—a doctor who was in love with a woman who only wanted to take, not to give. Doctors, Mr. Curtis, have easy access to poison. And this particular doctor has no alibi for the time of Mike's death. And he was here this afternoon. This afternoon that hypodermic was planted in Lucinda's bag. Why did he leave in such a hurry? A call from the hospital? Calls can be faked."

Caroline Semmer circled the coffee table, and came toward Susan, her eyes blazing, her face swollen with rage.

"Liar," she cried, and it was a Caroline none of them knew. "Liar! You know Linwood is guiltless as a little baby. You can prove nothing . . ."

Susan had whirled at Caroline's words. Still speaking in her deliberate fashion she interrupted:

"I can say I . . . saw Linwood . . . switch the capsule boxes . . . and fix the suicide note so it would fall out of Nancy's bag when she opened it. Can't I? You yourself, Caroline Semmer, testified that you saw it fall from Nancy's bag when she took out her box of capsules. Your own testimony has helped to build your brother's coffin . . ."

Caroline Semmer sprang for Susan as if she were determined to crush the words back into her mouth, but even before Curtis and Withers could intervene, she stopped short, and seemed to droop, as though the fight had gone out of her. Susan stood perfectly still, feeling a certain inner calm now in the necessity for playing her role through to the end. Her eyes were still fixed on the older woman's.

Curtis turned to the door and shouted: "Send out a radio call to pick up Dr. Linwood Semmer." Then he turned back to Susan and said bluntly:

"Do you swear to all this, Miss Yates?"

But before Susan could reply, Caroline Semmer wrenched herself free from Sergeant Withers and sprang for the table. It was like a cat's spring, swift and unerring. More quickly than their eyes could follow, she snatched the hypodermic from the table and pulled the plunger.

"Withers!" Curtis shouted and leapt. But it was too late. As Withers' hand closed on the gleaming shaft, the needle sank into Caroline Semmer's veined wrist, releasing the fluid.

"Get a doctor—quick!" Curtis shouted, and put out a hand to the beautifully dressed dowdy woman. But Caroline waved him away with a curiously imperious gesture.

"The doctor won't be able to keep me alive," she said. And suddenly there broke from her lips the same hysterical laugh that Susan had heard three times before. "I did it! I killed them, Nancy Pierce and that talkative waiter. I wanted to kill Susan Yates, too—she knew too much. I almost did. But Mr. Benchley interfered in Van Cortlandt Park—and I didn't have the hypodermic with me in the Grand Central shuttle. When it was the waiter's turn, I knew better. I stole the hypodermic from my brothers' office, but he didn't know anything about it. It was a sample I found one day—two weeks ago—about the time Nancy first threatened me. I found the box lying on his table. It hadn't even been opened but it said what it was on the outside. I knew he wouldn't miss a sample. . . ."

Between the burly detectives she was growing limp. Her voice had become a hoarse rattle. "I had the weed killer for my garden. The mud was on my stocking—not Linwood's. It was I Nancy Pierce was blackmailing. And it's true, I didn't go home last night, after I left the subway . . ." Suddenly then she seemed to revive. In almost her customarily apologetic tone, she said: "It's all in writing—in a letter to my brother. You'll find it in the Hamilton safety-deposit vaults. The wrapping of the sample hypodermic is there, too. I rented the box—for a year." She laughed faintly, and her voice began to fade again. "I wrote everything down, because if anything happened to me I wanted Linwood to know I had done it for him; because I loved him; because I would have done *anything* for him. So it's all there in the letter. . . ." With a jerk, Caroline's head fell forward on her breast. Sergeant Withers stooped, and, one arm under her knees, one under her shoulders, carried her into the hall.

CHAPTER THIRTY-FIVE

SUSAN'S EYES TURNED slowly from the hall door to Lyle Curtis. He was standing by the coffee table, staring at the empty hypodermic with bitter eyes. "He's blaming himself for her death," thought Susan. "But I can't be sorry she managed it. Even if some smart lawyer had concocted an insanity case for her defense, her feeble joys in living would have been over."

Curtis was motioning the now quiet and still horrified little group of people to sit down. He turned to Susan and made another vague gesture toward the hall, down which Caroline Semmer's body had been carried. "She told us the essentials, I suppose. But not much more. Do you know the rest?"

Susan's voice was low now and filled with the helpless incredulity they were all feeling. She said slowly: "Not enough to have proved her guilty without a confession. But I was convinced that she would tell the whole truth if her brother was convincingly accused; but, of course, she wouldn't have lifted a little finger to protect anyone else. He was her one love."

The assistant district attorney nodded. And Susan went on: "Her love for her brother was stronger than her instinct for self-preservation. She loved him better than anything else in the world—better than she loved herself. That's got to be said for her. Oh, there's lots to be said for Caroline Semmer. She had a frightfully bad emotional set up for this life. And then she was a poor little sparrow among us peacocks . . ." Susan sounded a little hysterical herself now. "Anyway," she went on, "the one thing she loved in the world being her brother, she couldn't stand it for Nancy Pierce to steal him from her. That's really why she murdered her. I think you'll find, too, though not in her letter, that Nancy was blackmailing her. That's the only thing that could make sense of that note. What is so baffling to me is what poor Caroline could have done to be blackmailed. . . ."

Susan was interrupted by the ringing of the doorbell, and they all turned to listen to one of Curtis' men saying: "Yes, Doctor—we moved her under the circumstances—this way." There were quick footsteps and an ambulance doctor passed by the open door going down the hall. They all sat waiting. Susan glanced up and to her great chagrin found that Howard Pierce was still standing in the library door—still in his shirt sleeves and suspenders, his expression hard and sharp. He was listening, too, to the quick footsteps. He must have heard what she had said of Nancy. Murder cases, she thought, put people in odd positions. Under normal conditions—well, she doubted if Howard Pierce had many illusions about his late wife.

Footsteps sounded again in the hall. The ambulance doctor stood in the doorway. He made a sidewise gesture with his right hand and said: "D.O.A."—police parlance for "dead on arrival," Susan recalled grimly.

Without glancing at any of them, Howard Pierce moved out of his trance as the doctor disappeared. He turned without a word and closed the library door behind him. Susan had a curious impression that he, too, in his own way, was glad Caroline Semmer had escaped as she had.

Curtis had gone to the telephone in the hall. He was speaking very distinctly: "Got the report on the books of the Tomorrow Club yet?"

The members glanced at each other with renewed incredulity. Coming back into the drawing room after a few moments, Curtis addressed Miss Peabody. "You people never had an auditor for the club books?"

With a queer look of self-blame, Vivian shook her head. "I never thought it necessary—" she began.

Lyle nodded. "Well, Miss Semmer has been doctoring your books for two years. I believe the method was to underestimate attendance at your banquets and shows, and overestimate expenses. Very simple, it seems."

Vivian shook her head in very un-Peabody-like bewilderment. "Caroline Semmer dishonest? But she was so—so meticulous; and she never had vast sums to handle. We're a nonprofit-making organization."

"Enough for defalcations to improve one woman's wardrobe," sighed Miss Yates. "That was a tip to me. I knew she must be spending more than she made from us. We didn't exactly pay her royally, Vivian. Not enough, at least, to compete"—she glanced hastily toward the still closed library door—"to compete with Nancy Pierce. Poor old thing, she thought it was Nancy's clothes and perfumes that attracted Linwood Semmer. Undoubtedly she thought that if she could dress glamorously her brother would notice and admire her more."

Colonel Gamberson looked distinctly shocked at this, as if nice young women didn't mention in public strange emotional attachments.

Susan went on: "I dare say Caroline managed to justify her pilfering to herself. You all know she was always talking about how hard she worked. She probably made herself believe she was more than worth the money she took, really entitled to it after a fashion. Of course when I first began to notice how well she was dressing, I assumed that her brother was providing the extra capital. Then when I saw the positive distaste in his expression the day they met in the bar—the day of Nancy's death—I wondered. When the suicide note began to seem so incomprehensible I began to wonder, too, if it had actually been written by Nancy as a blackmail note for someone else to sign—for I knew Caroline was the only one of us who could have 'planted' it. I thought perhaps she had been stealing directly from Nancy—providing she was stealing at all—and providing she was at all involved in the case."

Lucinda demanded breathlessly: "What do you mean, Caroline was the only person who could have 'planted' that note?"

Susan smiled wanly. "That note wasn't there when I first walked around Nancy after we found her unconscious. I looked at the floor to make certain I wouldn't step on your dog. I made a statement to that effect," she added, turning to Curtis, "on Tuesday afternoon, you know. But it didn't mean very much until it dawned on me that the note hadn't been on the floor at Nancy's feet until after Vivian and Tom—the only other persons except Caroline, the hotel doctor and manager who went near her—had moved away. After Vivian and Tom moved away Caroline went up to Nancy and tried to rouse her, reached down and dragged her shoulders back. Then the doctor came and as soon as he had reported her dead the hotel manager stepped in and found the note. It had to be Caroline who had planted it."

Everyone looked very thoughtful. Curtis said with a wry look: "We were convinced that the 'suicide note' was a shrewd victimization of a blackmailer by an intended victim. But why didn't you tell me it was Caroline Semmer who had planted it?" His tone was not nearly so stern as his words.

Susan shook her head. "How could I be positive? I had to make other things match, too. That hysterical laugh she gave this afternoon again, for example. I went around asking everybody horrible questions trying to scare that sound out of them again."

"For the love of sleuths past and present," shrieked Lucinda, "was *that* what you were up to, Susan Yates?"

Miss Peabody looked firm. Mr. Benchley broke the tension by laughing outright and demanding: "Did you think I was given to hysterical outbursts, pal?"

"I know you nearly scared me to death with the best of intentions," said Susan, but that story went untold for Hortense Culbertson interrupted to ask: "Why on earth should Nancy have cared about blackmailing poor old Carry for a little pilfering? Why didn't she just report it to us and have done with it?"

Susan glanced toward the library door again and studiously avoided the eyes of both Vivian Peabody and Colonel Gamberson. "I have no proof, of course," she said, "but I think perhaps—from something Caroline said to me one day this week—that she had discovered Nancy was no more faithful to her brother than to her own husband. Perhaps Caroline threatened to tell Linwood in a desire to cure his emotional attachment to Nancy. Perhaps Nancy wasn't ready for that to happen. She gave me the idea that she intended to keep him dangling."

Colonel Gamberson blew his nose with a Van Weck stentorian quality. Vivian sat, scarlet to the ears, playing with a beautiful lace handkerchief in her lap. And Susan thought again that murder cases certainly led nosy people into very queer situations. Yet all of them had a right to know as much as was necessary. She felt wilted, however, and miles away from the serene hazards of her designing rooms.

Ethan Van Weck was trying to ask a question. He labored over the first word: "H-h-h-ha! Q-question of c-c-counter threats, eh? Ha! B-but f-far as I'm c-c-concerned w-wouldn't f-feel safe t-threatening a w-woman l-like that Mrs. P-Pierce."

Lucinda glanced apprehensively at the library door, conscious, apparently, that tact was not Ethan's salient virtue.

But Ethan persisted: "N-no t-time at all and she'd been off with some other f-fellow and w-wouldn't have cared a t-tinker's d-damn w-what Sister Caroline t-told her b-brother."

"Exactly," sighed Susan. "That was the trouble. Caroline's threat to tell on Nancy was a temporary one at most. But what Nancy could tell Linwood and the world about Caroline's thieving was a different matter altogether. That, I believe, is the other reason she decided to kill Nancy. The main reason, I'll always believe, was to save Linwood and re-establish herself as the important woman in his life. This sort of thing apparently happens outside textbooks on psychology—a complete brother fixation."

Colonel Gamberson stopped looking red, and looked shocked again.

"Well, it's simply dreadful," Hortense Culbertson was saying.

"I suppose," Lucinda Mason interrupted, "that she had the poison all the time."

"Weed killer," nodded Curtis. "We found some at her house—in a bottle in her basement. She evidently thought it smarter to leave it right where her part-time gardener had seen it for months. But by the way, a number of you were well supplied with potassium of cyanide," he smiled. "You, Miss Mason, had a gallon of it in your garden toolhouse in the form of weed killer. You had it in a certain form for photography, Miss Culbertson. You had some for your penthouse flowers, Miss Peabody. Only Miss Yates, Colonel Gamberson and Tom Benchley slipped up on having a handy supply. Mrs. Pierce had some for jewelry work in the Pierce residence."

"Good heavens, so I have a gallon of it!" cried Lucinda, her green eyes amused. "Ethan, think what a chance that is to dispose of you."

Ethan began to stammer again, but the bent of what he wanted to say seemed to be that they had better dispose of Miss Yates first if they wanted to have any more murders in their club.

Susan shook her head. "I don't deserve any credit. Mr. Curtis would have had the case in his hat in half an hour more—once he got that report on the club books."

Curtis seemed to be on the point of insisting too vehemently to the contrary, and Susan abruptly interrupted. "This afternoon, when I was trying to sum things up with a feeble imitation of a professional, it worried me how Caroline had managed to plant the capsules—"

"Yes," demanded Lucinda, "how did she do that?"

"And," Miss Peabody asked in a horrified voice, "why did she want to kill you, Susan? I had no idea that attacks were being made on your life. I thought— Oh, it's horrible."

Susan closed her eyes for a moment, conscious that what Vivian had said was all too true—horrible. "Well," she sighed, "what I started to say wasn't that I was worried over how Caroline had planted the poisoned capsules—for I all but saw that—but how she avoided leaving fingerprints on the capsule box. You see, to go back a little—she must have seen the box on the stage. No one ever remembered whether Caroline was or wasn't present at any given time, unless there was some dull work for her to do. You supposed she must have been there but couldn't remember. Well, she evidently was, and after seeing how many capsules were left in the box, she must have found an opportunity to disappear—probably immediately afterward. I suppose she went to the Ladies' and fixed her box, wiping it clean of fingerprints, but then discovered she'd have to leave her own on it because she had dropped her gloves in the bar. I don't imagine she'd planned yet on the time when she would manage the transfer. By chance, she went back to the bar for her gloves, found her brother gone, Nancy's back turned, and Nancy's handbag on the divan past which she had to bend to pick up the gloves. Obviously, it was then she switched boxes—else why fear Mike and me both—and so—so violently? You see, at that almost exact moment I was standing outside the glass door leading to the bar from the lobby corridor. I didn't see what she did, but apparently I could have. So could Mike, only he actually came to her aid about the gloves a few seconds too late. She may have thought Mike had come up too late to see anything, but there was always the chance that he might have—that he might be holding back, perhaps to blackmail her afterward. She had experienced blackmail, you see."

Susan glanced again at the closed door to the library. "I don't suppose Caroline even saw that Mr. Pierce—and a guest—whom I now know were in the bar at that time. Even if she had, she would have known they were too far away actually to have seen what she had done. Anyway, when Mike and I began conferring, and Mr. Curtis began interviewing Mike and Lucien—the bartender—it apparently sealed the death warrants of both Mike and me. Evidently she had some reason for knowing Lucien couldn't have seen; and Nancy's and Mr. Van Weck's backs were turned."

"Thank God, she failed with you!" Curtis said with such emphasis that everyone turned and stared at him. Susan found herself blushing.

"Anyway," she said quickly, "the murderer's suspicion of Mike and me—and only us—is what really tipped me off. When I got down to brass tacks, I saw *I* must have heard or seen something Mike could have seen or heard. Perhaps I seemed doubly dangerous. Like a nitwit, I went around chattering about hysterical laughs and Nancy having kept a diary. Caroline also probably heard I'd reported there wasn't a suicide note at Nancy's feet when we first found she was unconscious."

Miss Peabody turned white. "I told her that myself," she whispered.

"Never mind," smiled Susan, "I'm a difficult person to dispose of!"

"You didn't finish the point about there being no Caroline Semmer fingerprints on the capsule box," Lucinda Mason reminded her; and Susan said that still puzzled her because Caroline had been carrying her gloves in her hand when she came out of the bar. Mike had seen her pick them up.

Curtis said softly: "She did leave fingerprints on the box. You've just forgotten that she took a capsule herself at the luncheon table— evidently because she remembered about the prints. It justified her finger marks being on the box."

Susan said: "I have a shoddy brain. Of course. That was it!"

Mr. Benchley's eyes had meanwhile been moving back and forth between Susan and Curtis as if he knew something no one else knew. He stopped looking wise and asked: "What did she mean about mud on her stocking?"

Smiling bleakly, Susan explained. "Today was dry and fine— both here in New York and out at White Plains where Caroline lived. I telephoned there to find out. Yesterday was slushy and muddy. Caroline, however, this morning had a splash of mud on one of her stockings. She was far too neat and meticulous not to have noticed and changed them if she had taken them off last night. It occurred to me she hadn't been home and hadn't been to bed."

Curtis broke in: "Her only alibi for the time of the waiter's death was that she had been seen going down a Grand Central Station platform. A conductor, in a muddled way, thought he remembered her getting on the nine-twenty train. She probably did—and off again."

"And probably," Susan said grimly, "when I mentioned the mud spot, she guessed I had suspected the worst. She was wrong. It took me the rest of the afternoon. I mentioned to her, too, that I'd come up to the club by way of the chauffeurs' parking space and the fire stairs—doubtless exactly the way she managed to hide out last night after stabbing poor little Mike—" She looked angrily down at the hypodermic.

Smiling at her gently, Curtis asked: "You didn't, of course, see her plant the hypodermic in Miss Mason's bag and not tell me as soon as I got here?"

Susan shook her head. "Oh no. That was just part of my extemporaneous build up against Dr. Semmer—part of my effort to make Caroline confess. What I had actually seen was only a straw in the wind. You see, she was standing on the edge of the crowd watching Mr. Van Weck do his trick at the library table. Her handbag was clutched in her hand—not suspicious in itself. But when you and your men arrived everybody began tumbling out here into the drawing room. I heard G. B. barking and glanced at him. He was barking at the door to the powder room. A split second later, Caroline came unobtrusively out of the powder room—without her handbag but with a very peculiar look in her eyes when our glances crossed. I was scared to death. Thought she was going to make for me then and there. I tried to look as if I hadn't noticed anything. She was watching me. Evidently, I put it over with dumb luck. Anyway, she must have missed your police matrons' entrance into the powder room from the hall by half a second, Mr. Curtis. And G. B., Lucinda, must have had a sixth-sense knowledge that she was touching something of yours."

At this, Miss Yates suddenly put her head back on Miss Peabody's damask-covered chair and burst into weary, very feminine tears. Vivian, Lucinda and Hortense all started for her from opposite sides of the room, but curiously Lyle Curtis already had a comforting arm around her shoulders. He was murmuring: "You broke the case for me, Susan." And she was sobbing: "Oh piffle."

"But you did!" Curtis repeated with louder insistence while the rest of them stared with sudden appreciation. "Without you, we might have gone into court, but you broke it with the confession inspiration, and everything else. And I let you in for terrible dangers. She might have killed you there at the club this morning when you spotted that mud—"

"Oh piffle!" sobbed Susan again. "What would she have done with the body?"

Mr. Benchley cleared his throat. "What I want to know is when you two are—ah—going into business together?"

Miss Yates stopped crying and blushed. So did Mr. Curtis.

COACHWHIP PUBLICATIONS

COACHWHIPBOOKS.COM

ISBN 978-1-61646-233-8

COACHWHIP PUBLICATIONS

COACHWHIPBOOKS.COM

MURDER OF
THE HONEST BROKER

WILLOUGHBY SHARP

ISBN 978-1-61646-211-6

COACHWHIP PUBLICATIONS

COACHWHIPBOOKS.COM

THERE IS
NO RETURN
THE ADELAIDE ADAMS MYSTERIES
ANITA BLACKMON

ISBN 978-1-61646-223-9

COACHWHIP PUBLICATIONS

NOW AVAILABLE

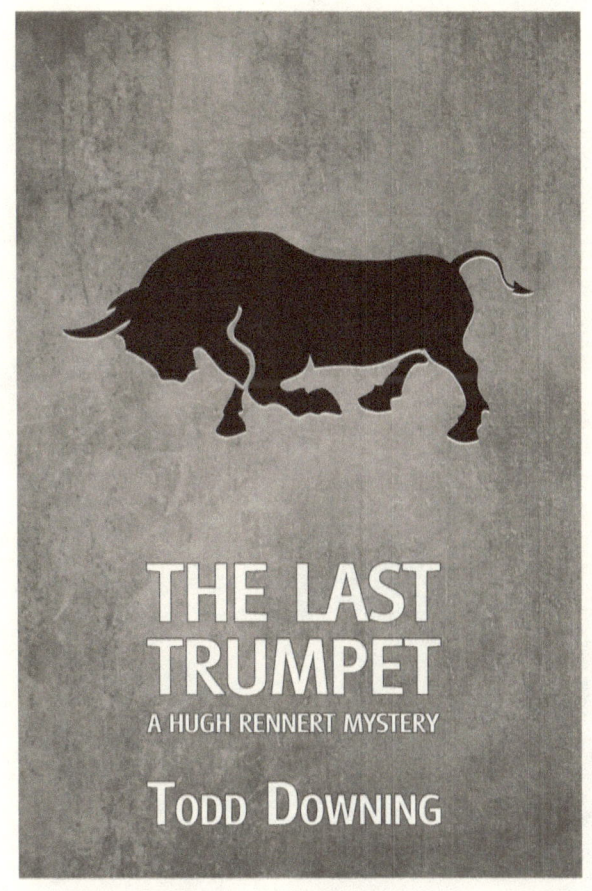

THE LAST TRUMPET

A HUGH RENNERT MYSTERY

TODD DOWNING

ISBN 978-1-61646-152-2